Mr. Sticks

sands press
Brockville, Ontario

Mr. Sticks

Jeffrey Hale

sands press

sands press

A Division of 10361976 Canada Inc.
300 Central Avenue West
Brockville, Ontario
K6V 5V2

Toll Free 1-800-563-0911 or 613-345-2687
http://www.sandspress.com

ISBN 978-1-988281-67-4
Copyright © 2019 Jeffrey Hale
All Rights Reserved

Cover Design by Kristine Barker and Wendy Treverton
Edited by Laurie Carter
Formatting by Renee Hare
Publisher Sands Press

Publisher's Note
This book is a work of fiction. References to real people, events, establishments, organizations, or locales, are intended only to provide as a sense of authenticity, and are used fictitiously. All other characters, and all incidents and dialogue, are drawn from the authors' imaginations and are not to be construed as real.

No part of this book may be reproduced in whole or in part, stored in a retrieval system or transmitted in any form or by any means, without the prior written permission of the publisher.

For information on bulk purchases of this book or any book published by Sands Press, please call 1-800-563-0911.

1st Printing April 2019

To book an author for your live event, please call: 1-800-563-0911

Sands Press is a literary publisher interested in new and established authors wishing to develop and market their product. For more information please visit our website at www.sandspress.com.

Chapter 1

Finley stood outside the cornfield, her fists clenched and her spine rigid. She could see through the first few rows, thanks to her Pontiac's headlights, but the space beyond was an amorphous tangle of darkness: black upon black upon black. Where one shade of blackness ended, another began, creating the illusion of an endless void—one which shuddered and eddied in concert with the spectral breeze.

For a moment, Finley thought she spotted a humanoid form among the stalks, but she quickly dismissed it as a product of her overactive imagination. The Pontiac's high beams were gauzy, and cast a multitude of shadows into the field. At any given time, there were a hundred shapes scuttling to and fro, tickling the peripheries of her vision.

Tucking a red and blue strand of hair behind her ear—an action she'd unwittingly adopted from her mother—she backpedaled to the Pontiac's driver-side door, doused the lights, and popped the trunk. She listened for any unusual sounds as she rooted through the storage compartment, but heard no overtly suspicious crackles or pops. Either she was alone or it was in no hurry to reveal its presence.

Content with the fruits of her labor, she shut the trunk and resumed her position before the field. Even though she could see the old Stenson Company grain elevator and the Great Western sugar plant—both boxy shapes against the pre-dawn horizon—she couldn't shake the notion that she was *elsewhere*. Not removed from her hometown, perhaps, but in a separate state of existence. All the usual sights, sounds, scents, and sensations were still there, but there was an emptiness about them. A factitiousness. She felt as though she were a patron at a bizarre zoo, and her hometown was the prize exhibit.

If she waited long enough, would someone appear and shoo her along? Would someone remind her not to fall too far behind her tour group? Would a gaggle of teenage girls point and whisper over the tops of their cell phones, the way they did at Eaton High?

Experiencing a sudden heat in her cheeks, Finley bent down and tugged at her shoelaces. She needed to stop putzing around—her father's words—and get on with it. The longer she delayed, the harder it would be to follow through.

Two weeks ago, she could have dropped everything and walked away without regret, but now…? Now she was in over her head. She was past the breaking point. She was *invested*. She couldn't *afford* to abandon her plans.

Ruminating on the sacrifices she had made, she removed her Chuck Taylors, set her socks and sneakers aside, and straightened once more, shifting her weight ever so slightly, to acclimate her soles to their new environs.

She had never liked the look of her toes, to tell the truth—she hated their stubbiness and the way they curved inward, giving the suggestion of some exotic musculoskeletal disease—but she didn't make a single move toward the amalgamation of rubber and fabric. She understood the rules.

"A second of pain for a lifetime of pleasure," she muttered, withdrawing the knife from her pocket; inspecting it beneath the sallow September moon. It wasn't a particularly impressive specimen, what with its corroded blade and its chipped and yellowed antler handle, but it was sharp at the point, and that was all that really mattered. Everything else was merely a matter of aesthetics.

Aesthetics.

That damned word again.

How had Destinee pronounced it in art class? *Ass*thetics? No. That wasn't quite right. The girl had sandwiched three words together, and had come up with something entirely new and entirely hilarious. The two of them had sat at their station and laughed until the teacher had sent them to the principal's office.

Finley wanted to derive some pleasure from the memory, but the experience at Eaton High suddenly seemed less than real. Once again, she was struck by a sensation of *otherness*—like she was an observer, separated from her native reality by a thick pane of glass. And that frightened her.

At the very least, there were rules in her native reality. If you did something bad—if you were caught cheating or shoplifting or defacing public property—you were disciplined. And if you did something good—if you helped an old lady across the street, studied an extra hour, or spent a day recycling aluminum cans—you were rewarded. The penalties and rewards might have been negligible, depending on the circumstance, but there were still *rules*. At the end of the day, doing good resulted in praise, and doing bad—dying Ms. Sheppard's dog the colors of the Jamaican flag, for instance—resulted in condemnation.

In this place, however, Finley wasn't sure there *were* any rules. She got the feeling that she was surrounded by forces much older—and much more apathetic—than she. When she looked up at the stars, she found herself wondering how many individual eyes were watching her; how many of them gave a shit about her very existence…and how many of them wanted to see her life actively snuffed out.

Knife in hand, she shuffled in a circle—once, twice, three times—then exhaled, and pressed the blade against her opposite palm. She hoped the cold would dull the pain when she eventually forced the tip downward and across, but she was disappointed. The moment the length of steel tore through her outer layer of flesh, she experienced a wave of red-hot agony, followed by nausea.

Blood.

It was the blood.

She'd never been a fan of the stuff.

Fingers trembling, curling and uncurling reflexively, dripping with hot and sticky plasma, she started toward the field. Halfway there, she realized she was still holding the knife, and she cast it into the dirt, revolted by the way her bodily fluids beaded on the oxidized finish.

Was she losing her mind?

The concept crossed her cerebral cortex as she separated the first row of stalks, but she didn't let it stop her. Sane or not, she was no longer the conductor aboard her life's train. She was merely a passenger. The engine would speed her along to the end of the line, with or without her consent, and then…

Ass-tit-hips, she thought, using her forearms to create a pathway through the corn. That was the word Destinee had used in art class. And when the teacher had asked Destinee to repeat the word, Destinee had complied. Happily.

The mental image briefly cheered Finley, but her exuberance was short-lived. Between rows fifteen and sixteen, she stepped on something sharp, and she stumbled. She tried to regain her balance by grasping one of the nearby shoots, but the plant wasn't up to the task. It crumpled under her weight, depositing her face-down in the next row.

Incensed, but too breathless to conjure more than a muted "fuck," Finley rose and rubbed the dirt from her wounded palm. She could feel something *inside* the cut, rubbing against the exposed nerves and blood vessels, but she couldn't bring herself to look at it. Even if it was a rock—and only a rock—she wouldn't have the wherewithal to excise it.

Teeth gritted, she pressed forward, careful not to plant her feet before her toes had a chance to test the earth. She tried to chart her progress by counting her steps and by traveling in—what she perceived to be—a straight line, but she was quickly disoriented. Even with the stars as a guide, she couldn't tell north from south or east from west. Which was unusual. She had grown up under the stars. Since the age of three, she'd memorized their constellations.

More proof that she had, somehow, slipped between dimensions? Or proof that her mental state was decaying, leaving her stranded in an ocean of uncertainty?

Finley made one more effort to locate Polaris, but abandoned the effort when she detected a disturbance to her left. Something had passed quickly, causing a small number of stalks to quiver. She could see the tassels swooning against the night sky, as if heralding the arrival of a foreign dignitary. Or a merciless conqueror.

No longer aware of the cold, Finley set her teeth and moved toward the disturbance. Any other night she would have done the exact opposite, as a presence in the midst of a vast and otherwise desolate cornfield was cause for alarm, if not full-blown panic, but she managed to reign in her apprehension.

This is it, a small voice said, from the bottommost depths of her skull. *This is what you've been waiting for. This is the moment of truth.*

The voice wasn't lying.

Twenty yards to the west—or was that north?—a low, mournful, warbling noise rose through the oceanic tide of cicada calls. It wasn't quite human, but it wasn't quite animal, either. It sounded *different*—like the death knell of a disemboweled elk.

Unable to pinpoint the source of the noise, Finley stopped; reevaluated her surroundings. She searched the dirt for footprints and the rows for displaced stalks, but her examination turned up little. So she changed her tactics.

"Hello?" she ventured, as loudly as her vocal chords would allow. "Are you there? If you are, please give me a sign."

She very nearly added the phrase "I'm ready," but "ready" wasn't entirely accurate. As much as she hated to admit it, she was afraid. She was frightened by the unknown *and* by the silhouette that abruptly materialized in her peripheral vision—the silhouette that seemed to swell amongst the darkness; that dissolved to nothingness as soon as she turned her body toward it.

Assuring herself that a combination of fear and paranoia was to blame for the apparition, she reigned in a breath, and pressed forward. She crossed one row, then two, then five, then…

Nothing.

Without warning, she stumbled onto a stretch of compacted, level earth, and her confusion caused her emergency brakes to engage. Her legs—simultaneously light with adrenaline and heavy with cold—ground to a halt, and both her hands tightened. She was tempted to fish the cell phone from her pocket and to use the onboard light, but she resisted the urge. There was nothing wrong, after all. She'd simply discovered one of the access roads that wove in and out of the corn.

Come on. Pull it together, Champ, she thought, standing in the middle of the pathway and flexing her toes. *You're letting the heebie-jeebies get the best of you.* Then: *The heebie-jeebies? For fuck's sake. You're sounding more like your mom every day.*

She wasn't a fan of the concept, but she didn't have to endure it for long. As she shuffled indecisively and contemplated her mother's favorite idioms, she detected a presence at the top—or was that the bottom?—of the road. She couldn't say, exactly, where the presence ended and the field began, as the thing was cloaked by a wall of fibrous stalks, but she could tell it was *there*. It wasn't merely a vision—a thing culled from the mire of her teenage desires. It had depth. Dimension.

Breath catching in her throat, Finley stepped in the phantom's direction. She expected it to react in some way—hoped it would react in some way, as even the slightest move would have helped define it; given it a concrete structure; stripped away the fangs and the sores and the crown of antlers—but it kept its place. It didn't crouch down, beckon to her, or even hiss.

Was it aware of her presence?

The closer Finley drew, the more she questioned her own senses. The thing seemed to expand and contract in time with her heartbeat, as if it was tied, somehow, to her own life force—as if her psyche was feeding it; giving it the power to manifest.

Unsure whether the ground beneath her feet was lengthening or whether her steps were shortening, Finley swallowed; ran her palms down her thighs. She wanted to assure herself that everything was going to be okay, but her internal voice was otherwise occupied.

Mr. Sticks, Mr. Sticks, master of tricks, she heard, from the depths of her consciousness. *Tall as a shadow and wide as a mouse. Call him and tease him, but don't disappease him…or you might end up stiff as Barb Klaus.*

It was a simple rhyme—a childish rhyme—but it was incredibly powerful. It reverberated in her head until it was more *real* than the rows of corn around her—until she could hear nothing else. But it dissolved as soon as she reached her destination.

The second her hand met the telltale wall of vegetation, everything in the world came to a screeching halt. The tassels stopped swaying, the cicadas stopped hissing, the coyotes stopped yowling, and the stars became a little less bright. It was as if a vortex had opened—as if an otherworldly proboscis had begun to suck the meat from reality's bones.

Unable to peel her gaze from the enigma, now less than six feet away, Finley groped blindly for her cell phone. It was a risky move, but she couldn't help herself. She had to share what she was experiencing. She had to let someone know that she *wasn't* crazy; that she'd been right from the beginning.

Temporarily blinded by the brightness of the LCD screen, Finley cued up a text message and typed out eleven words. She typed: *It's not a hoax. He's real. He's real and he's here.* Then a guttural laugh spread through the rows of color-bleached filaments, and Finley's phone plummeted to the earth.

Chapter 2

The town of Eaton greeted Lucia the same way it greeted the countless truckers, door-to-door salesmen, and traveling preachers who ventured across its borders. There were no parades, welcome banners, or even "glad to see you again; you've been gone for some time" smiles.

From the Eaton, Colorado: Our Happy Home Since 1892 signage to the used RV lot, which seemed more adept at growing weeds than soliciting the transfer of decade-old machinery, Lucia didn't spy a single sign of life. Unless rotting birds and coyote husks counted as "life."

Nauseated by the stench of a bisected skunk, Lucia rolled up her driver-side window and closed her air vents. She didn't want her brand-new Focus imbued with the odor of death and rectal fumes. It was on lease, so she was contractually obligated to keep it for a year. After that, well, the kind salespeople at Iron City Automotive could deal with the stench. Provided her sister didn't send her to an early grave.

Replaying their last conversation in her head, complete with the half answers and the inattentive sighs, Lucia grabbed for her cell phone. She knew she shouldn't be fiddling with the device while she was driving, since Eaton cops were sticklers about speed limits, and since, as the only major thoroughfare in town, Highway 85 was under constant surveillance, but she couldn't help herself. Her last five text messages had gone unanswered, and her sister's social media feed had been static since Saturday.

Two days, she thought, thumbing through her messages. *Two days, and no updates whatsoever.*

For a thirty-year-old man, two days of radio silence was par for the course, but for a sixteen-year-old girl—one who fostered accounts on Facebook, Twitter, Instagram, Pinterest, Tumblr, and YouTube—two days was an eternity. Finley might have been a tad bipolar—like her mother—but she had always kept her virtual presence up to date.

Finding no new information on the web, Lucia tossed her phone onto the passenger seat and focused on the highway before her. She could see the Stenson Company grain elevator and, beyond, the Great Western sugar plant, but she paid the structures little mind. Both had been abandoned for decades—so long they had come to symbolize the town and its "never say never" spirit.

In some ways, Eaton's unchanging nature was comforting...but not all of Lucia's memories were of the cute-and-fuzzy variety. Many of the sights transported her to a darker place. A place she had spent time and money to exercise.

Regardless, the picturesque swaths of corn brought a smile to her lips. Whenever Cozzens Lake—known locally as "Kissing Cozzens Lake"—had failed to alleviate the pressures of high school or home, she had taken solace in the seemingly endless rows.

Out there, in the midst of the stalks and the dirt and the silk, she had been able to *disappear*.

Startled by the horn of a passing trucker, Lucia jumped; checked her gauges. According to her speedometer, she was going forty-five miles an hour—ten under the speed limit. And she was traveling in the left lane, to boot.

Waving sheepishly at the trucker's rearview mirror, Lucia merged into the slow lane and shifted her focus to the west—to the warehouses and manufacturing plants that dotted the highway. She knew a couple of them were permanently shuttered, but she couldn't rightly tell the active from the inactive. For better or worse, business owners in Eaton tended to abide by the "it ain't broke, so don't fix it" mentality—even if the object in question was broken, and in need of fixing.

At 5th Street, the warehouses gave way to manicured lawns, budding trees, and modest, turn-of-the-century churches, but the gentrification was severely limited. A block to the west, the lots lost their polish and luster. Grass was replaced by gravel, flower beds were replaced by weeds, and model-year SUVs were replaced by incapacitated fifth wheels. There was a sugar beet field visible near the end of the road, where the pavement doglegged south and wound into more respectable neighborhoods, but it was overshadowed by a large—and somewhat disconcerting—jumble of mobile homes.

Distinctly aware that her Focus was the nicest car in the area, but determined not to be intimidated by that fact, Lucia pulled to the curb, killed the engine, and studied her reflection in the vanity mirror. She'd visited her hair stylist the previous day, and had added highlights to her shoulder-length brown hair, but she now questioned whether the addition was too much. Did it make her look, well, *floofy*? Lucia hated the term—it was a word her mother used to describe hoity-toity, overly-groomed out-of-towners—but it had become ingrained in her personal vocabulary. Much like *wuss, janky*, and the *heebie-jeebies*.

"Shit. You're doing it again. You're over-thinking it," she told herself, when her self-appraisal turned to her pencil skirt, button-up blouse, and open-toed heels. "You just need to step outside, and get on with it. You don't live here anymore. You got out."

Hadn't she?

The moment she opened her door and inhaled the heady mixture of compost, pollen, and prairie dust, she experienced a rush of nostalgia, and her heart stumbled in her chest. Even though she hadn't ventured down these streets in years, she felt an uncomfortable pull. It was as if the town was calling out to her; wrapping itself around her; begging her to stay.

Hoping her Estee Lauder makeup was sufficient to conceal her anxiety-deepened eyes, she stepped out of the Focus and took in her mother's lot—the lot with the dilapidated fence, the plastic patio furniture, and the olive-green single-wide, complete with the cardboard-covered living room window. She wanted dearly to walk, unencumbered, to the front door, and to show her mother how far she'd come, but she didn't have that much faith in herself.

Releasing a desultory sigh, she reached past the center console and withdrew her Dirty Secret. It wasn't anything more than a matte black cane with a Fritz handle, but the mere sight made her bristle. To her, it was a sign of weakness. It was a painfully visible reminder that she was not *normal*—that, centimeters beneath the surface, there was something fundamentally *wrong* with her. Something that a thousand layers of Estee Lauder-brand makeup couldn't conceal.

Armed with her least favorite accessory, she closed her door, locked up, and started for her mother's pitiful excuse for a front yard. In years past, the woman had kept a hot tub around back, and had spent whole days in its bubbling waters, drinking champagne and watching her "stories" on a twelve-inch television, but the hot tub was no longer in service. Lucia could see the thing from the curb—could see the mud-smeared cabinet and the leaf-filled shell. Given a stick of dynamite, she would have gladly blown the thing sky-high. Then she would have turned to the house proper, and asked for another.

There was nothing remotely endearing or welcoming about the residence. The paint on the exterior was old and chipped, the roof was shedding shingles faster than a mange-stricken dog, and the few undamaged windows were foggy and dotted with Christmas stickers.

Lucia was fairly sure that, in three thousand years, archaeologists would pull the remains of the trailer from the dust, and would declare the Santa Claus likenesses an advanced form of hieroglyphic.

Was Lucia secretly pleased by her own apartment's superiority? Yes. Of course she was. But she was saddened as well. She was disappointed that her own mother could find contentment in such filth. Didn't the woman have standards? Wasn't she repulsed by the raccoon feces and the wasps' nests and the general aura of decay?

Making sure to avoid any substances that might stain and/or leave a lasting odor on her person, Lucia ascended the rickety steps and knocked at the door. She was certain her mother was home, since the woman's 1989 Jeep Grand Cherokee was outfitted with two all-terrain tires and two cinder blocks, and since Mike's Place didn't open until four o'clock, but she detected no noises from within.

Following thirty seconds of stillness, she tested the doorknob, found it unlocked, and gave it a shove. She was worried, initially, that the barrier would rebound off a wall, or otherwise betray her presence in the neighborhood, but her fears were quickly put to rest. There were so many pizza boxes, milk jugs, and soda bottles scattered across the floor that the door couldn't open more than a few feet.

Swallowing her revulsion, Lucia stepped across the threshold... and immediately released a squeal of terror. She regretted the noise as soon as her brain identified the brown blur as a mouse and not an oversized spider, but by then the shriek was already echoing into nonexistence.

"Little Red? That you?" a disoriented, sleep-thickened voice said from the master bedroom. "If it is, turn that damned TV down. How many times have I told you to keep it quiet during Mommy's nap time, huh?"

"Not enough, apparently," Lucia remarked, using her cane to sift through the gossip rags that cluttered the coffee table. "Also, it's not Little Red. It's your other daughter. The one you haven't seen since Thanksgiving. Of 2012."

It wasn't the sharpest barb in her arsenal—she had a number of scathing critiques, which she kept in a shoebox, and which she revisited and revised whenever she was feeling blue—but it was good enough to earn a moment of stunned silence.

"Lucia?" the voice croaked at last. "Lucia Cameron Corvi?"

"The one and only," Lucia replied, seconds before the voice's owner appeared at the end of the hallway, clad in a fluffy pink robe and matching slippers. "Surprised?"

"No. Not surprised. *Delighted*," the woman said, hurrying across the carpet as fast as her razor-burnt legs would allow. "How long has it been? A year?"

"Five, actually," Lucia started to say.

She was cut off by a wild, bear-like hug.

"Whatever the case, it's been too long," the woman concluded, burying her face in Lucia's neck. She smelled of menthol cigarettes, gin, sweat, and body odor, but she didn't seem to notice. She prolonged the embrace until Lucia finally managed to free her arms.

"Glad to see you, too, Mom," Lucia lied as she edged in the other direction. "But I'm not here to socialize. I'm here because I need to talk to Finley."

"Finley?" Her mother frowned. "Why on earth do you want to

talk to *her*? She hasn't done anything *illegal*, has she?"

"No. At least...not that I'm aware of," Lucia said, using her free hand to brush a strand of hair from her forehead, then to straighten her blouse. "I last heard from her on Saturday. You don't happen to know where she is, do you?"

"No. I'm afraid not," her mother said, while patting absentmindedly at her pockets. "Your sister is...ah...a bit of a free spirit. She comes and goes as she pleases. Some nights she stays at your father's, and others...well...she doesn't."

"Which means...?"

Her mother shrugged, pressed a cigarette between her lips, and flicked at a dime-store lighter. "Your guess is as good as mine, darlin'," she said between puffs. "Hell, you remember what it was like to be a teenager. All those hormones rushin' around, makin' a mess of things. Not to mention high school."

A pause.

When the woman's voice returned, it was more relaxed. Sedated. As if the nicotine was singlehandedly taking over her system; transforming her into a middle-aged zombie.

"I learned a long time ago that it's best to step back and let nature take its course," she continued. "When I was a girl, my mother—"

"Was a tyrant. Yes. I've heard the story a million times," Lucia interrupted. She was losing patience with her mother—with those glazed, half-present eyes, thin lips, and tangles of fiery red hair—but she had to keep her cool. She couldn't afford a Thanksgiving 2012-level meltdown. At least...not until she found her sister. Once everything was sorted out, and her worries were put to rest, she could open the floodgates and really let her parents have it. But patience was key.

"Look. I'm only here for Finley," she said in the lowest, most controlled tone she could muster. "I think she may be in trouble. The faster I find her, the faster I can get back to the city."

"Then you've got your work cut out for you," her mother smirked. "I haven't seen her since Friday. No...Thursday. I was on my way home from work, and I passed her. She was walkin' on the side of the road."

"Alone?"

"No. She was with someone."

"Who?"

"I didn't get a good look. One of her friends, I think."

"And you didn't bother to say hello?"

"Are you kidding?" the woman laughed, jettisoning wisps of smoke into the air. "I'm her *mother*. If she had money, she'd *pay me* to not speak to her in public. The last time I waved to her, downtown, I thought she was going to have a heart attack. Besides, she might've been with a boy."

"And that's relevant because…?"

"Sex, of course," Lucia's mother said, with an apathetic wave. "Finley's a young woman. Do *you* think she wants her mother to know who she's sleeping with?"

The woman attempted another laugh, but it wasn't a genuine article. It sounded wooden and desperate, perhaps due to the look that crystallized on Lucia's face.

"She's *sixteen*," Lucia deadpanned, feeling her eyebrows draw gradually downward. "That makes her a *girl*. Not a *woman*. She's not even old enough to *drive*. Does she…"

Lucia cut herself short. As much as she wanted to inquire about birth control, she had to maintain her focus. She wasn't the girl's legal guardian, after all. If Finley wanted to have sex, and Finley's mother supported that decision, there was little Lucia could do about it.

Frustrated, but resolved not to let the depth of her frustration show, Lucia thanked her mother for the information, and took her leave. She half expected the woman to swoop in for a farewell hug as she navigated the front steps, but her mother was too busy fishing for another cigarette. She *did* hear a shrill, "Don't be a stranger, now!" as she slipped into her Focus, but she refused to acknowledge it.

Somehow, the scent of her mother's robe was stronger and more repelling than the odor of the dead skunk.

Chapter 3

Two blocks to the west, and two blocks south, Lucia pulled to a stop. She was in a better neighborhood—an older neighborhood, complete with maple trees, picket fences, and dainty bungalows that looked as though they had been plucked from the same mail-order catalogue—but she still double-checked her surroundings before she stepped outside. She didn't want someone from her past spying her and striking up an overly long and overly personal conversation. There was a reason she'd chosen the big city over a small town. In the city, you could operate with a degree of anonymity. You could shop and eat and relax without fear of being recognized. In a town—especially a town of 4,500—you were constantly in one limelight or another.

While that small-town sense of community was appealing, from time to time, Lucia didn't miss the gossiping or the backbiting or the petty squabbling. Because everyone knew everyone in Small Town, USA, and because everyone was on a first-name basis, there was no such thing as a private matter. Every victory and defeat—every accomplishment and embarrassment—was subject to public scrutiny and opinion.

There were different cliques in Eaton, of course, but each was interconnected, and each was insufferable in a unique and terrible way. The churchgoing crowd was stuffy and moralistic, the atheists were sanctimonious and snobbish, the farmers were grumpy and isolationistic, and the jocks were, well, the jocks. They all managed to live together on the same 1.9-square-mile piece of land, but they were never quiet about their differences, whether politically, religiously, or otherwise. They seemed to draw strength from the insignificant local events that divided them.

Mr. Sticks

Noticing movement in a window down the street, Lucia locked her car—with the key, not the fob, to avoid the telltale *bleep!*—and hurried toward her father's house. She'd opted to park on the opposite curb, since her father's lot was bordered by rusted boats and trailers, so she didn't see the woman in the red hat until the woman was halfway down her father's front walk. At that point, she could've said hello, but there was something odd about the woman's posture and pace.

Was the woman simply preoccupied, or was she anxious to leave?

Unable to tell, one way or another, Lucia watched the woman drive away. Then she went straight to her father's door, and snapped her cane against the knocker.

She wasn't alone for long.

"Couldn't wait for round two, huh?" her father called as he tugged at the barrier. "Can't say I blame you, really. If I was in your shoes—"

"Yes?" Lucia said expectantly, locking eyes with the man who had taught her to fish, to drive, and to cuss—albeit with the grace and sophistication of a little lady. "What's this about *round two*?"

"It's…ah…it's nothing. I thought you were someone else," her father stammered, while discreetly making sure his fly was zipped. He looked a touch older than she remembered him, but not excessively so. If anything, the touches of gray at his temples added to his roguish charm.

"Still trying to pull off the goatee, I see," she remarked, in order to keep the awkward silence, which seemed to follow her around like a puppy, at bay. "Hasn't anyone told you that the greasy pirate look went out of style in the mid-nineties?"

"No. And for your information, I'm not *trying* to pull it off," her father said, absent a trace of irony. "This facial hair is a tribute to manliness, and I've been successfully pulling it off since the year 2000. But that's enough about me. What brings you back to our happy little town? That English teacher of yours finally kick the bucket?"

"Mr. Freeland? No. He has more lives than a cat," Lucia grinned. "I'm actually looking for Finley. Mom said she may be over here. You haven't seen her since Saturday, have you?"

"Since Saturday? Nope. Can't say I have," her father said, retreating from the doorway and beckoning for her to follow. "She did spend the night on Tuesday and Wednesday, but we didn't talk much. She said she was busy—studying for finals and all that jazz."

"Was she with anyone?"

"No one but her shadow."

"You're sure?"

"What am I, an omniscient guard dog?" her father's voice echoed from the living room.

By the time Lucia caught up to him, he was sprawled in his favorite recliner, and he was thumbing through the *North Weld Herald's* sports section. There was an uncomfortably musky odor to the place—an odor that could only be created by two consenting adults with vigorous libidos—but Lucia chose not to mention it. Instead, she took a brief tour of the room, reacquainted herself with the barren walls, the painfully outdated drapes, and the perpetually-stained carpet, and asked about Finley's temperament.

"Did she seem worried, anxious, or afraid?" she inquired as she paced. "The last few times we talked on the phone, she sounded...I don't know...*listless*. Like she was preoccupied with something."

"Schoolwork, maybe?" her father volunteered, flipping from one page to the next.

Lucia shook her head. "No. Finley's never been one to fret about homework. Maybe she's having boy problems. Or maybe she's—"

"Hit that age where it's no longer cool to have hour-long chats with her older sister?" her father guessed, adding a "Have you considered that line of reasoning, Sherlock?" look for good measure. Lucia doubted that he meant to offend with it, but she experienced a pang of resentment anyway.

Ever since Finley had turned fourteen, Finley had been gradually pulling away. Both from her parents, and from Lucia. To bridge that gap, Lucia had been placing regular phone calls, sending regular text messages, and instigating regular Skype sessions. But her parents? Her parents had been too busy bickering and slandering to notice the growing chasm. To them, Finley was an object to squabble over; another reason to scream when they crossed paths in the grocery store.

"Whatever the case, I'm sure your sister is fine," her father concluded, at long last. "She may not have Corvi blood running through her veins, but she's damned headstrong. Just like you. I'm sure she'll turn up in a day or two."

"And if she doesn't?" Lucia retaliated.

Her father didn't react in kind.

With leisurely, deliberate movements, he folded up the paper, placed it on the side table, leaned forward until his forearms were resting on his knees, and said: "Do you have any idea how many times that girl has gone missing in the past twelve months? I stopped counting in February because it was a biweekly occurrence. She turns up and disappears like a damned fairy. But she never goes far, and she never stays missing for long."

"Maybe not...but she's *sixteen*," Lucia reiterated. She was beginning to sound like a broken record, but she couldn't help it. Her parents were treating their teenage daughter like a grown-ass adult. Or worse—like a stray cat. Neither of them seemed particularly concerned, or the least bit inclined to remedy the situation.

"Tell you what?" her father said, rising from his chair in response to her bunched eyebrows and flaring nostrils. "Why don't you stay here for the next few days? That way, when Finley does show up, you can be the first to interrogate her. Or you can use this as your base of operations, and you can track her down yourself. Either way, you're welcome to the bedroom down the hall. Deal?"

Lucia swallowed. Her knee-jerk reaction was to say, "Thanks, but no thanks," and to hightail it to a motel in a nearby town, but who was she kidding? She couldn't afford a motel room on top of her rent payments, utility payments, car payments, insurance payments, and college loans. She was barely making it as it was.

"Fine. We have a deal," she relented, following a Doberman-sized intermission. "On the condition that, when I find Finley, you'll buy a shock collar, and help me put it on her. Can you do that?"

"As long as the pet store has her size in stock. No problem," her father grinned. "I should warn you, though: these walls are thin. You may hear some strange noises, late at night, and you may be tempted to call the police. But you shouldn't follow through. It's—"

"None of my business. I get it," Lucia interjected, before her father could share too much information, and forever transform her remaining sweet dreams into unmentionable nightmares. "If I hear anything after seven o'clock, I'll take a sleeping pill and put a pillow over my head."

It was a simple solution to a simple problem, but her father favored her with a "that's my girl" laugh, regardless, and led her down the hall, to the spare bedroom. To his credit, he did his best to make her comfortable—he dressed the bed with fresh sheets, emptied out the wastebaskets, and warned her about the hot water knob in the shower—but there remained an unspoken barrier between them. She felt it ebb when he made a comment about her career, but it returned the moment he asked about Michael.

"Dad, Michael and I haven't been an item in *years*," she said as the two of them straightened the comforter. "I dumped him after I caught him sleeping with my roommate."

"The blond one?" her father frowned, as if the color of the roommate's hair might, somehow, explain the indiscretion, and make it all okay. It was the type of free-spirited, devil-may-care response that made middle-aged women swoon and insecure husbands bristle, but it had a different effect on Lucia. It made her *sad*. It reminded her that her father had not been a part of her life in quite some time.

Following fifteen minutes of polite, if mundane, conversation, Lucia excused herself and retreated to her Focus. She couldn't endure an entire afternoon of yes and no questions. She had to get out. Before she went off the deep end.

Chapter 4

The Eaton Police Department headquarters was, not surprisingly, the newest and most impressive building in town. It was positioned on the corner of 1st and Maple, as if to assert its dominance over the cars and people who frequented the intersection, and it made the entire block look decrepit in comparison.

It was sad, Lucia thought, that the town relied so heavily on income from speeding tickets and parking violations, but then, the local economy wasn't exactly booming. Half of the buildings on 1st Street, between Maple and Elm, were vacant, and the other half were old-as-dirt mom-and-pop shops that averaged two sales a week and kept the most bizarre hours imaginable. One shop, surreptitiously called The French District, even had a sign in the window that said: "We are now Closed. We will open when the owner feels like it. Please have a good day."

That small town "What the hell?" mindset drove Lucia crazy, but she resisted the urge to make her opinions known. She simply parked in front of an animal sanctuary, which may or may not have doubled as a serial killer's weekend lair, and made a beeline for the police department's front door. She probably shouldn't have jaywalked as she did so, but there were precious few squad cars in the lot. Besides, the streets were nigh empty. She could have changed clothes and jump roped in the middle of the intersection without incident.

Inside the lobby, she soaked in the floor mosaic, which depicted a badge, a mountain range, and the phrase "To Serve and Protect," and proceeded to the big Formica-topped desk, which took up two thirds of the far wall. Everything was very clean and very polished, but the whole place lacked *identity*. Either a robot had been the lead designer, or the city had contracted with the least imaginative human on the planet.

As if to add weight to the robot theory, the officer at the front desk—Maria Gonzalez, according to her nametag—failed to look up until Lucia cleared her throat. Then the officer smiled a plasticine smile and said: "Hello, there. How can I help you today?"

"Well…I'm here in regard to my sister," Lucia began, transferring her cane from hand to hand. "She hasn't been seen in forty-eight hours, and—"

"Name?" the officer interrupted, producing a clipboard, and jotting a date onto an official-looking form. Her movements were crisp and professional, but her voice was steeped in boredom. She couldn't have sounded less enthusiastic if she'd tried.

"It's…ah…Finley. Finley Corvi," Lucia said, working overtime to keep her tone even and respectful. "Her home address is 313 Park Avenue."

"And you say she's been gone for forty-eight hours?"

"Yes. That's right."

"Which makes you…?"

"Her sister. Or rather…her half-sister," Lucia said. Then she realized the officer was no longer adding detail to the form, and she stopped herself. "Is something wrong?" she inquired, when it became apparent that the officer was not about to explain her actions.

The officer answered Lucia with a sigh and a half-completed eye roll.

"No. Nothing's wrong," the officer said, clicking her pen shut and stowing it in her breast pocket. "It's just…your sister has a reputation. A bad reputation. She—"

"Has a tendency to run away from time to time. Yes. I'm aware," Lucia said. "But this time's different. This time, I think she's in trouble. My mother—"

"Has a reputation of her own," the officer said, proving once and for all that she possessed the interpersonal skills of a sociopathic butcher. "Just last week, we brought her in for disturbing the peace. She was standing in the street, drunk as a skunk, screaming your father's name. Along with a number of expletives. But that's nothing compared to your sister.

"Last month alone, we booked Finley for three separate crimes. The first was petty theft. She was caught stealing three-two beer and cigarettes from the gas station on Collins. Then she was brought in for possession of a controlled substance. One of our officers found her smoking a doobie behind the high school. And the third? Well...she was apprehended for painting Ms. Sheppard's poodle green, yellow, and black."

"Damned thing *still* looks like a creature from another dimension," another officer said, emerging from the hall behind the desk. He was tall and tanned and possessed the lean-but-muscular figure of a seasoned cattle hand, and he tipped his hat as he approached the station.

"The name's Dan," he said, without taking his eyes from Lucia. "My friends in Nebraska call me *Steely Dan*, on account of my profession and my appreciation for classic rock, but you can just call me Dan. I'm the community service officer. I guess you could say that it's my job to maintain good relations with all our fine citizens."

"Then you've interacted with Finley?" Lucia said, experiencing a spark of hope. She suspected that the entrance was an act—that she was supposed to be taken off guard by his easy smile and laid-back charm; that he'd employed the method on countless other young women, with excellent results—but she was willing to give him the benefit of the doubt. Especially if he was able to point her to her sister.

Dan didn't disappoint.

"Of course I've interacted with her!" the man chuckled. "Her freshman year at Eaton High, she attended all my presentations. She even volunteered for my Twenty-One Means Twenty-One anti-underage-drinking campaign and footrace. She was quite a lightning rod. Then she started hanging out with that Cutler girl, and her personality changed. She stopped showing up for events, and she started skipping out on classes; hanging with the stoner crowd."

"The stoner crowd?"

"Yeah. You know: kids who smoke Mary Jane, steal whiskey from their parents' liquor cabinets, vandalize buildings, and generally cause a nuisance?" Officer Gonzalez said.

Lucia chose not to dignify that with a response. To Dan, and to Dan alone, she said: "How many kids are a part of the stoner crowd? Do you know their names?"

"All of them? No. But I know the ringleaders," Dan said. "There's Eddie Tate, Jack Thompson, Marissa Pyle, and—of course—Destinee Cutler. Most of them hang out in the school parking lot after class, and most of them are pretty familiar with the inside of our cells. I doubt many of them are as close as Destinee and Finley, though. Those two do everything together. They're a cuter version of Butch Cassidy and the Sundance Kid."

"In other words, the Cutler girl is a good place to start," Lucia murmured, more to herself than to the officers behind the desk. Then she straightened and said: "You wouldn't happen to have a picture of the Cutler girl, would you?"

"Outside of a booking photo? No. But she's hard to miss," Dan said, hands on hips. "She's the only girl in the entire school with blue hair. You find the chick with the black T-shirt, the military boots, and the blue hair, and you've found Destinee."

Chapter 5

While Lucia was frustrated by the interaction in the police station—by Officer Gonzalez' indifference to the news of her sister's disappearance, and the department's refusal to file a missing person report—she was, nevertheless, thankful for Dan's assistance. The man had given her more information than her mother and father combined, and he'd done it with consummate professionalism. Which led her to wonder...

Had her off-the-cuff estimation been wrong? Had Dan not been hitting on her? Had the "aw shucks" personality and charismatic smile been genuine? Or had he finally noticed her cane, and decided to cut the mating dance short?

To her chagrin, she kept thinking back to his dimpled cheeks and his understated country boy drawl. She made an effort to direct her concentration elsewhere but, sitting in the high school parking lot, her car shut off to save the battery, there wasn't much to concentrate *on*. The school itself was a drab utilitarian structure, and the fields beyond were all but empty. There was a single maintenance worker in the midst of the grassy space, laying twine, but he seemed about as thrilled with his job as Officer Gonzalez was with hers.

Feeling an uncomfortable weight in her bladder, Lucia shifted; twisted the key in the ignition just long enough to read the time on the dashboard monitor.

3:20 p.m.

Based upon her knowledge of Eaton High, the last classes of the day would let out in ten minutes. She didn't expect many parents to arrive, since most of the students lived within walking distance of the school, and since most of the parents commuted to work, but she kept her head on a swivel anyway. With her luck, one of the paranoid parents would arrive, peg her as a suspicious individual, and call the cops.

Seeing Officer Gonzalez' smirk in her mind's eye, Lucia leaned back, and watched the first few chauffeurs enter the lot. They opted to form a line outside the front steps, rather than to take a parking space, so she didn't get to witness the doors opening or the initial wave of students bursting forth. But the visual wasn't necessary. Between the sound of the bell, the hoots of excitement, the rustle of paperwork, and the pitter-patter of a hundred feet, she knew precisely what was taking place.

Okay. Assuming Dan is on the ball, Destinee will be showing up at any moment, she thought, scanning the rows of baggy pants, baseball caps, and zit-covered faces.

Some of the students clumped together on the sidewalks and talked, upon leaving the building, but most fanned out and went their separate ways—made tracks for bikes and cars and pickups.

Ten years earlier, when Lucia had attended the school, there had been roughly three hundred students. Now, there appeared to be four hundred and fifty...if not five hundred. She made a halfhearted attempt to count the teenagers as they swarmed around her, but the identical letter jackets—red wool, with cream-colored leather sleeves and rib-trimmed collars—made the effort incalculably harder.

"Does everyone in this damned school play sports?" she muttered to the emptiness in her passenger seat. Then she noticed a flash of pale blue amongst a pocket of black, and she jerked forward. Were her eyes playing tricks on her, or...

No.

She wasn't mistaken.

There, next to the bicycle rack, surrounded by boys in dated leather jackets and girls in fishnet stockings, was a chick with shoulder-length blue hair, a black T-shirt, and military boots. The shirt itself was a recent purchase, as the dye was vibrant and the material was unmarked, but the hair was another matter. It appeared, from a distance, as though she had run out of blue coloring in the middle of the process, but had soldiered on, regardless.

A nice touch, Lucia thought. *Nice, but unconvincing.*

Thanks to her tenure in the city, Lucia knew the difference between punks and posers. And Destinee was a major poser. Real punks didn't wear foundation, own designer jeans, or rock jewelry from Hot Topic. Real punks didn't have manicured nails, or carry wallets embroidered with the anarchist symbol. Real punks were dirty and broke and—frequently—high on a substance other than life.

From the get-go, Destinee struck Lucia as a scene kid; a Disneyfied version of the real enchilada; a suburban princess with a rebellious streak. She had no doubt that several years of hard living could transform the girl from chic to freak, but she also doubted that Destinee would ever stoop to such a level. One taste of the real world and Destinee would return to her white, middle-class roots.

Steeling herself for the impending confrontation—and it would be a confrontation; posers were automatically insecure, and therefore defensive—Lucia stepped out of her car. She heard someone yell something about the superiority of trucks—about how all car owners were gay—as she withdrew her cane, but she dismissed it out of hand. High school students were, in her estimation, no more than overgrown toddlers. If you didn't give them the time of day, they would inevitably tire and turn their miniscule attention spans to other subjects.

Thankful that her own high school experience was safely in the rearview mirror, Lucia followed Destinee and her minions to the far side of the lot, where they gathered around a Buick station wagon of indeterminate age. She was worried, at first, that they would pile into the rust bucket and peel away, but they were in no hurry to leave. A couple of them sat down on the hood, while a couple of others made themselves comfortable on the roof.

In short order, a lighter was produced, and a pack of cigarettes was passed around, along with a few that were hand-rolled, and that looked about as legitimate as a pyramid scheme run by wealthy ex-convicts.

While the acrid, no-brand cancer sticks were pungent, they couldn't quite overpower the stinky-sweet odor of marijuana. Lucia caught a whiff as she closed upon the rag-tag group, and she resisted the compulsion to cough.

What the kids were smoking…it wasn't marijuana proper. It smelled like a mixture of resin and stems, collected from better harvests. Too much of that, and everyone in a twenty-foot radius would wind up with one hell of a headache.

The kids didn't seem to notice.

"Hey. Who's this?" one of the female lackeys said, when Lucia drew within ten yards. The girl was dressed in a frilly skirt and a low-cut top—standard fare for her generation—but her platform boots and her limited color pallet betrayed her social identification. She could have passed as a smaller, less charismatic Harley Quinn. With acne.

"She the new counselor?" inquired a boy with a lip ring and a peach-fuzzed chin. Lucia pegged him as the primary drug procurer, due to his missing teeth, receding gum line, and half-present gaze, so she didn't direct her response toward him, or even to Ms. Quinn. She spoke directly to the queen bee.

"Actually, I'm not affiliated with the school at all," she said, towing the line between authoritarian and friendly. "I'm here because of Finley."

"And…?" Destinee said, flicking a finger of ash from her cigarette. "As you can see, Finley isn't here right now. You'll have to try back later. Unless…" She emitted a self-satisfied cluck. "You aren't *blind*, are you?"

"No. I'm not *blind*," Lucia returned, shrugging off the pointed glances at her cane, as well as the round of subdued laughter. "I'm Finley's sister. Lucia. Lucia Corvi."

"Ah! The one with MS!" Destinee exclaimed. "That's right. Finley's told me all about you. You're quite a celebrity around these parts."

Another round of laughter.

"I hear they ran a newspaper story on you and everything," Destinee continued, when the chuckles and giggles and playful nudges subsided. "I haven't read it myself, but I'm sure it's inspirational. How old were you when you were diagnosed, again? Eighteen?"

"Seventeen," Lucia said. "I had my first attack the day before a swim meet. Ruined my chance to compete for the state title. But that's old news. Right now, I'm looking for my sister."

"Then why are you still here?" a boy in a battle jacket said. He opened his mouth to continue, but Lucia wasn't in the mood to hear his opinion.

"I'm here because Finley is missing, and I was told that one of you could help me track her down," she explained, quickly and professionally. A part of her wanted to use the marijuana angle as leverage, to achieve her desired goals, but another part pumped the brakes. In a social setting, threats were unlikely to get her anywhere. Threats would only make the kids puff out their chests, and further alienate them.

Perhaps sensing Lucia's powerlessness, Destinee's minions began extinguishing their cigarettes, and leaving in groups of twos and threes. A few muttered something about a "harsh vibe" while stalking off, but Lucia didn't press the issue.

Her moment of opportunity was narrowing.

"I'm not interested in getting Finley in trouble. Honest," she continued, when Destinee ground her own cigarette under her heel, and tugged at the station wagon's passenger-side door. "I just want to make sure my sister is alright. Can you *please* help me out?"

It was a last-ditch appeal, bordering on desperation, but Lucia didn't have any other options. She hoped—no, *prayed*—that Destinee would hear the sincerity in her voice, and take pity on her. After all, Finley was Destinee's best friend.

Wasn't she?

Based on the look of boredom that crossed Destinee's face— on the way she slumped into the passenger seat and pushed the windswept blond and blue hair from her face—the girl was wading in a pool of apathy. There wasn't a glimmer of concern or sympathy in her aristocratic baby blues. But she didn't order Peach Fuzz to toss the old Buick into gear. Rather, she looked Lucia up and down, and said: "How much you got?"

"As in...money?" Lucia stammered. "I...I don't have anything on me…but I should have a twenty in my car. Why?"

Destinee and Peach Fuzz exchanged glances.

"That'll do," Destinee concluded. "But don't consider it anything other than a onetime fee. If you need something else down the road, it'll cost you extra."

"Double," Peach Fuzz chimed in.

Destinee released a dramatic sigh. Then she plucked a rolling paper from the glove compartment, scrolled a name onto it via permanent marker, and said: "Here. This is Finley's boyfriend. If I were you, I'd pay him a visit. The two of them are probably having sex as we speak."

"And if they're not?" Lucia inquired, waiting patiently for the scrap of paper to move in her direction. "Am I entitled to a refund?"

In response, Peach Fuzz snorted. For an entrepreneur, he wasn't particularly interested in customer satisfaction.

Chapter 6

Exhausted by the conversation in the high school parking lot, but no less determined, Lucia approached the West Weld Feed and Tack. The building may have been modeled after a barn, down to the red and white color scheme and the gambrel roof, but the interior was surprisingly clean. The epoxy floors, though dated, were expertly polished, and reflected the fluorescent lights, which hung from the rafters, and which emitted a continuous buzz. Said buzz wasn't particularly loud, but was noticeable in the gaps between the country hits. When there wasn't a full-size diesel truck idling outside, of course.

Absorbing Merle Haggard's "Workin' Man Blues," Lucia wandered through the aisles, poking this and prodding that. There were cabinets near the checkout lanes, which displayed cattle roping trophies, signed photos, scarred chaps, and other bits of paraphernalia, won and collected by enterprising locals, but she didn't move to take a closer look. She'd seen them before. Hell, she'd *dusted* them before.

During her high school years, the cabinets had been unlocked, but something had clearly gone sideways in the interim. Now, each display was fitted with a chain and a padlock. She could see no cameras in the corners, but there was definitely a security device inside the front doors. It was big and bulky and gray, and it looked distinctly out of place among the horse blankets, the bags of feed, the dog toys, the saddles, and the lawn fertilizer.

I guess Bob Dylan was right, she thought as she passed a cardboard standee of John Wayne. *The times really are a-changin'.* Then she heard a rustle near the back, where the boots and fishing rods were kept, and she angled toward the source of the noise.

As she walked, the odor changed from grain and straw to leather and rubber, freshly manufactured, but she staved off the related memories. Unlike her father's house and her mother's trailer, the Feed and Tack retained a soft spot in her heart, and she wanted to keep it there. She didn't want her own stilted recollections to poison it. For the record—

"Can I help you, miss?"

The voice came from above her, and she jerked to a halt, relying on her cane to stop her forward momentum. Or…she relied on her cane until it slipped on the polished epoxy. Then she threw her arms forward and grasped a display shelf, to keep from falling flat on her face.

Once her footing was secured and her balance was again under control, she looked up, and found a young man on a ladder. She should have noticed him earlier—he was clad in a green apron, with a stack of cowboy hats in one hand and a hammer in the other—but she chalked the oversight up to her distracted state of mind.

"Oh. No. I'm just browsing," she said, pretending to admire the items on the display shelf, which may or may not have saved her life seconds before. "You hung one of those pegs off-center, by the way. It's making the whole thing look wonky."

"Wonky?" the young man returned, flashing a crooked but attractive grin. "Is that one of the five-dollar words Mr. Freeland taught you?"

"No. I'm borrowing it from my mom's vocabulary," Lucia said, stepping to the side so the young man could descend the ladder. And in response to the crackle of laughter that followed: "I guess you've probably heard about what she did last week, huh?"

"Yeah. I have," the young man admitted, placing the cowboy hats on a bench and slapping ineffectually at his dusty apron. "But to be fair, so has half the town. I'm pretty sure her voice carried all the way to Lucerne. Which makes her—and by extension, *you*—a bit of a celebrity."

"According to who?"

"Anyone who matters, really. The cops. The mayor. That coyote who lives under Mr. Ander's porch."

"He's still there?"

"You better believe it."

"And that godawful hen that used to hang out in front of the hardware store?"

"Long gone. Mr. Harvey found it in the street one morning, dead as a doorknob."

"Foul play?"

"I doubt it. There were no other chickens in the vicinity."

Lucia nodded somberly. Then the joke hit her, and she lashed out with her free hand, catching the young man on the shoulder before he could twist away. That was precisely his style: to lure her into a seemingly innocuous conversation, to make a pun, and to maintain a perfectly straight face until she finally caught on.

"That's bad," she admonished as he rubbed theatrically at his shoulder. "That's the kind of lowbrow humor you were known for in high school. But I guess I'm not surprised. Not much has changed around here. That old Marlboro Man advertisement is still up in the window, and you're still stocking shelves."

"When I'm not making schedules, ordering products, auditing inventory, or hiring employees," the young man said, plucking the nametag from his shirt, and flipping it in Lucia's direction.

Lucia caught the tag with minimal difficulty—in her case, fumbling and nearly dropping it—and turned it over in her palm.

"Brian Van Pelt, Store Manager," she recited. "Looks like someone scammed his boss into a promotion." Then she handed the tag back and said: "Congratulations. How long have you been captain of this fine ship? A month?"

"More like twelve of them. Times four," Brian said. "There's no water on the main deck because we have a pump running, twenty-four seven, down below."

"Ah. So the ship isn't exactly sinking. It's just leaking profusely," Lucia smirked. "Knowing you, it's probably held together by duct tape."

"And bubble gum," he corrected. "Don't forget the bubble gum!"

"I wouldn't dare," Lucia snickered. Then she realized she was doing the thing she used to do in the presence of high school crushes—she was standing with one leg slightly bent, one shoulder cocked, and her head tilted back just enough to highlight her high cheekbones—and she shifted into a more neutral stance.

She wasn't in town to strike up any old friendships or to explore any long-dormant relationships, but she had to admit, chatting with Brian was still as easy as breathing. The guy had a way of putting her at ease, which she couldn't entirely explain. She'd expected their nine years apart to drive a wedge between them, so she hadn't bothered to prepare for...*this*.

Brian must have noticed her sudden discomfort.

"Anyway, what brings you to the humble Feed and Tack?" he said, giving the last three words a physical flourish, which he pulled off with a mix of self-deprecating charm and charisma. "I hear you work at a marketing firm now. In the big city."

"Yes. But it's not as glamorous as it sounds," Lucia said, in a much more guarded tone. "I mostly answer phones, open letters, and prepare documents."

"Sure, but you got *out*. That's no small feat," Brian offered. "Plenty of our classmates have tried, and failed. Remember Glenn Roseland? In twelfth grade, he swore he was going to move to Los Angeles and make it as a musician. Well...he gave it a shot...and he now lives in his parents' basement. Broke as shit. Word on the street is that he's waiting for his big break, but I don't see one happening."

"Yeah. Me neither," Lucia said listlessly, transferring her cane from hand to hand. She half wished he would break down and tell her what she needed to know, without prompting, so she could gather her wits and leave, but he was clearly on a different train of thought.

"Cards on the table...I'm only here because I'm looking for Finley," she said at last, trying her hardest to keep her gaze steady. "I haven't heard from her since Saturday, and I'm worried about her."

"Then why aren't you at her house?" Brian frowned. "Or her school? Her friends—"

"I tracked them down already," Lucia interrupted. "And they sent me here. With this."

She raised the rolling paper.

Brian didn't react one way or another.

"Looks like a scrap of paper. With my name on it," he shrugged. "What's it mean?"

"It *means* that you've been sleeping with my sister. My *sixteen-year-old* sister," Lucia said, feeling anger, resentment, disbelief, and sadness well inside of her. She wanted to scream, cry, flee, and punch something simultaneously, but she was determined to keep her composure. She had to hold it together. At least until her fears were verified. "According to Destinee, you two have—"

"Wait. Your information is from the *Cutler* girl?" Brian said, taking a tentative step toward her. "That girl is the least reliable source in the whole *county*."

"So you deny any kind of relationship with my sister?" Lucia said, folding the rolling paper into her palm, and squeezing it against her thigh. "You've never *once* taken her out on a date?"

"No. Of course not! With our age difference, that's not even *legal!*" Brian insisted. But there was something off about the way he laughed in the aftermath. To her ears, the outburst sounded fake. Nervous. *Desperate.*

She decided to push him.

"Maybe not, but my mother sure as hell saw you two walking last Thursday night," she said. "Can you explain that?"

Some of her—a bigger portion than she cared to acknowledge, either to herself or to anyone else—hoped that Brian would deny the allegation outright, and then crack a joke to lighten the mood, but she was disappointed. The second she said "Thursday night," his face fell and his eyes lost their youthful shine.

"I...I never meant to hurt anyone. Least of all...well...*you*," he fumbled, once he was sure the two of them were well and truly alone. "The truth of the matter is...yes...we have been seeing each other. But it's not—"

"How long?" Lucia demanded. If she had possessed quills, every single one of them would have been standing on end. She couldn't believe that, minutes earlier, she had been happily conversing with the man—no, the *thing*—standing before her.

Brian took her question in stride.

"Six months," he said decisively. "We've been dating for six months. It started at a movie theater. On Thanksgiving Day. Neither of us had anywhere to go or anything to do, so we watched three showings together. It was completely organic. It's not like I went out of my way to—"

"Have you two had sex?" Lucia interrupted again. And again, she was served a quick and straightforward answer.

"No. Fuck no," Brian reiterated. "We've made out, but that's the long and short of it. I would never...you know...take it that far. Not until she's—"

"Of legal age?" Lucia said, pinning him with her pupils. She would have gone on, but short outbursts were all she could muster, under the circumstances. Anything more and her emotions would have gotten the best of her.

For what it was worth, Brian didn't dodge her accusation.

"Yes. Yeah. I mean...we're going to go public eventually," he said, scratching the back of his neck. "We just...we both agree that now isn't the right time. What we have...we don't think it's wrong, but we don't think our neighbors are ready for it. You know what the people in this town would do if they found out a twenty-eight-year-old was seeing a sixteen-year-old. They'd tar me, feather me, and drive me out of the state with pitchforks!"

"And that would be bad because...?"

"Because Finley and I are in *love*," Brian said, in a lower and more forceful voice. "You might not approve of our age difference, but you, of all people, should want to see your sister happy. And she is happy. When she's with me. You should see the two of us together."

"I'd rather not."

"When it's just the two of us, she's a different person," Brian continued, despite Lucia's deathly glare. "She's not angry, frustrated, or troubled. She becomes this incredibly mature and quirky young woman."

"And you seriously think you're meant to be together?"

"Yes. Without a doubt," Brian said, moving even closer, as if to better communicate his sincerity. "I'd gladly stand before a judge, any day of the week, and defend what we have."

"Good. Because that's precisely what you'll have to do," Lucia concluded. Then she cracked a mirthless "go fuck yourself" smile, turned on her heel—which was more than a little difficult, considering her impaired coordination and balance—and started for the door.

Not surprisingly, Brian hurried after her.

"Wait!" he called. "Where are you going? I thought we came to an understanding!"

"We did," she returned, without looking over her shoulder. "You understand that what you're doing is illegal, and I understand that it's my duty to bring this information to the police. You can come along if you want. Or you can wait for the cops to show up with an arrest warrant. Either way, you'll end up in the same place."

"Yes…but if I'm in jail…there's no way you'll find your sister," Brian cautioned.

The revelation may have been nothing more than a frantic, eleventh-hour attempt to tilt the board in a more favorable direction, but it *did* succeed in stopping Lucia.

"Excuse me?" she said, halting a foot away from the steely security gates. "Is that a *threat?*"

"No. It's not a threat. It's a promise," Brian said, breathlessly skipping around the display cabinets. "The last few months, she's been obsessed with this game—this *scavenger hunt*—on the dark net. I think she may have gone too deep and gotten involved with some shady people."

"What kind of people?" Lucia hissed.

Brian didn't have a good answer.

"Maybe drug dealers, maybe hit men, maybe sex traffickers… maybe none of the above," he said, hunching his shoulders and letting them fall. "The point is…the dark net is filled with predators…and I'm worried about her. The last time I heard from her was Saturday night. She sent me a text. This text."

Brian lifted his cell phone; displayed a single message. It wasn't anything more than black font on an orange background, but it sent an electric current up Lucia's spine.

It's not a hoax. He's real. He's real and he's here, she recited inwardly. Then she swallowed, collected herself, and said: "If that's authentic, and you're truly in love with my sister, why haven't you gone to the police?"

"For the same reason the two of us haven't made our relationship public," Brian said, stuffing the phone back into his pocket. "If I told the police, they'd inevitably start asking questions, and those answers would put me in a prison cell."

"And you can do more good outside a cell than in one. Am I right?" Lucia ventured.

Brian nodded briskly. "Yeah. Exactly. Aside from that Cutler girl, I'm her closest friend in the world. I know more about her than her parents and the police combined. Together, you and I stand a chance of finding her. But we have to work *as a team.*"

There, he dropped his hands, sighed, and said: "I get it. You want to see me rot. And I don't blame you. But the fact of the matter is… we need each other. The longer Finley stays missing, the higher the odds that she'll never turn up. Or worse…."

Brian let his words trail off. Neither of them wanted to picture the teenager in a ditch, her skin waxen and her body bruised; her milky eyes staring up at a bloated September moon. But it was that mental image that ultimately pushed Lucia over the line.

"Fine," she huffed, after a solid minute of Waylon Jennings-infused silence. "I won't turn you in. But in return, you have to make me two promises. First, you have to promise to do everything in your power to help find my sister."

"Done."

"And second, when we do find my sister, you have to end it."

"Come again?"

"You have to swear that you'll cut off the relationship," Lucia said, in no uncertain terms. "If you so much as text my sister after this ordeal is over and done with, I'll contact the police department, and I'll make sure your name is on a sex offender registry for the rest of your natural life. Are we clear?"

Brian hesitated. She could tell he wanted to alter the terms of the agreement, but he didn't have a leg to stand on. It was she who controlled the deck. For once in her life, she was judge, jury, and executioner.

To his credit, Brian saw the futility of an appeal.

"Yes. We're clear," he muttered, with all the enthusiasm of a condemned man.

Chapter 7

After the showdown in the Feed and Tack, Lucia needed a break. At home, in Denver, she would have stopped for soup at one of the hole-in-the-wall eateries, drawn a hot bath, and lit a couple of scented candles, but she was seventy miles from her adopted city. To relax, and to avoid contracting a rare skin condition from her father's turn-of-the-century tub, she would have to think outside the box.

Driving down Highway 85, she encountered a pizza shop, a steak house, a Chinese restaurant, and the town's one fast-food burger chain, respectively, but she didn't stop at any of them. She wasn't in the mood to fraternize with locals or to fill her stomach with synthetic beef. She needed comfort food, and she needed peace and quiet, so she swung over to Oak Drive, passed a cluster of storage units, a couple of warehouses, a half dozen asphalt lots, and accelerated toward a squat structure, trimmed in neon lights.

Uncle Rudy's wasn't the oldest drive-in diner in America, or the most flamboyant, but it was, for Lucia's money, the most authentic. It had all the original appointments, down to the clunky and oversized order boxes, and it had undergone minimal refurbishment. The steel poles, which supported the overhang, were painted the original shade of yellow, and the windows of the diner proper were filled with sun-bleached advertisements from the establishment's glory days.

During Lucia's tenure in high school, the drive-in diner had been frequented by both old farmers and young hipsters, who drank coffee and smoked cigarettes and complained about the state of American society, but the demographic had changed in her absence.

When Lucia pulled into the lot, she didn't notice any young people. There were a few pickups parked downwind, but they were all plastered with NRA bumper stickers; occupied by bitter-looking men and women with gray hair. Either the place had become too popular for the hipsters or the old farts had organized a coup and banished anyone under the age of fifty-five.

Happy she'd chosen the car with the tinted windows, Lucia parked and took in the menu—the varieties of burgers, hot dogs, sodas, and milkshakes.

In her estimation, only the prices had changed. Everything else… it was precisely the way she remembered it.

Settling on a grilled cheese sandwich and a vanilla malt, Lucia speared the call button and waited for a metallic voice to echo from the speaker. When none surfaced, she hit it again. Then she gritted her teeth and—

"May I take your order, ma'am?"

The inquiry echoed through her cab via the passenger-side window, and nearly made her lose control of her bladder. She jumped, and simultaneously twisted toward the perceived threat, her fists clenched and ready for action. But the face hovering outside her window was the opposite of menacing.

"Peter? Is that you?" she said, lowering the glass so she could better see the man in the clownish yellow and green uniform. "I thought you were living in Florida. When did you move back here? And when did Rudy's hire you to frighten their female clientele? Also…is the moustache-and-sideburns combo required for your current position?"

"To answer your first question: one year ago," Peter said, before she could go on. "The cost of out-of-state tuition was just too high. I thought I could convince Mr. Wells and Mrs. Fargo to cover my costs, but it turns out that they have their limits. As for your second question: Senior Female Frightener is my unofficial title. My official position is Male Roller Skate Waiter Number One."

"But you're not wearing roller skates," Lucia pointed out. "Are they in the shop?"

"In a manner of speaking," Peter said, clearing his throat. "My second week on the job, I tried to jump over a curb, and I may or may not have landed on my face. Details aside, I wound up with a broken collarbone and an order not to wear skates on company property."

"Which explains the shoes…but not the facial hair," Lucia smirked. "Either you're *trying* to resemble a Polish Jack the Ripper, or you're suffering from Evil Genius Follicle Growth Syndrome. Which is it?"

"Neither," Peter said. "Although I do appreciate your commitment to genre movie and television tropes. The truth is, I met a girl while I was down south."

"Go on."

"She was this cute little thing, and she was obsessed with *Sgt. Pepper's Lonely Hearts Club Band*-era John Lennon."

"What girl isn't?"

"Most of them, actually. But that's not the point. The point is, I figured I could impress her. Thus…" Peter gestured at the meticulously-crafted whiskers that unspooled beneath his nose and trailed up his jaw line. The combination wouldn't have looked bad on, say, a porn star from the 1970s, but it didn't do her former classmate any favors. The ebony hairs merely accentuated his already angular features and olive complexion.

"Well…did it work?" Lucia ventured, after a moment of probing stares and—what she interpreted to be—meaningful eyebrow movements.

"No. Not at all," Peter concluded, quick as a hyena on cocaine. "We went out for a week, then she dumped me for a member of the football team. Not a starting player, either. He was a walk-on. A part of the practice squad."

"Bummer."

"You're telling me! He wasn't even tall!" Peter exclaimed. "He was five-foot-nine. You know what that means, don't you?"

Lucia shook her head.

"It means that, without my scoliosis, I would be two inches taller!" Peter ranted, as if all life's problems could be chalked up to the curve of his spine. Then he took a step back, released a deep breath, and apologized.

"It's just…it's been a year and a half, and I haven't had a real relationship since," he explained. "How pitiful is that? A twenty-seven-year-old with no life and no prospects. I'm like a character from a Judy Blume novel."

"Then you're in good company," Lucia snickered. "My own love life hasn't been exactly active, of late. When I'm not working, I'm paying bills. And when I'm not paying bills, I'm stressing over my sister."

"Finley?" Peter frowned. "I haven't seen her around in a while. How's she doing?"

"I wish I could tell you," Lucia sighed. "No one seems to know where she is or why she's gone. Her boyfriend thinks she's gotten herself wrapped up in this weird deep web scavenger hunt, but at the moment we're still in the dark. We know about as much as you."

"Well, if you need any help, I'm more than happy to lend a hand," Peter offered. "I've been messing around with encrypted search engines for the past ten years. I'm not much of a hacker—social or otherwise—but I know my way around. I know what's safe and, more importantly, what's *not*.

"Under the surface net, it's a literal maze," he continued. "There are no indexing sites like Google to guide you. To get to the lower levels, you have to hop from site to site. Occasionally you can find what you're looking for in a chat room, but that comes down to blind luck—being in the right place at the right time." Then he paused and, in a lower voice, said: "Your sister isn't into...ah...*cheese pizza*, is she?"

"*Cheese pizza?*" Lucia repeated. "What does cheese pizza have to do with anything? Is that something you can buy on the deep web?"

"Oh yeah. It's all over the place," Peter confirmed. "But I'm not talking about the *food*. I'm talking about *child pornography*. That's, arguably, the most bought and sold product on the entire internet. Bigger than weapons and drugs *combined*."

"You're shitting me."

"I wish," Peter sniffed. "The University of California, Berkeley? They estimate that there are over seventy-five thousand terabytes worth of data on the deep web. That means *four percent* of the internet is available to surface browsers. The rest...that's locked up below. Sometimes *very far below*. It would take a hundred lifetimes to see everything the deep web has to offer. Or longer. Like the surface web, the deep web is always growing."

"Yes, but *kiddie porn?*" Lucia said, suddenly regulating the volume of her own voice. "There's no way there's a big market for *that.*"

"Not at Walmart," Peter agreed. "But the deep web isn't a digital Walmart. The deep web is our equivalent of the Wild West. According to the UN, child porn is a twenty-five billion dollar industry." And in case that wasn't enough: "At any given second, there are *eight hundred thousand* people on the internet, trading…well…you get the picture."

Peter proceeded to qualify that statement by rattling off a number of figures and sources, but Lucia didn't catch much of his spiel. She was too busy picturing eight hundred thousand people on their personal computers, uploading and downloading content; salivating at unclothed boys and girls; giddily waiting for the next folder to appear; joking and bragging about recent conquests. How many of those people had abused a child themselves? And how many of them were planning to molest a child in the near future? How many of them were networking with experienced pedophiles; building the courage to act on their compulsions?

Disgusted by the idea that her sister might be in the presence of such degenerate men and women, Lucia cleared her throat and thanked Peter for his concern.

"If I find myself in need of a deep web tour guide, I'll definitely hit you up," she assured him. "But for now, can I please have a grilled cheese sandwich and a vanilla malt? My stomach is killing me."

"Preaching to the choir, sister," Peter chuckled. "You wouldn't guess it from looking at me, but I'm always hungry. Just this morning—"

"Peter."

"Yeah?"

"I'm not making polite conversation. I'd literally like to order a grilled cheese sandwich and a vanilla malt," Lucia deadpanned. She didn't mean to sound bitchy, but she remembered how conversations with Peter progressed. She remembered that a five-minute conversation could easily become a half-hour visit, and she didn't have the mental fortitude to undergo a commitment of that nature. She needed to get her food, and get to a quiet place—a place where she could find her center. Already, her head was throbbing and her peripheral vision was going soft.

Fortunately, Peter heard her message loud and clear.

"One grilled cheese sandwich and a vanilla malt. Got it," he said. "Oh, and it's good to see you, by the way. You may not realize it, but this place isn't the same without you." Then he patted the roof of her car, as if it was a faithful steed in need of recognition, and jogged back to the diner.

Chapter 8

Footsteps.

Lucia detected footsteps in the house, but she couldn't tell, in her sleep-addled state, where they were originating, or where they were going. One moment they seemed to be at the far end of the living room, and the next they were in the hall—directly outside of her bedroom. They weren't loud, but they weren't necessarily stealthy, either.

Was her father to blame?

Groggily, Lucia sat up and rubbed her eyes. She made an effort to read the clock next to her bed, but her pupils refused to comply. Bright red numbers cut in and out of focus, doubling and tripling.

In high school, the bouts of double vision had confounded and frustrated her, but she'd since grown accustomed to them. She'd learned that they were temporary nuisances, and that they would go away if she remained calm.

Taking a deep breath, Lucia leveraged her legs to the edge of the bed and groped about for her Dirty Secret. On an up day, she could have navigated the room without assistance, but she could tell that she was not at the threshold of an up day. She could tell that her balance was slightly off and that her coordination—especially in her left leg—was lagging.

"Come on. Where are you?" she muttered, feeling along the side of the mattress, then along the bedside table. The last evening was a blur, but she was positive she had left the walking stick right there—right on the edge of her bed. Had she kicked it over in the middle of the night...or had someone *taken* it?

Distracted by another set of footfalls, Lucia straightened; tilted her head toward the doorway. There weren't many thugs within city limits, but then, homegrown hooligans weren't the only source of trouble. The highway, which ran through the middle of town, occasionally provided another kind of criminal. A *worse* kind.

Remembering the Wilson family tragedy of '96—the ambulances, the crime scene tape, the headlines, the police cruisers, the men in the black tactical garb—Lucia decided to test her maneuverability. To do so, she leaned forward until the pads of her feet touched the floor. Then she eased herself upward, turned in a circle, and shuffled from side to side.

While her movements were stiff, she was reassured by her range of motion. She was fairly sure she would be able to travel up and down the hall without issue. She wouldn't be able to run, or to effectively defend herself in a pinch, but she didn't intend to incite an attack. If her fears were confirmed, and there *was* an intruder in the house, she would simply return to her room, lock the door, and call the police. Easy peasy.

Right?

Assuring herself that Eaton was a hundred times safer than the big city, she stumbled to the wall and felt her way east, toward the lone entrance. The old wallpaper crackled under her fingertips as she moved, hand over hand, but it wasn't the crackling of the wallpaper that caused her to pull up short of the door. Her hesitation was spawned by another crackling—a dry, rhythmic crepitation; the sound of cicada shells crushed under a vulcanized heel—which whispered from the ventilation system, and which immediately painted her forearms in gooseflesh.

No longer certain that she was, in fact, awake, and safe from the ungodly beings that haunted her subconscious, she gripped the knob and counted to five. Then she twisted, ever so carefully, and eased the door open.

Outside, the hallway was long and dark; empty and indistinct. She blinked twice in an effort to bring it into focus, but it, like the alarm clock, remained hazy. It would've made her feel like a patron in a funhouse, given some garish neon signs and a splash of calliope music, but the whole place was near dead. If not for the glow of a neighbor's flood light, which crept through the picture window, and which swayed across the walls in time with the half-drawn blinds, the place could've passed as a vampire's crypt.

On the one hand, Lucia wanted to say her father's name and end the charade once and for all, but on the other, she was afraid of what she might discover. She was afraid that a man in a silicon mask might storm around the corner, a cleaver in his gloved fingers and a swath of blood across his rubber apron. That was what the Wilson family had encountered, after all. They'd awoken, in the middle of the night to the sound of lamps breaking and furniture being overturned. And when they'd gone to investigate the clamor, they'd been pursued by a hulking figure. Or…that was the story, at least. The police had never released a full report.

Working to purge the leaked crime scene photos from her mind, Lucia crept through the hall. She no longer detected the squeal of displaced floorboards, but that wasn't necessarily comforting. If the killer—*No. Not* killer. *Person*—was still on the premises, that meant he was *listening*. And if he was listening, that meant he was aware of her presence.

Heart crashing against her sternum, Lucia made it to the mouth of the hall, but didn't peer around the corner. Instead, she flattened herself to the wall and willed her body to relax. To her chagrin, her symptoms weren't easing up. They were building. Her peripheral vision was receding, the left side of her face was tingling, and her inner ear was spinning.

She needed to act.

Throwing caution to the wind, she pulled herself into the open and looked from one end of the living room to the other. She couldn't make out many details, because her brain was processing a limited amount of information from her rod cells, but she could see *shapes*. She could make out the lamp, the coffee table, the recliner, the sofa, and—

A loud *bang!* redirected her attention to the front door.

Someone had, a second before, slipped onto the porch.

Mind racing, Lucia limped toward the picture window. Going was slow, since she wasn't intimately familiar with her environs, and since her inner ear was spinning, but she managed to weave from the wall to the recliner, from the recliner to the coffee table, and from the coffee table to the windowsill.

At her destination, she swiped the blinds aside and pressed her nose to the glass. There was an early-morning chill in the air, which radiated through the pane and across her face, but she barely noticed it. Her concentration was centered on the figure who was, at the moment, hurrying down the sidewalk.

To her surprise, the figure wasn't large *or* intimidating. In fact, it wasn't even a *man*. The shoulders were too narrow and the hips were too wide.

It's a woman. A young woman, Lucia thought, following the stranger's progress toward a gold pickup.

While the latter was vaguely familiar, Lucia couldn't see enough to give it a positive identification. The bumper stickers were blurry, and the decorations on the dashboard were little more than suggestions. Until the woman hopped into the cab, and drove the truck past the front of the house. Then everything became incredibly clear.

"Deborah?" Lucia whispered, glancing from one Greenpeace sticker to the next. "Deborah Hollinger? What the hell—"

She didn't get a chance to finish her sentence. As the pickup and the bottle-blond beauty accelerated for the main thoroughfare, her father stepped out of the hallway and muttered a question of his own. He asked what his daughter was doing out of bed; why she was plastered to the window.

"It isn't Christmas time yet," he pointed out, making sure his robe was cinched around his waist as he plodded for the kitchen. "Even if it was, Santa doesn't deliver presents to children unless they're asleep. You should know that by now."

Lucia didn't respond straight away. She waited until the pickup was out of sight, then she said: "Deborah Hollinger. Have you seen her lately?"

"Who?" her father returned, clattering from one cupboard to the next.

"Ted and Melinda's daughter," Lucia clarified. "The two of us went to high school together; graduated together. We used to study in the back yard when we weren't—"

"Practicing for swim competitions," her father affirmed. "Yeah. I remember her. She has blond hair, doesn't she? Works at her parents' café on 1st Street, if I'm not mistaken."

"But you haven't seen her recently?"

"Can't say I have."

"Then why was she in your house this morning?"

"*My* house?" her father laughed, appearing with a cup of coffee and a slice of toast. "I have no idea what you're talking about. Are you sure you're not…you know…"

Her father wiggled his fingers about the side of his head. The gesture was supposed to humorously convey the concept of a flare-up, but Lucia found it neither humorous nor endearing.

"Dad. I have multiple sclerosis. I'm not insane," she growled. "I saw Deborah leaving the house. I saw her pickup truck. She was *here*."

"Then I hope she pruned the bushes out back. Those things are starting to get wild," her father said with a wink. He proceeded to place his dishes on the coffee table and to gently take her arm, but she shrugged him off.

"I'm fine. I don't need help," she hissed.

She was lying, of course, and she suspected that he *knew* she was lying, but he backed away regardless, palms raised in a placating manner.

"Okay, okay. I get it. You're a grown-ass adult. You can take care of yourself," he said. "I just thought—"

What? That you should finally say sorry for missing all my swim meets? her inner voice demanded. *For sending cards, rather than showing up for my birthday parties? For not coming to the hospital after I collapsed? For not being there to hold my hand while I was diagnosed? For all the nights I lay in my bed, alone, and cried because I couldn't move my toes? For the milestones in physical therapy that you missed? For each of the times that you cheated on Mom? For the fact that we have a broken family? For the hollow text messages you send every other month?*

She wanted, more than anything, to release the molten craters of pain and resentment that were bubbling up inside her, filling her with noxious and poisonous fumes, but she stamped down the inclination. She knew that, the minute she started to unload, she would break down, and she was determined not to cry in front of her father. Tears were a sign of weakness—a message that she was not a strong or a well-adjusted woman. So she kept herself cool.

"I appreciate your concern, Dad, but I'm good," she assured him, moving uncomfortably from the window to the opposite wall. "I'll be back out after I shower. You don't have to wait up for me."

"Well, if you're sure," her father said, standing far enough away to avoid impeding upon her personal bubble, but not so far that he couldn't sweep in and catch her if she began to fall. "There's coffee in the pantry and bacon in the refrigerator, by the way. You may have to wash a skillet, but you're more than welcome to whatever food you can find."

"Thanks," Lucia mumbled. But her heart wasn't in it. She was solely concentrated on the task at hand—at traveling through the living room, down the hall, and to her bed. She felt like a circus freak, putting on a private performance for a wealthy businessman. She managed to keep a stiff upper lip, though. She kept her legs moving and her eyes on the prize until she drew alongside her twin mattress. Then she collapsed to the floor, and let her emotions overtake her.

She probably would have cried for fifteen minutes straight if she hadn't glanced to the left, and seen the black-and-white backpack stuffed under the box spring.

Chapter 9

In the lot behind the Feed and Tack, Lucia paced. Her face was still a bit tingly from the morning's attack, but her eyesight and her balance were restored. She felt well enough to undertake a cross-country road trip or to go nine rounds with the first person who commented on her cane. A few motorists had already slowed down, and a few joggers had already given her quizzical looks, but no one had dared to ask the million-dollar question. Maybe it was the expression on her face. Or maybe it was the way her eyes narrowed when she met their gazes. Whatever the case, Lucia's inner monologue was interrupted when the Employees Only door swung open.

"Hey. Sorry about the delay," Brian said, brushing straw out of his hair and dust from his apron. "I got your text fifteen minutes ago, but I was with a customer. He needed my help to load up a bunch of shit. What's up?"

"My question exactly," Lucia returned, snagging the black-and-white backpack from the trunk of her car, and lobbing it into the center of his chest. "That look familiar to you?"

"No. Should it?" Brian said, turning the canvas accessory over in his hands. "No offense, but I wouldn't buy this thing from a dollar store. Looks like it's been to Hell and back. Is it yours?"

"Close," Lucia said. "Check the book inside the front pocket."

Brian did as he was told. He unzipped the outer pouch, tugged at the science textbook, saw the name scrawled across the top corner, and said: "This stuff belongs to Finley. Where'd you find it?"

Lucia didn't respond to the inquiry. Instead, she instructed him to open the main compartment, and she remained motionless while he complied. It was hard for her to stay still, but she'd gone over the interaction a thousand times in her mind. She needed him to see for himself. She needed him to understand where he stood.

Her patience paid off.

In seconds, Brian's look of friendly self-assuredness was gone—replaced by a mask of terrible comprehension.

"I...uh...I can explain," he stammered. "This isn't what you think it is. It has a perfectly innocent—"

That was as far as Lucia let him get. Fast as she could move, she closed the distance between the two of them and punched him in the face. Hard. So hard that Brian lost his grip on the backpack, and the packet of birth control pills—half used—skipped out, onto the pavement.

"How *dare* you," Lucia fumed, even as she wavered and cradled her bruised knuckles. "First you lied to my face, and now *this*? Who the fuck *are you*?"

"I just...I don't know...I'm sorry," Brian said, pinching the bridge of his nose in a feeble attempt to stem the flow of blood. "I didn't want you to worry. Everything I said the other day, I said it to protect you. To protect *us*. If I had told you the truth at the start, you would have—"

"What? Overreacted?" Lucia cried. "You're fucking a teenager, for goodness' sake! How in the world is someone supposed to react to that information?" And, when Brian failed to supply a defense: "Did you really think I wouldn't find out? Did you really think you could get away with this shit forever?"

"Forever?" Brian grimaced, his front teeth stained red. "No. Not forever. Like I told you before, we were going to come clean. When she turned eighteen, we were going to tell everyone. We were going to tell *you*. It wasn't supposed to happen like this."

"Well, it is. So get used to it," Lucia growled. Some of her anger was pacified by the strings of sticky plasma that hung from his lips and chin, and that rolled down his forearms, coloring the sleeves of his collared shirt, but not all of it. Not nearly enough to eliminate her desire to hit him again; to see his skin pucker with yellow and purple welts.

In truth, the passing traffic was the only thing that stopped her from landing another hook. She was sure that, if she connected a second punch, one of the many rubberneckers would rush to the police station and tattle on her. After all, it wasn't every day that a woman beat up a man in the Feed and Tack's rear parking lot.

Perhaps sensing her hesitation, or perhaps thinking—mistakenly—that there was still a way *out*, Brian straightened and said: "If it's any consolation, she had the prescription before she met *me*. I think she got it when she was fifteen. At the time, she was going out with—"

"I don't give a shit who she was dating," Lucia interrupted, yet again. "High school students are stupid because they're *high school students*. They're not fully matured. *You* don't have the same excuse. You should've known better. I mean...she's *sixteen*."

"Yeah. She is," Brian retaliated, growing indignant for the first time. "She *is* sixteen. And you know what else? She's a whole fucking lot like you, when you were her age."

"What the hell are you talking about?"

"I'm talking about *you and me*; the relationship that *we* used to have," Brian roared. "Up until junior year, we were thick as thieves. We used to do everything together. We used to smoke behind the bleachers during football games. We used to spray paint the pavilions at City Park. We used to swim laps around Cozzens Lake. We used to bum three-two beer from the gas station off Factory Road, and drink them inside the old sugar plant. Then the attack happened...and you changed."

"Oh. So *your* poor decisions are *my* fault. Is that it?" Lucia contended. "You chose to stick your dick in a teenager because your girlfriend in high school dumped you and moved to another city? That's some pretty fucked-up logic right there."

"On the surface, yes," Brian conceded. "But you *did* change. When I was fourteen, I fell in love with this anarchist rebel—this girl who laughed at funerals and cracked jokes at weddings. Back then, you were spunky and daring and full of life. You made every day into an adventure. A *good* adventure. But all that came to an end when you were diagnosed. That self-confident anarchist I loved so deeply...she disappeared. She became this resentful, angry, bitter shadow.

"Remember the day after the attack?" he continued, spitting a wad of crimson-flecked phlegm onto the concrete. "Sandy and Deborah and I tried to visit you in the hospital and you had us run out. Hell, you refused to talk to any of us for the next three weeks. By the time I finally got to see you, I had four dead bouquets in the back seat of my car. When one would die, I'd buy another, because I wanted you to realize that someone out there cared about you; that you weren't all alone. But you didn't even care enough to face me. You strung me along. And then you told me to get lost."

"Maybe in *your* twisted little world," Lucia snorted. "Here, in *reality*, everything was mutual. We both agreed that our little...whatever we had...wouldn't work. It wasn't a spur-of-the-moment decision."

"No. On that, we're in agreement," Brian admitted. "I spent *months* reaching out to you, trying to bridge the gap. I left voicemails on your phone until the damned thing was full. I dropped cards and balloons outside your room. I offered to wheel you out to Cozzens Lake each day, after school, so you could have some time away from it all. And then, out of the blue, you ended it. With a text message."

There, he exhaled, and let his blood-drenched hands fall to his sides.

"I'm not telling you all of this because I expect you to forgive me," he said, in a more plaintive tone. "I know I fucked up, and I know I fucked up bad. I just want you to understand where I'm coming from. My relationship with Finley...it started exactly the way I told you it started. I didn't realize that she was so much like you—the younger you—until that Thanksgiving at the movie theater. To be honest, I'd forgotten what *our* relationship was like. I'd blocked it out. But Finley brought it all back.

"Maybe I'm crazy," he said, venturing within Lucia's reach, "but your sister has more Lucia in her than the Lucia who's standing right in front of me. Finley's funny and quirky and headstrong and resilient, and she makes me want to become more than...well...*me*.

"I guess my main sin was thinking I could have what the *real* Lucia and I *used* to have," he concluded, despite the blood that continued to trickle from his nose.

It was an uncharacteristically candid admission, and it didn't just catch Lucia by surprise. It actually sucked the wind from her sails; left her dizzy and conflicted.

Yes, Lucia wanted the man to pay for his transgressions, but her desire to see him humiliated was waning. She no longer wanted to witness his arrest or to read the headlines that followed. He may have been unreasonably stupid and in need of a lengthy verbal thrashing, but he wasn't a remorseless monster. She could tell that he was genuinely in love with Finley, and that level of affection was worth something. How much, she couldn't say, but one thing was certain: Finley would be easier to find *with* his help than *without* it.

Brian must not have noticed the subtle shift in her mood.

"So...that's it," he said, when the silence threatened to stretch into a full minute. "That's my story. If you're going to call the cops, have at it. I won't stop you. I probably deserve it. I probably deserve all of this."

"Yes. You do," Lucia agreed. "But I'm not going to call the cops. Not yet. Not as long as you *swear* to uphold the terms of our bargain."

"Are you serious?" Brian gaped. "You're going to give me a second chance?"

"Yes. But you better behave yourself. And you better not lie to me again," Lucia said, flexing her injured hand. "By now, Finley's been gone for almost seventy-two hours. That means our odds of finding her are already slim. We need to pool our resources and make some headway before the trail goes cold."

"Then the Cutler girl should be stop number one," Brian said, using his forearm to wipe at the clumps of semi-coagulated blood that clung to his nostrils. "If I'm not mistaken, she's the one who introduced Finley to the deep web game. If anyone can point us in the right direction, it's her."

Chapter 10

"How do I look?"

"You look fine."

"Normal?"

"Define 'normal.'"

"Well, in this case, like someone who hasn't been mugged by a featherweight boxing champion?" Brian said from the Focus's passenger seat.

In response, Lucia sighed and tore her gaze from the high school's utilitarian façade. She wasn't in the mood for banter, as she was busy plotting her line of questioning, and waiting for the telltale pitter and patter of teenage feet, but she supposed that a word or two couldn't hurt.

At the moment, Brian was daubing at his chin—using a box of tissues and a bottle of water to scrub the stubborn streaks of blood from his face. He looked much better than he had at the beginning of the drive, but there wasn't much he could do about the purple crescent beneath his left eye. For the next few days—a week, tops—he would resemble a down-on-his-luck prizefighter.

"I'll be honest. Your mug has seen better days," she said at last, noting the place where her pinky ring had split his lip. "You look about as put together as Joshua Stuckey after he fell off that bull. Also, you could use a new shirt. That one's ruined."

"Seriously?" Brian grimaced. "I just bought it last week, to replace the one I tore the week before. If things don't change, my entire wardrobe will need to be replaced by Halloween."

"And that's a shame because…?"

"Because clothes are expensive," Brian concluded. "And because my collection of T-shirts is priceless."

"Sure. If by 'priceless' you mean 'devoid of value,'" Lucia smirked. "Somehow, I doubt collectors will ever scramble for Nirvana reproductions or for nu metal bands of the late nineties."

"Mid-nineties," Brian amended. "And I seem to remember that you were fond of a particular Limp Bizkit T-shirt during sophomore year. Some mornings, that was the only thing you wore, aside from—"

Brian wisely cut himself off. Either he noticed the "that's enough, Brian" expression that cut across Lucia's face, sharp as a razor, or he saw the high school doors opening. Regardless, Lucia was thankful for the dead air that intervened. She wasn't sure how to react to the "you and me" talk. On the one hand it was flattering, and on the other, insulting. She would've felt more comfortable in a terrarium, surrounded by poisonous spiders.

Eager to leave the confines of the compact sedan, Lucia opened the door and stood; let her gaze sweep across the unspooling mass of students. There was a stiff wind in the area, which disheveled her hair and pulled at the hems of her pea coat, not unlike the hands of an eager former lover, but she paid it little mind. In Eaton, wind was as common as the rodents that burrowed in and out of the undeveloped prairies. It often arrived in the afternoon and died out in the evening, leaving relocated tumbleweeds and runaway umbrellas in its wake.

"See her?" Brian inquired, joining Lucia near the front of the car.

Lucia shook her head. "Not yet. The other day, she.... Wait. Is that her?"

"Sure is," Brian verified, watching the blue-haired girl and her black-clad minions emerge from the sea of red letter jackets. He opened his mouth to make a follow-up statement, but Lucia didn't stick around long enough to vet his point of view. She made a beeline for the dated station wagon, intending to intercept the group before they could spark any of their lighters or break out their flasks.

She was almost successful.

"Hey. Look who's back," Battle Jacket said, following a pull from a belt-mounted container. "It's the MS chick."

"And she's got backup. How cute," Ms. Quinn contributed.

Both Lucia's Irish side and her Italian side wanted to teach the pipsqueaks a modicum of respect, but she managed to subdue the inclination. She'd already punched one person that day, and one was her self-ascribed limit. Besides, her favored hand was injured. She wouldn't be able to use her fists to their full potential until she was somewhat healed.

"Firstly, he's not my backup. I can take care of myself," she said, staring down each and every one of Destinee's lackeys. "And secondly, I'm not back by choice. I'm here because I need more information."

"Fair enough. Then I need another twenty dollars," Destinee returned, sashaying to the front lines. She was wearing black lipstick and heavy eyeliner for a change, but the dark colors didn't make her any more intimidating. If anything, they highlighted her pale complexion and made her seem even more feeble: like a goth with a D-vitamin deficiency.

Lucia didn't break rank.

"I don't have another twenty dollars. Not on me," she said, straight-faced as a pallbearer. "So you're going to give me this tip free of charge. We understand each other?"

"Actually, no. We don't," Destinee said, to a round of "oohs" and "ahhs," and other cracks from the peanut gallery. "One of us must be deaf—or dumb—because we've already established the price of cooperation. Either you have twenty dollars, or this conversation is over. So which is it?"

"Do you want to talk, or do you want to walk?" Peach Fuzz chimed in. Judging by the glaze in his eyes, he was already well on his way to Woodstock—or wherever the hell potheads went when they were too high to function in polite society—so Lucia wrote him off as a minor inconvenience and stepped straight up to the Cutler girl.

"This isn't a game, sweetheart," Lucia said, through barred teeth. "Your best friend—and my sister—is *missing*. She's not skipping school; sleeping in or huffing paint in some shitty little apartment. She's *gone*. Which means that you have two options. Either you can tell me everything you know, or I can—"

"What? Hit me in the teeth?" Destinee said, ever defiant. "Go ahead and try it. I dare you. We're on school property and I'm a minor. If you so much as touch me, I'll have you thrown in jail so fast that your head will spin. You *and* your creepy boy toy over there."

It was an artless low blow, clearly crafted to offend and to provoke an extreme response, but Lucia almost fell for it, nonetheless. She started to say "He's not my boy toy," then she registered the alligator grin on Destinee's face, and she mentally checked herself. She was letting her emotions take the wheel. To get what she was after, she had to be smarter. She had to convince the Cutler girl that it was in her best interest to play ball. But how? She couldn't afford to buy the stoners' loyalty, and she knew that threats would go nowhere fast.

For once, Brian was a step ahead of her.

"Why don't the three of us discuss this in private?" he said, gesturing toward the industrial trash compartments that flanked the high school's west side. "After all, this is a personal issue, and I'd hate to muddy the waters with *more* personal issues."

"Such as…?" Destinee leered. She seemed to think he was blowing smoke up her ass, but her attitude changed the second he brought up a particular Comfort Corner pharmacist. It was a subtle change, which she attempted to cover with a strategic cough and a raised eyebrow, but it registered loud and clear on Lucia's radar.

"Yeah. Dr. Brewer is a regular at the Feed and Tack," Brian continued, with a congenial shrug. "He loves to chat about his horses and his collection of Civil War memorabilia, but he loves to talk about his customers *most*. He won't shut up about them. Just the other day, he came in for a rain sheet, and he told me—"

"Okay. Fine. Let's talk. But this better be quick," Destinee said, passing a crumpled pack of cigarettes to Battle Jacket and starting for the trash compartments. She wore an expression of exasperation as she stomped north, across the parking lot, but it was her eyes that betrayed her. It was her eyes that revealed her discomfort and alarm.

Once safely out of earshot, she turned on her heel, looked from Lucia to Brian, and said: "Time to cut the shit. How much do you know about my prescriptions? And what the hell do you plan to do with that information? You're not a couple of right-wing Bible-thumpers, are you?"

"No. We're not. But we know enough," Brian assured her. "As long as you cooperate, here and now, we'll make sure that your secret doesn't get out."

"Because you're magnanimous. Is that it?" Destinee chuffed.

That was Lucia's signal to intervene; to deescalate the situation.

"We're not out to vilify anyone," she said, quickly and evenly. "We just want to find Finley. We're worried about her. We have reason to believe that she's gotten herself mixed up with some bad people. Possibly through a game on the internet."

"You mean *Mr. Sticks' Labyrinth*?" Destinee said, showing a crack in her cold and calculated veneer. "*Mr. Sticks' Labyrinth* isn't real. It's a Creepypasta."

"A what?"

"A *Creepypasta*," Destinee repeated, with significantly more teenage disillusionment. "*Creepypasta* is this website where people submit scary stories. It's basically a collection of urban legends."

"And it's updated daily?" Lucia inquired.

Destinee's pupils did a circular loop. "Daily? Weekly? Yearly? How the hell should I know? The point is, none of it's legit. All the stories are made up. Some of them are more convincing than others, but that doesn't change the fact that it's a bunch of BS."

"According to *you*," Lucia pointed out. "It sounds like Finley started to take this Mr. Sticks legend seriously."

"As gonorrhea. Yeah. She did," Destinee confirmed. "I played along for a while because…you know…why the hell not? But Finley went off the deep end. She was convinced that the story was real—that if she followed the clues, she'd reach the end."

"And what, exactly, is supposed to happen at *the end*?" Lucia ventured.

Destinee's shoulders did a vertical leap.

"No one knows for sure," the girl admitted. "The ultimate goal of the game is to summon Mr. Sticks. Some say he's a type of genie who will grant a single wish. Others say he's a demonic spirit who will drag you into the deepest bowels of Hell. One way or another, he's supposed to solve all your problems and make all your worries disappear."

"Like a rich old grandfather," Brian mumbled.

Lucia tuned him out; asked whether Finley had been playing the game on the night she disappeared.

"In my opinion?" Destinee said. "Yes. Without a doubt. When she wasn't at school, or smooching it up with Brian there, she was crawling around the internet; digging up clues. The last time I talked to her, she told me that she was getting close. She said she only needed one or two more pieces to complete the puzzle."

"And...?"

"And what?"

"Did she say anything else?"

"To me? No. Hell no," Destinee frowned. "I told her that she was crazy. I told her to drop the damned game and join the rest of us in the real world."

"And that was that?"

"For the most part," Destinee said, fumbling through her jacket for a cigarette, realizing she'd given the pack away, and kicking absently at a cluster of rocks. "She ended up calling me a cunt; telling me that I wasn't a real friend. She said a real friend would've supported her. She said that..." The girl took a breath. "She said that Mr. Sticks would find me and make me sorry."

"She threatened you?"

"If you call that a threat," Destinee said, regaining a measure of her youthful defiance. "Like I said, Mr. Sticks isn't real. He's a *fiction*. He can't do anything out here, in reality."

Maybe not directly, Lucia contributed internally. She was reminded of a case that had taken place a few years prior, where a couple of high school girls had lured a classmate into the woods and stabbed her half to death in order to gain the approval of another supernatural being, but she kept that information to herself. She didn't want to unduly scare Destinee. The Cutler girl was exactly that. A *girl*. Beneath the layers of greasy makeup and the leather jackets and the torn jeans, she was a typical seventeen-year-old. She was desperate for approval, for acceptance, for love. But above all, she was trying to find her place in the world. She didn't understand how everything *worked*—where she was supposed to go, or what she was supposed to do. She was an extremely tiny fish in an extremely large ocean, and she was just beginning to grasp the enormity of her natural habitat.

Lucia was sympathetic to the girl's plight. Not long ago, Lucia had been in the same pair of shoes. Hell, there were some days when she wondered if she wasn't *still* in those shoes.

"Anyway, that's all I know," Destinee concluded, crossing her arms to project an air of composure—and to keep her fingers from fiddling. "Am I free to go now, officers? Or would you like me to bend and spread?"

It was precisely the kind of crack that would have initiated a wave of laughter from Destinee's confederates, and made it difficult to pose a follow-up question, but the peanut gallery was too far away to intervene, and Lucia was less than amused by the remark.

"As a matter of fact, there is one more thing you can do," Lucia said, relying on her cane to keep her upright amidst a sudden gust of cold wind. "You can tell us how to start this game. After that, you're good to go."

"Are you serious?"

"Serious as a heart attack," Brian promised. "You can walk out of here free and clear."

"No. Not that," Destinee scowled. "You guys seriously want to play that damned game? For the millionth time, *it's a hoax*. There's nothing real about it. It's a story that some creepy yahoo made up to scare kids during camping trips. The clues don't lead anywhere. If you really want to find Finley, you should wait her out. She'll come crawling back here as soon as she finds out that Mr. Sticks is a myth."

"Maybe so," Lucia said, "but I'd rather run around in a circle than sit at home and do nothing. Besides, one of the clues may lead us straight to her."

"Yeah. Maybe," Destinee said, in her most patronizing tone. But she didn't ignore the directive. Whether out of fear of reprisal or out of a genuine desire to help, she unlocked her smart phone, accessed her email application, and scrolled through her messages until she came across what she was looking for. Then she cued up a document, highlighted a block of text, and held the phone out to Lucia.

"That's it," the girl said. "That's the URL. That's how you start *Mr. Sticks' Labyrinth*. Just don't let anyone know where you got it from. Legend goes that, if you share the website, and if Mr. Sticks finds out, you'll wind up in a creek. With a hundred pins in your eyes."

That said, she lowered the phone, put a finger to her lips, and glanced around her, as if afraid that someone might be lurking nearby. Then she laughed, slapped her knees, and jogged past Lucia, eager to be reunited with her friends.

Chapter 11

"You sure this is the place?" Lucia said, standing before the house on Carriage Drive. "Looks too nice to belong to a glorified waiter. This thing must be two thousand square feet."

"Or more," Brian said, looking up at the arched second-storey windows and across at the attached three-car garage. "One of my warehouse guys used to work as a drywall installer and he says these houses are prime. Some of the nicest in the city."

"Then let's take a tour," Lucia said, leading the way up the drive, past the immaculately-placed shrubs, and to the recessed doorway. From there, she could only see manicured lawns, blue skies, budding trees, and fresh-laid pavement, and she forgot—briefly—that she was still in Eaton, Colorado. There were no rusted-out trucks, no fields awash with corn, no barnyard cats rooting through garbage…. The neighborhood was a microcosm within a microcosm—a place where the scent of new turf and latex paint overwhelmed the aroma of dust and pollen. Lucia was sure that, in time, the development would be consumed by the surrounding city—that the polished edges would lose their shine; that the roads would crack and the lawns would dry out and the windows would become glazed in allergens—but she tried to not think that far into the future.

At the door, she paused, collected herself, and jabbed at the bell. She expected a shrill buzz to accompany the action, as most of the houses in the older parts of town were fitted with the same system, but she was pleasantly surprised. The sound that drifted onto the porch was both soft and melodic—a happy sound that, somewhat magically, melted the knots from her shoulders.

She didn't have to wait long for an answer.

"Yes?" a kindly old woman said, opening the door wide and favoring her guests with a warm—if questioning—smile. "Can I help you?"

"Actually, I'm not sure," Lucia said, taking a small step backward. "We were told that Peter Janowski lives here. Are we at the wrong place?"

"Oh, no. No, no, no. You're at the right place. I'm Bernadette Janowski. Peter's mother," the woman said. "Peter lives down in the basement. We don't have a separate entrance, though, so I understand your confusion. Are you friends of his?"

"Something like that," Brian said, attempting to hide the bloodstains on his shirt by holding one hand across his chest, and cradling his chin in the other. "Is Peter in, by chance? We need his help with a…ah…technical matter."

"A technical matter, huh?" Mrs. Janowski tittered. "If you're having trouble with something computer-y, my Peter is definitely the person you want. His room is *filled* with new-fangled thingamajigs. He probably has more gizmos than NASA. Just last week, he reset the satellite receiver for the television and he fixed the…ah…. Shoot. What is that little internet doodad called? The one that hooks into the phone line and sends out—what do you kids call it? *Wee fee?*"

There, Lucia and Brian traded glances.

"Are you talking about an *internet router*?" Brian said at last.

"Yes! That's it! That's the gizmo!" Mrs. Janowski laughed, causing her tight white bob to bounce around her neck. She was a peculiar old bird—shaped, quite literally, like an oversized duck—but then, Lucia was used to dealing with peculiar people. Her first job in the city had been at a call center, where she'd fielded calls from technologically inept customers. While not a high point in her career, that job had taught her a number of valuable skills, which she had refined and utilized in subsequent positions.

Calling upon her reserves of patience, Lucia negotiated an invitation to the living room, where the topic of discussion turned to dot-com millionaires, cell phone towers, and politi-corporate corruption. Mrs. Janowski was one of those later-in-life naturopaths who believed that doctors were in league with pharmaceutical companies, that non-organic food should be collected and shot into space, and that the government was irradiating its people in order to shorten lifespans and to boost the economy via cancer treatments and medications. She also had some unique views about the apocalypse and about Rosh Hashanah, the Jewish holiday, but Lucia wasn't forced to form any on the spot opinions about those topics. As Mrs. Janowski prattled on about Benjamin Netanyahu, the Israeli Prime Minister, Peter appeared, and surreptitiously cleared his throat.

Two minutes later, Lucia, Brian, and Peter were in the basement, and Peter's bedroom door was locked behind them.

"Sorry about that," Peter said, gathering up scattered magazines, placing books on shelves, containerizing dirty laundry, and straightening the comforter on his bed. "My mom is…well…my *mom*. She doesn't get out a whole lot anymore. Not since my dad moved out."

"Yeah. My parents are divorced, too," Brian said, soaking in the bank of computer towers and monitors that dominated the north wall. "Happened when I was thirteen. How about you?"

"Oh…my parents aren't divorced," Peter returned quickly. "Eight months ago my parents bought a project house in California, so my dad's been over there, fixing it up. He's retired, so he can come and go as he pleases." A pause. "I am sorry about your parents, though."

In response, Brian shrugged. Then he shot Lucia a look that said: "Who the fuck *is* this guy? We don't have *any* other options?"

"No. We don't. So sit down and behave yourself," Lucia communicated, via arched eyebrows and a terse nod.

Displeasure conveyed, Lucia unlocked her phone, brought up a memo with the text "9v99yw.onion," and placed the device, face-up, on Peter's workstation.

"What's this?" Peter said, glancing from the phone to Lucia, and back again. "My first guess is that it's connected to our discussion the other night. My second guess is that you're a postmodern visual artist, and that this is your idea of an installation."

"Door number one," Lucia confirmed, without delay. "We have it on good authority that Finley was playing *Mr. Sticks' Labyrinth* on the night she disappeared, so we believe—"

"Hold up. *Mr. Sticks' Labyrinth?*" Peter interrupted.

Lucia inclined her head. "Yeah. Have you heard of it?"

"Never outside of deep web chat rooms," Peter said, taking a seat before his panel of computer equipment and booting up one of the bigger, flashier models. "*Mr. Sticks' Labyrinth* has been a part of—pardon the expression—cyber lore for years. To the best of my knowledge, it sprung up in the early oughts, and it's been floating around ever since, frightening greenhorns and journeymen. Most think it's a myth that some tech geek created to keep kids from going too deep, but there is a small faction of believers—people who swear that Mr. Sticks is real, and that it's possible to reach him by getting to the end of the game. Personally, I fall into the first category, but then again, I've never seen any actual proof. If this website is the real deal…"

Peter didn't bother to finish the sentence. He let his fingers do his talking for him. In a matter of seconds, he had a Tor browser open and Destinee's deep web URL plugged into the search bar. He explained the finer points of the Tor web browser as he pressed Enter and waited for the desired page to load, but Lucia only caught bits and pieces of his diatribe. She didn't particularly understand how proxies worked, or how secure browsers differed, so she stood back and muttered "uh-huh" and "hmm" until there was something on the screen to digest.

She wasn't disappointed.

Once Peter's computer made the connection to the site's server, his screen went black and a single phrase appeared, flanked by two MS-DOS style buttons. The phrase read: Mr. Sticks welcomes you. Would you like to play his game? And the buttons followed suit. One read Yes, while the other read No.

"Looks pretty real to me," Lucia mumbled, looking from one side of the monitor to the other. She half expected another block of text to appear or a selection of links to materialize in the margins, but the screen didn't flicker.

Yes or no. Those are our options, she thought. *We can either go forward, right now, or we can call it off. The decision is up to us.*

Brian must have been reading her mind.

"So?" he said, peering over Peter's shoulder. "What is it going to be? Are we going to do this, or not? I vote yes. We've come this far, haven't we?"

Yes. We have, Lucia thought. But she was unable to force any words through her vocal chords. The majority were stuck in her belly—mired in acid; unable to navigate the knots in her trachea. She tried to remedy the situation by re-inflating her lungs, but the excess oxygen seemed to leak out of her, not unlike a punctured balloon.

There was something strange and unappealing about the website itself, she determined. The minimal details and the outdated imagery contributed to a sensation of *wrongness*. In the day and age of flash plug-ins, animated GIFs, and embedded videos, the website seemed distinctly out-of-place—as if it should not exist; as if a time warp had absorbed it in the mid-nineties, and deposited it into the deepest bowels of the modern net.

Peter wasn't nearly as creeped out.

"What's the verdict?" the young man said, while shifting his cursor between the two buttons. "In the words of the Clash, should we stay or should we go? If we go there could be trouble…"

"But if we stay there could be double," Lucia concluded. She didn't intend to picture her sister at that moment—didn't intend to visualize bruised limbs, duct-taped wrists, zip-tied ankles, or tendrils of sticky-wet hair—but she did. And that image prompted her to say: "We're going. We don't have a choice. Let's do this."

"Down the rabbit hole it is," Peter said, clicking the button marked Yes and cracking his knuckles. He added that he would've followed the link later on, regardless, but Lucia wasn't particularly reassured by his machismo. She had a leaden weight in her gut before the video window appeared—again, against a black background—and she had a leaden weight in her gut after the video started playing.

She shouldn't have been disturbed by the old-timey cartoon character who skipped down the old-timey cartoon street, swinging his arms to a lively carnival tune, but then, there was something *off* about the animation. The look on the cartoon character's face was empty. Despondent. As if he didn't care where he was going or how long it took him to get there.

To compound the sense of otherworldliness, there was a limited number of buildings in the background. Every few seconds, the scrolling animation would repeat, giving the impression that the goofy mouse was making precious little headway.

"What is this?" Lucia finally asked, following five minutes of uninterrupted, unchanging footage. "Is this some kind of a joke?"

"No. I don't think it's a joke," Peter muttered. "I think it's the first clue in the game. Look at those buildings."

"What about them?"

"Do you notice anything interesting?"

"Other than the fact that the artist ran out of patience?" Brian chimed in.

His observation went unanswered.

"There are ten numbers, total," Peter said. "The first building is marked *fifty-one*. The second is marked *seven*. The third? *Two*. The fifth? *Eighteen*. The sixth? *Thirteen*. The eighth? *Zero*. And the ninth?"

"*Three*. Yeah. We can read," Lucia said as the cartoon character picked up speed; as his lips peeled back, forming a rictus grin; as the tempo of the music became fevered, and the chords dissonant. "What does it mean, though? Is it another deep web URL?"

"No. Deep web URLs contain a random combination of numbers and letters, to make them harder to track down and harder to remember," Peter said, while scratching the digits onto a scrap of notebook paper. "If I'm not mistaken, this is a phone number."

"You're kidding me."

"Maybe I am, maybe I'm not. There's only one way to find out," Peter said, handing the sliver of paper over to Lucia, and fixing her with an expectant look.

A part of Lucia hoped that Brian would take the lead and dial the number himself, as the activity on the computer monitor and the cacophony streaming from the speakers was making her feel physically ill, but Brian didn't make a move toward her. He remained where he was, as if he was rooted to the floor—unable to lift his boots or even crack a reassuring smile. "Well?" his eyes seemed to say. "Are you going to do it, or aren't you?"

Determined to not look weak for a second time in one day, Lucia snagged her cell phone, dialed *-6-7, to block her own number, and punched in the row of handwritten digits. She hadn't bothered to block her number in years—hadn't since the summer Deborah Hollinger had acquired a voice changer and a local phone directory—so she wasn't entirely comfortable when she pressed the speaker to her ear. She felt like a clumsy teen again, psyching herself up for a string of prank calls.

"Hello, sir. Is your refrigerator running? It is? Well, then, you should probably go catch it!"

That line had been Deborah's favorite. The girl had laughed hysterically every time Lucia had said it. Deborah had tried it herself a few times, but had broken into a fit of giggles before the end, effectively ruining the result.

How many summers had Lucia and Deborah spent together, before The Attack? Seven? Lucia had vague memories of the two of them competing in middle school. Deborah had been faster on the track, but Lucia had been faster in the pool. By freshman year, their coaches had begun calling them "the Dynamic Duo."

The Dynamic Duo.

Funny… Lucia hadn't thought about that in a coon's age. Not since—

Lucia froze. There was a voice on the line. A woman's voice. But it didn't belong to a flesh-and-blood human. It was a recording. It advised Lucia that she'd reached a number that did not exist, and invited her to hang up and try again. So she did. And she was rewarded with the same message.

"Shit," she sighed, suddenly aware that the video was no longer playing on the monitor. "It's no good. Are you sure the numbers are in the right order?"

"As sure as I can be, given the circumstances," Peter said. "While you were dialing, the cartoon mouse collapsed and…well…it's gone."

"What's gone?"

"The video player...the file...all of it," Peter said, swiping his cursor across the black screen. "I can't find it anywhere."

"He even looked in the source code," Brian contributed. "No luck."

"Then what are our options?" Lucia said. She didn't *want* to revisit the video in her mental theater—didn't want to re-expose the darker side of her psyche to the haunting sepia tones, the dizzying melody, the startling and disturbing rictus grin—but she was willing to unspool the film reel, if necessary. She was willing to comb through every individual frame if it meant unearthing a clue that might, eventually, lead to her sister.

Perhaps seeing her desperation, Peter swiveled and said: "My advice? We should sleep on it. One of us might remember something that the others missed. Failing that...we can try the link again tomorrow. The video may have a one-play-per-day maximum."

Or there may be something monitoring the page; making sure the rules of the game are enforced, Lucia thought. She wasn't sure why she thought it, or why she thought "some*thing*" rather than "some*one*," but she could already tell that she was treading water in a very deep—and a very *dark*—lake.

Chapter 12

For an hour, Lucia lay in her father's guest bedroom and Googled the phrase "Mr. Sticks." There weren't many results on the surface web, and those few results she did come across were conflicting and excessively fantastic. One site—hosted on a free server—claimed that Mr. Sticks was a reimagining of Thanatos, the Greek god of death. Another asserted that Mr. Sticks was, in actuality, a woodland fairy who had been captured and distorted by witches. A third attempted to further the notion that Mr. Sticks was a living shadow who dwelt in a subterranean castle and who ventured out each night to harvest children. That particular author didn't provide any foundation for his claims or explain *why* a shadow would need *children*, but he seemed sincere in his beliefs. In the comments section, he vehemently defended his position, going as far as to threaten dissenters with slow and painful death.

Disappointed, and underwhelmed by the childlike depictions of amorphous squid men, Lucia closed her browser window and stared up at the ceiling. She tried to occupy her mind by searching out faces and shapes in the plaster textures—something she'd done as a child, to put herself to sleep—but she couldn't focus. All she could see was the cartoon mouse. Each time she blinked, he became sharper and more detailed. First, she saw she circles that formed his torso, his head, his ears, and his eyes. Then she saw his spaghetti-like arms and legs. The buttons on his old-timey overalls appeared next, but her attention was drawn to the lines on the cartoon mouse's face—the downturned lips and the rheumy, half-present pupils.

Hearing her father in the kitchen, Lucia sat up and ran a palm across her stomach. She was hungry, but she was afraid that, if she sat down with a plate of food, the meal would turn to cardboard in her mouth. It was a silly fear, but she couldn't shake it. Images of cartoon eggs, cartoon ham, and cartoon Brussels sprouts filled her head.

Was she going crazy? No. She wasn't going crazy. She was just tired and worried and paranoid. The nebulous nature of the internet made Mr. Sticks' existence seem possible, if not plausible. But then, wasn't that the case with most urban legends? Even the most outlandish stories could obtain a veneer of truth, following a lengthy game of telephone.

Releasing a languid breath, Lucia leveraged her body to the edge of the bed and plucked the sliver of notebook paper from the nightstand. She wanted to believe that the numbers held a clue, but her optimism was fading. She couldn't glance at the handwritten digits without Destinee's zealous denial echoing in her skull.

"You guys seriously want to play that damned game?" she heard, followed by: *"There's nothing real about it. It's a story that some creepy yahoo made up to scare kids during camping trips."*

But that wasn't all Destinee had said. Destinee had also said that, according to legend, Mr. Sticks was an escape; that, one way or another, he delivered his acolytes from their troubles and cares. In the eyes of his disciples, he wasn't a monster from another realm. He was a type of father figure; a protector.

Maybe that's my problem, Lucia thought, sitting up straight. *Maybe I've been wearing the wrong pair of glasses since the beginning. Maybe the mouse in the video is supposed to represent a believer. And maybe the end of his journey isn't madness and death. Maybe that's the beginning.*

Played backwards, the video wouldn't depict the mouse's demise. It would show the exact opposite. It would show the mouse rising up; becoming progressively more relaxed. Which meant…

Equal parts excited and anxious, Lucia reversed the digits on the sheet of notebook paper and punched the resulting number into her phone. She didn't want to get her hopes up prematurely, but her hunch felt *right*. There was a logic to it. A crazy logic, sure, but a logic nonetheless.

Her heart skipping and her fingertips tingling with nervous energy, she pressed the phone to her ear and breathlessly counted the seconds.

At "six Mississippi," the call connected.

First, she heard a click, then a whir, then the sound of wet lips parting and a tongue slipping from the roof of a well-moistened mouth.

It was another recording. But it wasn't the same message she'd reached before.

"Mr. Sticks, Mr. Sticks, master of tricks," a man recited, from the depths of his chest. "Tall as a shadow and wide as a mouse. Call him and tease him, but don't disappease him…or you might end up stiff as Barb Klaus."

As the message played, Lucia imagined a man in his late twenties, hunched over an antique writing desk, a cassette recorder pressed to his lips and an oil lamp burning before him. She imagined his beard, neatly trimmed, and his hands, scarred and calloused from hard labor. She didn't imagine the room around him, but rather, she imagined that he was perched amidst an ocean of blackness. Sticky blackness that pulsed and receded like cancerous tissue. Or like the fibers of a giant spider's web. Then the message ended, and the vision disappeared. Just like that. One second it was there, and the next it was gone.

Unsure what to make of the limerick—or verse, or whatever the hell it was—Lucia called the number again, and transposed the words onto a spare sheet of paper. That done, she hung up, and punched the first few sentences into her phone's web browser. She had never been a student of poetry, but she had rubbed elbows with it enough to know that context was everything. Without context, poetry was nothing more than a collection of nonsensical alliterations.

To understand the poem, she had to understand the author.

Fortunately, the latter had a web presence.

"Travis St. John," she muttered, locating a handful of his poems on a site called ArtistArchive.org. According to his bio, he was a twenty-five-year-old poet and painter from Philadelphia who enjoyed fine wines and long walks in the fall. But his profile hadn't been updated in years. His last poem had been submitted on January 9, 2012, and his personal information had been revised not long after.

Curious, Lucia backtracked to the search results and scrolled further down the list. She looked, briefly, at a review of Mr. St. John's work, which appeared in a low-budget e-zine, and at a book, which contained one or two of Mr. St John's earlier efforts, but her attention wasn't arrested until she brought up her search engine's second page.

There, underneath a paid advertisement for a self-publishing company, lay a newspaper article with the headline: "Local Man Found Dead in Wissahickon Valley Park." It wasn't a new article—it was dated February 6, 2012—but it caused the breath to catch in Lucia's throat, regardless.

Was Travis St. John to blame for her sister's disappearance? Had he killed a man in 2012, fled, and aligned himself with the legend of Mr. Sticks, in order to lure unwitting teenagers into his arms? To continue his reign of terror? To sate his lust for blood?

While the theory sounded good on paper, it was seriously flawed.

Two paragraphs into the article, Lucia learned that the headline referred not to a victim of Mr. St John's, but Mr. St. John himself. Apparently, Mr. St. John had ventured into the park late on February 4, wearing nothing but a light sweater, had handcuffed himself to a tree, and, during the course of the night, had succumbed to hypothermia. A jogger had found him early the next morning and had contacted the police straightaway. The first detectives on scene had suspected foul play, due to Mr. St. John's ruined fingernails and the scratch marks on the tree, but foul play had been ruled out when a note had been found in Mr. St. John's pocket. Through the note, and through contact with Mr. St. John's father, police had determined that a schizophrenic break was to blame. According to a police spokesperson, Mr. St. John had been diagnosed some years before, but had refused to take his medication as prescribed. In the days leading up to his death, he'd grown excessively paranoid and fearful.

But paranoid and fearful about what? Lucia wondered, upon reaching the end of the article. She would have killed for a picture of the crime scene or for a transcript of the alleged suicide note, but the article was vague in those regards. The author seemed more interested in the big picture than in the nitty-gritty. Perhaps his reservation stemmed from the grisly nature of the case. Or perhaps the details had been purposefully withheld, to keep public interest at a minimum.

With no other resources to satisfy her interest, she forked over twenty dollars for a background check on the deceased poet, and browsed through the list of known relatives. She was looking for a brother or an uncle—someone who could provide some objective answers—but there were no brothers or uncles on file. There was only a woman named Diana St. John.

Travis St. John's mother.

Shit.

Unsure whether she would be able to coax anything out of a bitter sixty-four-year-old woman, Lucia punched Mrs. St. John's number into her phone, pressed Send, and mentally ran through a number of platitudes while the call connected. She didn't want to come off as overly apologetic, but she couldn't afford to sound indifferent, either. She had to walk the line between forceful and understanding. She had to—

"Hello?"

"Mrs. St. John?" Lucia said, faster than she intended. "My name is Lucia Corvi, and I—"

"Who?"

"Lucia Corvi," Lucia repeated. "I'm from Colorado, and I—"

"Do I know you?"

"Personally? No. You don't. But I knew your son," Lucia lied, praying that the old woman's mind was sharper than her voice. Over the phone, Mrs. St. John sounded anesthetized and frail. Either her grief had prematurely aged her or she'd gone through some sort of a physically disabling disease. She could have easily passed as a ninety-year-old with a respiratory condition.

"You knew Travis?" the old woman said, perking up ever so slightly. "That's lovely, dear. Just lovely. Did you make it to the wake?"

"No. I didn't. I was away. At school. Overseas," Lucia said haltingly. "I'm sure it was wonderful, though."

"Yes. It was. It was wonderful," Mrs. St. John cooed. "It was precisely what Travis would've wanted. We had wine and music and crackers…and we all wrote something in his dream journal. Have you seen his dream journal, dear?"

"No. I haven't. Which is why I'm calling," Lucia riffed. "I'm hoping to learn more about him. About his last days, I mean. I hear he was…*troubled*."

"Who? Travis?" Mrs. St. John said. "No, no, no. Travis was never troubled. Travis was a happy and talented young man. It was those doctors' fault."

"Those doctors?"

"Yes. The men who gave my son those nasty pills," Mrs. St. John confirmed. "Travis never had any problems before those pills. He said they made him feel strange. But when he stopped taking them, he *saw* things."

"What kinds of things?"

"All kinds of things. Things that shouldn't exist. Things that *couldn't* exist."

"He told you that?"

"No. But he didn't have to. He said it through his poetry," Mrs. St. John swallowed. "The last thing he wrote was…"

She didn't continue. And Lucia concluded that it was in her best interest to not press the issue. The woman was clearly losing control of her emotions. If Lucia didn't tread lightly, there was a good chance that she'd wind up burning her bridge.

"Is there someone else I can contact to learn more about his poetry?" she inquired, when she judged the silence to be sufficiently sympathetic. "Maybe he had a girlfriend or a—"

"No. No girlfriends. Travis was a very private person," Mrs. St. John interjected. "He *was* active in this one group, though. He called it…he called it a *collective*. Isn't that silly? Makes me think of a beehive. A big old beehive, bustling with activity." A pause. "Have you ever seen a real-life bee farm, dear?"

"No. I'm afraid I haven't. But I am interested in this collective," Lucia said, struggling to keep her tone light; to keep the train from jumping the tracks. "You don't happen to remember what the group is called, do you? A name would go a long way."

"Oh, I understand, dear," Mrs. St. John said. "The trouble is… my memory isn't what it used to be. I suspect that it's affected by one of my medications, but I take so many that I can't keep them straight. That's what happens when you get old, I suppose. Things don't work the way they used to. But that's neither here nor there. A young thing like you…" Mrs. St. John stopped herself. "What were we talking about, again?"

"The *collective*," Lucia said, more vehemently. She felt like a preschool teacher, trying to draw an answer out of an easily-distracted student. Only she didn't have a juice box to incentivize cooperation. All she had was her voice.

Fortunately, a juice box wasn't necessary.

"Oh. Yes. The collective. They sent me such a lovely card when they learned of my son's passing," the old woman said. "I keep it on the dining room table, along with all the other cards. Would you like me to read it to you, dear?"

"If you wouldn't mind. Yes. Yes please," Lucia stammered. She was a little shocked by the turn of events and she wanted to thank the woman profusely, but she held off. She could thank the woman after she had her answers. Anything she said in the interim would jeopardize her odds of success.

Chapter 13

"What's this?" Peter said, peering through the Focus's driver-side window and studying the image on Lucia's phone. It was only nine o'clock in the morning, but he was already dressed in his Wednesday best: yellow and green button-down, paired with navy slacks; his black hair tastefully parted. "You do realize I'm on the clock, don't you?"

"Yes. But this is important," Lucia said, snatching the large coffee from his hands and depositing it in her cup holder. "Last night, I made a breakthrough."

"A breakthrough?"

"A breakthrough," Lucia parroted, suddenly wishing she'd ordered a croissant to go with her coffee. "I reversed that number we got from the mouse video, which led me to a poet named Travis St. John. Have you heard of him?"

"Unless his alter-ego is Robert Frost, no," Peter said. "I don't really keep track of that scene. Too dramatic. I went to a poetry slam once and all it did was make me wonder if I was in a weird musical."

"Okay. Then I'll make this brief," Lucia said. "Back in the winter of 2012, Travis killed himself."

"Metaphorically or literally?"

"Literally. He walked into the middle of a state park, handcuffed himself to a tree, tossed the keys into a bush, and let the cold finish the job."

"Holy shit. Why?"

"That's the million-dollar question," Lucia said, ignoring the looks she was accumulating from the diner's regular patrons. "The cops say he was a lifelong schizophrenic and that he was driven by depression, but that doesn't explain the handcuffs. Or why he attempted to escape during the night."

"It doesn't?"

"No," Lucia said. "Think about it. There are a million ways to kill yourself. Travis could've slit his wrists, overdosed on pills, hung himself, or jumped off a bridge. But he chose to *handcuff himself to a tree*. Doesn't that seem unusual?"

"Sure. To you and me. But artists don't function on the same wavelength," Peter shrugged. "Salvador Dali...Sylvia Plath...Hunter S. Thompson...they're not exactly pillars of sanity. Maybe Travis killed himself to prove a point. Maybe he thought he could achieve more notoriety through his death than through his life."

"Maybe," Lucia allowed. "But I chatted with a few members of his artistic collective and they said Travis *wasn't* suicidal. They said Travis *did* suffer from schizophrenia, but that he never discussed suicide on their message boards. They said his favorite subject was—care to guess? No? Fine. *Mr. Sticks*," Lucia concluded. "According to his collective buddies, he was obsessed with the mythology. He spent most of his free time researching the phenomenon and composing poems about its central figure. He was convinced that Mr. Sticks was real and that it was possible to summon him."

"Wait. *Summon*?" Peter said. "Like a demon?"

Lucia inclined her head. "At the beginning of his research, he believed that Mr. Sticks was a benevolent—or at least apathetic—creature. After a few months, though, his opinion changed."

"Why?"

"He came to the conclusion that Mr. Sticks was following him," Lucia said, lowering her voice progressively as she spoke. "He believed that he'd poked the bear, as it were, and that Mr. Sticks was stalking him; breaking him down; looking for *a way in*. He started to see Mr. Sticks everywhere—on the bus, at the park, on the street.... Even in his own apartment."

"And you learned all this from his internet buddies?"

"No. Not all of it," Lucia admitted. "I got some of it from the horse's mouth."

"How?"

"Two parts luck, two parts womanly intuition, and six parts determination," Lucia said.

Apparently, that wasn't enough of an explanation.

Following several seconds of expectant silence, she sighed and said: "I may have harassed the collective until they handed over the URL to Travis's deep web blog. And I may have spent three hours figuring out that encrypted web browser of yours. Happy?"

"Impressed," Peter said, wiping a spot of sausage grease from his nametag. "You've taken to this detective thing faster than a fish to water. Are you sure you weren't a KGB agent in a former life?"

Knowing that any kind of answer would lead to a discussion about the Soviet Union, which would lead to a diatribe about Russian politics, which would lead to a critical—and lengthy—examination of Cold War propaganda, Lucia wet her lips and said: "Crazy or not, Travis St. John handcuffed himself to that tree to keep Mr. Sticks at bay. He was convinced that Mr. Sticks was trying to possess him, and he was convinced that, if Mr. Sticks succeeded, more than one person would die. And now he's become a part of Mr. Sticks' mythology."

"In what way?" Peter inquired. His tone was changing—becoming more guarded—but she could tell that he was struggling with the details. He couldn't see the bigger picture because the puzzle pieces were spread out before him in no particular order.

To clarify things, Lucia brought up her phone one more time and jabbed a finger at the image on the display. "This is a screen capture from Travis's blog," she said. "It's actually the second to last post he ever made. In it, he talks about a videogame that he found on a dark net server. A lot of what he says is loopy, but I believe the link at the bottom of the page is legit. I believe the videogame is the next clue. And I believe we can reach it tonight, at one."

"Why so late?"

"Travis writes that the videogame is only live between three o'clock and four o'clock, Eastern Time," Lucia explained. "He says that, if you attempt to log in too early, your IP address will be blackballed."

"Okay, but he also says that homosexuals are from another planet and that black people are related to the gods of the underworld," Peter pointed out. "He doesn't really sound like the most reliable source of information. Why don't we take a step back and—"

"No."

"No?"

"I'm not taking a step back," Lucia said, wanting to stand up so the two of them could be on the same level. "I may be spinning my wheels, but as long as I'm spinning my wheels, I'm sure as hell going to spin them in the right direction. My sister is *out there*, Peter. She's out there and I'm not sure how long I have to find her. If something happens to her…and it happens because I'm over here, second guessing myself…I couldn't live with that. Could you?"

"I—" Peter began. Then he thought better of it and he pursed his lips; drummed his fingers on the roof of her car. He was split. In any normal situation, he would have told her to cool her heels. He would have reminded her that patience was a virtue, via a number of artful euphemisms, and he would have warned against foolhardy, emotionally-charged decisions. But he wasn't in a normal situation. Lucia could tell that her trepidation was affecting him.

"Twelve o'clock," he said at last. "Brian, you, and I should meet up an hour early so that we can share notes and make sure we're on the same page. How does my place sound?"

"Perfect," Lucia said, experiencing a subtle warmth in her chest. "I'll bring the coffee. Do you take yours black or with cream and sugar?"

"Neither," Peter said, straightening and brushing at his shirt, as if the action might rid him of the horrible yellow and green stripes. "I stopped drinking coffee shortly after high school. Makes me sleepy. I prefer a nice green tea. But it has to be jasmine-infused, and it has to be full-leaf. Know what I mean?"

Lucia didn't, but she didn't let on. She figured she had time to track down Peter's tea of choice while she waited for midnight to roll around.

Chapter 14

While shopping had never been one of Lucia's favorite activities, she was thankful for the distraction it provided. She was thankful for the bright lights and the linoleum floors and the garish product labels. It all reminded her that the world was still spinning—that the vast majority of people were going about their boring, everyday lives.

To the men and women she passed in the grocery store aisles, Mr. Sticks was a nonconcern. At best, he was a form of boogeyman: a shapeless figure who cast a shadow over their dreams. She could tell in the way they bustled past one another, filling their carts with cat food and shaving cream and chocolate pudding. A few of them might have been dealing with serious personal issues, but the rest? The rest were coasting—stressing over leaky faucets and the latest celebrity breakups.

Following a brief visit to Cynthia's Emporium—a natural goods outfit which used the terms "locally sourced" and "renewable resources" nearly as much as "non-GMO;" which occupied the lower portion of a house that would have made the Munsters proud—Lucia ventured downtown and drove past the rows of mom-and-pop shops. She could have burnt more time by parking and walking from one door to the next, but she wasn't in the mood to socialize. She didn't want the owners smiling and hugging her; asking about her cane; inquiring about her family; reminiscing about The Good Old Days; offering unsolicited advice; telling her what a gorgeous woman she'd become. She didn't want any of it. But she didn't want to spend the rest of the afternoon in her own head, either.

Spotting a tea display in the Old World Café, Lucia parked, checked the street for any familiar vehicles, and started for the glass double doors. She hesitated outside when she saw a flurry of movement behind the register, but she didn't recognize the teenage girl responsible, so she pressed forward.

Her arrival was heralded by a less-than-enthusiastic greeting.

"Hello and welcome to Old World, where our tea is divine and our coffee sublime," the girl said, without looking up from her fashion magazine. "Have you been here before?"

"Yes. I have. But it's been a while," Lucia said, inhaling the heady aroma of freshly-roasted coffee beans and exotic spices. "You do have green tea, don't you?"

"Oh yeah. We have green tea, black tea, white tea, yellow tea... even something called *oolong tea*," the girl muttered. "Most of them are on that shelf over there. We may have some more in the back, if you'd like me to check."

"No, no. There's no need for that," Lucia assured the girl. "I'm sure I'll be able to find what I need out here. I'm an expert at browsing."

"You and everyone else," the girl seemed to say, licking her index finger and flipping from one page to the next. Her lackadaisical attitude may have bothered some of the town's older and more conventional residents, but Lucia was grateful for the lack of attention. For the first time in days, she felt *anonymous*.

That feeling didn't last.

Halfway through the first row of tea tins, she heard a door creak open, a sudden intake of breath, and her name, paired with the phrase "Is that you?" and she turned to find Deborah Hollinger in the storeroom entrance. The woman had put on some thirty pounds since her senior year in high school, but she wore it well. The weight accentuated her feminine curves and gave her extra volume up top, which she further accentuated with a low-cut blouse and a rather aggressive push-up bra. Lucia thought the woman could've passed as a vapid reality television starlet, given a personal trainer and a tan, but she kept that opinion to herself.

"Oh my gosh, girl! I haven't seen you in ages!" the woman gushed, hurrying across the floor and wrapping Lucia in an impromptu hug.

Lucia was taken off guard by the gesture, considering the way she'd left things, so she wasn't ready with a rejoinder when the hug ended. Not that Deborah gave her much of an opportunity.

"How are you these days? Still living in the city?" the woman said, mere seconds after their bodies parted. "I hear the housing market in Denver is crazy. Doug—you remember Doug, don't you? Dirty Doug? Pizza face Doug? Anyway, he ran an article about real estate forecasts last week. I guess the whole Front Range is a hot commodity right now. Prices are supposed to quadruple in the next ten years. Isn't that insane? To me, that's insane." Then she realized that she was the one doing all the talking and she stopped; apologized.

"It's just…I had no idea that you were back in town," she blathered. "Have you been here long?"

"No. Not long. A couple of days," Lucia said, attempting to camouflage her surprise and confusion by mimicking the smile on her former friend's face. "I finally accrued some vacation time, so I figured, why not? Life can get hectic in the city."

"I bet," Deborah gushed. "I spent a weekend in Chicago for a relative's wedding and I was blown away by the size of it all. The buildings seemed to go on forever. And the people? There was never an empty street. Or an empty train. I was in a crowd the whole time I was near the…ah…what's it called? That place where all the lines come together?"

"The Loop?" Lucia guessed.

"Yes! That's it! That's the one!" Deborah laughed. "Hard to tell I'm a small-town girl, isn't it? It's amazing that I didn't get lost during our trips to Thornton. Remember our first night in that hotel, sophomore year? I went down to the lobby to get an extra pillow and somehow I ended up in the parking garage."

"Yeah. *Somehow*," Lucia said. "I saw you bumming drinks from that bartender while coach's back was turned. How many more shots did you do before you went to the front desk for your pillow?"

"Three," Deborah said, with a wink. "But they weren't straight up whiskey. And they didn't have anything to do with my ending up in the garage. That hotel was plain confusing. It had three sets of elevators, three sets of staircases, and four different entryways. Any fifteen-year-old farm girl would've gotten turned around."

"Sure. Whatever you say," Lucia smirked. She considered following that up with a question about Deborah's love life, as Deborah's presence in her father's house still struck her as unusual, but such an inquiry would've been awkward and out of place. Such an inquiry would've made Lucia sound suspicious, which would've, in turn, raised Deborah's internal alarms.

Deborah might've been a bottle blond with a breast obsession, but she wasn't stupid.

Opting to err on the side of caution, Lucia gestured around her and said: "At any rate, this is impressive. Really changed the place around. Different flooring, different color scheme, different layout. Even the ceiling's been renovated."

"Yeah. That was my idea," Deborah said, looking up and about with the pride of a new mother. "Took a while to convince my dad, but he's a sucker for the sad princess routine. Besides, I told him I wouldn't manage the store unless he gave the place a facelift."

"So you blackmailed him. Smooth," Lucia said, wishing the woman would volunteer some pertinent information.

At the moment, Lucia felt like a pirate, floating in the midst of a glassy sea, waiting for a breeze to catch her sails so that she could set her ship on a more favorable course. She was—honestly—happy to see the woman again, and she was happy that the two of them were getting along, but she had too many unanswered questions to be completely at ease.

On the bright side, the years had dulled Deborah's psychosomatic sensitivity.

"*Blackmailed?*" the woman beamed. "No, no, no. It's not blackmail if the victim has more to gain from the transaction than the criminal. I prefer the term *coerced compliance*. It sounds better. Less…1950s Chicago. But that's enough about me. What are you up to? You're certainly looking well. Is there a man in your life? A boy toy, maybe?"

"No. On both counts," Lucia said, twirling her cane; wondering if this was her opening. "At my office, most of the men are already taken. Those that aren't taken…well…let's just say there's a good reason."

"Slobs, huh?" Deborah said, the way that women did when discussing competition, members of the opposite sex, children, or disobedient dogs. "In my experience, the younger the stud, the bigger the mess. You should keep your eyes open for an older guy. Not *old* old, mind you, but experienced."

Like my dad? Lucia thought.

Again, she kept her mouth closed.

"Forty-five might *sound* ancient, but it's actually not that bad," Deborah continued, oblivious to the scenarios running through Lucia's head. "Guys who keep it tight at that age are keepers. They're good in bed, they generally have money, and they don't give a shit if you come home hammered at two in the morning. There's really no downside. Except the ED," she amended. "You do have to watch out for that. That can be a bummer."

"Noted," Lucia said. Then she casually brushed a strand of hair from her forehead and inquired about Deborah's own romantic entanglements. She tried to make the question sound cool and off-the-cuff, but she'd never been an extraordinary actor. To her, the words were wooden, as if they'd been pulled from the pages of an unfinished script.

For what it was worth, Deborah didn't blink.

"As a modern woman, I do my best to keep two or three names on my booty call list," she said, with a "know what I mean?" elbow to Lucia's ribs. "A couple of years ago I had a half dozen, but that was too much work."

"Because they were all out-of-towners?" Lucia followed up.

Deborah shook her head. "No. Not all of them. A few, yes, but I always keep a stable of locals. For that last-minute fuck. Nothing is worse than being horny and having to drive halfway across the state."

"Yeah. I imagine a commute would make things difficult," Lucia contributed, while searching Deborah's pupils for signs of evasion. As adolescents, pre-teens, and teenagers, the two girls had been in synch. They'd been able to read each other's moods flawlessly, through nonverbal communication. They'd been able to say more through a raised eyebrow than some people could through a megaphone. But those days were no more. Time and space had worn that connection thin.

"Speaking of commutes…how is your family?" Deborah said, without missing a beat. "I see your mom and your dad now and again, but not Finley. Is she doing well?"

"We hope so," Lucia said, as objectively as she could. "She's actually gone missing, these last few days. We think she's—"

Kidnapped, her brain screamed.

Her mouth opted for a less fantastical option.

"—run away," she concluded. "The police are looking for her as we speak."

"Are you serious?"

"I wish I weren't."

"That's horrible."

"Yeah. It is."

There, the conversation petered out and the sound of passing traffic—of all-season tires on heat-softened blacktop—intervened. The latter was slightly better than absolute silence, but it still left Lucia wishing that she could click her heels and transport herself into another dimension. Preferably, a dimension filled with kittens and puppies and all-you-can-eat ice cream parlors.

"Well…wherever Finley is…I'm sure she's just fine," Deborah offered, when it became apparent that there was little left to say. "If she's half as smart as her older sister, she's probably hiding out; partying it up; hitting the old baseball field on Friday nights."

"But there aren't any baseball games on Friday nights," Lucia pointed out.

"Exactly," Deborah returned, a finger to her nose.

Chapter 15

After dark, none of the houses on the Janowskis' block looked, strictly speaking, *real*. They looked like giant dollhouses, plopped on identical plots of land, fronted by perfect rectangles of sod. No lights twinkled in the windows and no vehicles hibernated in the driveways.

It was the sameness of it all, Lucia concluded, that made the whole development seem artificial. As she approached the Janowskis' front porch, she wondered whether the adjacent houses weren't occupied by mannequins. She wondered, if she were to slip in a cracked window, if she wouldn't discover a plastic family at the dinner table; if she wouldn't stumble upon a plastic housewife in the bathtub. The concept was ridiculous, without a doubt, but it left her with a nagging dread, regardless. The thought of faceless beings, posted sentry-like at second-storey windows, made her walk a bit faster and clutch her cane a bit harder.

At the Janowskis' front door, she rang the bell, and she fidgeted while she waited for someone to answer. The street behind her was vacant, but she couldn't shake the sensation that someone was watching her; that she was surrounded by innumerable eyes. Or…a form of eyes, at least. The impressions she received were unfamiliar and ambiguous, as if she were in the presence of something not strictly *human*.

Hearing a distant thrumming, followed by a yowl, Lucia checked her phone.

12:43 a.m.

She was running behind, thanks to an unexpectedly long nap, but she wasn't *that* late. Both Peter and Brian should have been expecting her. They should have been lounging on the other side of the door, talking about vaginas or beers or cars, or whatever the hell men discussed when they were alone.

Had they abandoned her?

The thought popped into her head as she watched one minute bleed into the next, but she refused to entertain it. Both Peter and Brian were dedicated to her cause. They weren't the type to throw up their hands and walk away. Still...the silence concerned her.

Confident that she could fight off a full-grown man with her Dirty Secret, she left the porch and edged along the house's northern façade. She tried to see through the arched living room window, but the space on the other side of the pane was black as pitch. She couldn't make out anything beyond her own reflection—beyond the girl with the sleep-darkened eyes, the moisture-sapped lips, and the disheveled hair.

Lord. She really was a sight.

Reprimanding herself for not checking her appearance in the car, she crept to the house's northeast corner and peered into the back yard. The Janowskis had a five-foot picket fence around the southern portion of their property, which lowered visibility, but Lucia could see something beyond the eggshell-white panels—something of amorphous shape and consistency, which drifted amongst the darkness. She couldn't tell what it was, exactly, but she could tell that it was more than a mirage. She could tell because it froze as soon as she centered her pupils upon it. And then it moved in her direction.

Breath catching in her throat, Lucia took a step away from the apparition, turned, and nearly unleashed the loudest scream of her life.

There, standing no more than six feet away, was Brian Van Pelt.

"Hey. What the hell are you doing out here?" the young man inquired, using the light on his phone to illuminate Lucia and her immediate environs. "Peter and I have been waiting for the past forty-five minutes. Did you get lost or something?"

"No. I...uh...I fell asleep," Lucia stammered, willing her heart to slow. "Did you see...?"

She cut herself off. Not only was the apparition *gone*, it suddenly seemed *less than real.*

"See what?" Brian said, while Lucia scoured the darkness around her. He didn't sound angry, but he didn't sound calm and collected, either.

Lucia's skittishness was putting him on edge.

In an effort to deescalate the situation, Lucia shook her head and said: "Nothing. It's nothing. My eyes are playing tricks on me, that's all. Is Peter downstairs?"

"Yes. And it's nearly one o'clock, so the two of us should boogie," Brian said, placing a hand on her lower back and guiding her toward the porch. Under any other circumstances, she would have found the gesture annoying, if not outright offensive, but she was thankful for the connection, however fleeting. It helped to calm her nerves, and it replaced the knot in her stomach with an unanticipated warmth.

*****

At one o'clock, on the dot, Peter plugged the videogame's URL into his encrypted browser and hit Enter. Lucia half expected a sound effect to accompany the action—a creepy scream, perhaps, or an evil laugh—so she was relieved when the woofers remained static.

"So good so far," Peter said, scrutinizing the grainy menu that filled his monitor. "Some of the instructional text is in Portuguese, but it looks like the gameplay mechanics are boilerplate. Direction keys to move, and the W, A, S, and D keys to look around. Easy peasy."

"Sure. If you're a tech addict," Brian mumbled. "What is this thing called, anyway? There's no title."

"No. There's not," Lucia confirmed. "On his blog, Travis St. John wrote that he played through the game multiple times, and he never reached a definite end. He came to the conclusion that the game was designed to drive a person mad."

"Well, that's reassuring," Brian clucked. "If I would've known earlier, I would've brought my tin foil hats and my necklaces strung with garlic."

"Really?" Peter frowned. "Tin foil and garlic is a strange combination. We'd only need both if we were dealing with aliens *and* vampires. Are you sure you don't mean garlic and mustard seeds?"

A beat passed. Neither Lucia nor Brian spoke. Then Brian leaned forward and said: "Why the fuck would we need mustard seeds?"

Peter must have anticipated such a reaction.

"For the same reason we would need garlic," he said, quick as a hare. "According to lore, vampires are repelled by mustard seeds. You sprinkle them on your roof for protection." And in response to the scowl that materialized on Brian's face: "Hey, don't blame me. I'm just trying to keep our tactics consistent. You'll thank me eventually."

"No. I won't. Because we're never going be attacked by vampires," Brian scowled. "Because vampires don't exist. What we're dealing with here…it's not supernatural. We're dealing with some very screwed up human beings. Right, Lucy?"

"Yeah. Absolutely," Lucia said. But the words didn't come out with any conviction. A white supremacist could have said "Martin Luther King Jr. is my hero," and sounded more sincere.

To her relief, no one pressed the issue. Brian sat back onto Peter's bed, and Peter clicked the button to start the videogame.

In a matter of seconds, the three friends were staring at a low-def horizon, painted in monochromatic shades of gray. There appeared to be a kind of maze ahead, but the edges of said maze were difficult to define. Due to the videogame's limited color pallet, the maze blended with the ass end of the horizon. The thing may have been massive, stretching out in all directions like a deranged serpent, or it may have been extremely limited. There was really no way to tell.

Peter took the spectacle in stride. Without consulting his cohorts, he spread his fingertips over the keyboard and urged his avatar forward, toward the mound of blackness. The sound of footsteps— of hard soles on stone—accompanied the action, and Lucia found that it matched the rhythm of her own heartbeat.

What—if anything—awaited them, within that darkness? Would they find another clue? A virtual map, perhaps? Or would they be treated to another strange video? While Lucia was proud of herself for deciphering the last set of clues, she preferred not to revisit the sad mouse or his bizarre cartoon reality. She still caught glimpses of his strained smile when she blinked—when her eyelids flashed before her pupils and blanketed her world in blackness.

Determined to stay in the moment, Lucia shook her head and refocused on the computer screen. She could make out a rectangular entrance ahead, but she couldn't tell whether it led up, down, left, right, or any direction in between. The inside of the rectangle was dark as the world around it.

Dark as a sarcophagus within a thousand-year-old crypt.

Lucia wasn't sure why that particular image sprang to the forefront of her thoughts, but it did, and it caused her fists to tighten until her fingernails left angry red crescents in her palms.

Peter must not have made the same association. He casually led his avatar into the crevasse while cracking jokes about the low frame rate, and he muttered "eenie meenie minie moe" at each intersection. He even smirked at the sound effects that wafted from the gloom—the moans and the snarls and the palpitations of indeterminate origin.

Brian was less patient.

"Anyone have any idea where we are?" he said, at the eighth turn. "Because I'm pretty sure we're going in a circle."

"And I'm pretty sure you're wrong," Peter said, without breaking his avatar's stride. "Games like these...they don't have sophisticated engines. If we were going in a circle, we'd trigger the same sound effects over and over."

"But that doesn't necessarily mean that we're going in the right direction," Lucia contributed. "We could be headed for a dead end."

"Yes. That's a possibility," Peter allowed. "But I really don't think that's the case."

"Why?"

In response, Peter eased off the directional keys and made his avatar pivot in place.

"Because we're being followed," he concluded, the instant that a spectral child appeared on the screen.

While there was nothing outright threatening about the child's appearance, Lucia still experienced an extreme physical reaction to the narrow shoulders and the downturned face. The sight of something so innocent in the midst of the all-consuming blackness seemed wrong. Not just aesthetically wrong, either. *Morally* wrong. She felt, in the innermost chambers of her being, that such a creature should not exist in such a world; that the child's very presence was an abomination; that the game's designer should be punished for simply allowing such content to exist.

Brian's response was no less visceral.

"Whoa. What the fuck is that thing? And how long has it been there?" he said, leaning forward until his ass was no longer touching Peter's mattress. "It can't hurt us, can it?"

"No. I don't think it's meant to hurt us," Peter said. "I think it's a sign."

"A sign?"

"That we're on the right track," Peter specified. "Or that someone out there is keeping an eye on us. Either way, it means we're making progress. We should keep going."

"No. We shouldn't," Lucia blurted, in a moment of clarity. "Think about it. Travis St. John played this game for weeks, and he never found an ending. Why? *Because the maze itself never ends.* It keeps replicating, over and over and over, until the player inevitably quits."

"Then what should we do?" Brian frowned. "Should we stay in one spot and hope something happens?"

"No. We should make contact," Lucia said. "We should say hello."

"To what?"

"Him."

"The kid?"

A nod.

"That's crazy."

"As crazy as anything else that's happened recently?" Lucia demanded. "Last night, the three of us were standing around this same computer, watching a cartoon mouse die. That isn't strange to you?"

"Well...yes...but..."

Lucia didn't wait for the rest of Brian's halfhearted defense to unfold. She reached over Peter's shoulder, pressed the up arrow, and guided Peter's avatar directly into the child. Or...she intended to make contact with the child. At the last possible moment, the pixilated rendering disappeared, and the screen went white. Then a bevy of pictures flashed across the monitor. Lucia was able to make out a staircase bedecked with stag horns, a bridge draped in moss, a sewer pipe infested with spiders, an access road flanked by dead trees, and a two-storey house choked by vines, but it was the whitewashed church with the sagging bell tower and the weather-beaten cross that caught her attention.

"There! See that?" she exclaimed, seconds before the monitor went blank. "That's the next clue!" And in response to her companions' blank stares: "It's the old Baptist church, outside Drake. Haven't you guys seen it? It's a local landmark."

"Is it?" Peter said, unable to get the web page to reboot. "None of those photos looked familiar to me."

"Me neither," Brian offered. "Are you sure you're not...you know..."

"Seeing what you want to see?" his hands communicated.

Lucia wasn't amused.

"I'm not mistaken," she assured him. "When I was younger, my parents used to drive through Drake to get to Rocky Mountain National Park. We passed that church once a month. That's the next clue. I'm sure of it."

"Fine. Okay. I believe you," Brian said, using his hands to make a different, but equally infuriating, gesture. "First thing tomorrow—"

"Tonight."

"Excuse me?"

"We have to go tonight," Lucia said, straightening to her full height. "If we take the highway south to 34, we can make it to Drake in an hour."

"Sure, but it's one o'clock in the morning," Brian reminded her. "The three of us are tired, it's dark, and we have no idea what's waiting for us in that church. There could be booby traps...men with guns... you name it."

"He's right," Peter contributed, however sheepishly. "It's not safe to go now. None of us are familiar with the area, and we really don't know what's out there. It'd be best to go in the daylight. That way we're—"

Peter finished his sentence with "prepared," but by then Lucia was halfway to the door. She couldn't believe that her friends were trying to shut her down. She understood their reservations, to a point, but it was her sister's life in the balance. She didn't have time to follow procedure—to cross her *T*s and dot her *I*s. She had to move fast, and cover as much ground as she could, when she could.

Not many words were traded on the staircase or in the living room, since Mrs. Janowski was sleeping, and since no one wanted to be responsible for rousing the woman, but the gloves were taken off as soon as the three comrades spilled across the front porch.

"Don't do it, Lucy!" Brian shouted, perhaps hoping that the volume and timbre of his voice would be enough to stop her in her tracks. "The three of us can go tomorrow, at dawn! We can make a day of it! Hell...we can tear the damn building to pieces, if we have to!"

It was a seductive offer, in all honesty, but Lucia was done bartering. Her mind was made up. Without another word, she slumped into her Focus, jammed her key into the ignition, threw the transmission into gear, and pushed the gas pedal to the floor.

Chapter 16

While the town of Drake was small, and while it boasted a humble shopping district, paired with a stretch of asphalt dubbed "Main Street," it was very different than Eaton. Or any of the towns out east. Its borders began in the foothills and ended in the foothills, which made it seem huge, yet insignificant. Especially when juxtaposed with the regal Rocky Mountains.

Lucia knew there were countless dirt roads and four-by-four trails that cut through the hills—trails that led to remote hunting cabins and scenic vistas and untouched lakes—but she wasn't about to stray off the beaten path. She was neither a skilled navigator nor an experienced off-road driver, and her Focus was seriously lacking in the clearance category.

Remembering the sour look on Brian's face as she'd driven away, she released a "hmmph" and glanced at her phone. She'd promised herself, at the beginning of her journey, that she wouldn't unlock the device until her work in Drake was done, but she felt a pressing need to communicate her disappointment to her colleagues. It was a selfish desire, driven by emotion rather than logic, but then, she wasn't in an entirely rational state of mind.

At a hiking trail pull off, she threw her car into Park and quickly glanced through her notifications—through the dozen missed calls and text messages urging her not to go it alone.

At her core, Lucia was thankful for the concern, but it was neither the time nor the place to get sentimental. She had to stand up for herself and go through with her plan. Before her better judgment got in her way.

"In Drake now," she typed, in response to Brian's last text message.

"Call you guys after I get done at the church."

She considered adding "Everything is going to be fine," to put his fears at ease, but ultimately decided against it. Her friends deserved to worry after the way they'd treated her—after the way they'd dismissed her. They deserved every second of lost sleep. After all, it was their fault that she was alone. It was their fault that she was idling in the middle of nowhere, surrounded by pines and peaks and innumerable flashing eyes. It was their fault that the darkness was gradually closing in upon her, waiting for the perfect moment to pounce; to embrace her with its cold, sinewy arms; to drag her, kicking and screaming, into a realm of pixilated madness—a realm where predators lurked in the margins, licking dry and flaking lips; where the screams of lost children echoed for all eternity, punctuated intermittently by peals of depraved laughter; by the sounds of—

Lucia's concentration was broken by a rapping at her driver-side window.

Catching a glimpse of a black leather glove, Lucia flinched; instinctively jabbed at the master locking button. She would've driven off right then and there if her phone hadn't illuminated the badge on the man's chest; if she hadn't glanced in the rearview mirror and seen the police motorcycle hunched in the shadows.

Had the officer been parked behind her the whole time?

Cheeks flushed and heart racing, Lucia lowered her window.

"Sorry, officer," she said, craning her neck in order to meet the mustachioed man's gaze. "I didn't see you back there. I must have been...um...." She wiggled her cell phone. "Anyway, how can I help you? I'm not in trouble, am I?"

"No. Not as long as you have your license, your registration, and your proof of insurance," the man said, hands on hips. "Not many folks come out this way, this time of the night. Not much of a reason to. Restaurants and bars close at ten." He hesitated. "You haven't been drinking, have you?"

"What? No. Not at all," Lucia said, a touch too hastily. "I'm... ah...I'm actually looking for someone."

"A friend?"

"A place," Lucia amended. "I misspoke. I'm looking for a place that a friend told me about. It's a church."

"A church."

"An old church," Lucia confirmed. "I think it's a bit west of here, off the highway."

"An old church, off the highway."

"That's right," Lucia said. She was aware that the officer was no longer asking questions—that he was, in fact, parroting her own words back to her, as if expecting to catch her in a web of half-baked lies—but she tried not to take the skepticism personally. Thus far, she'd done nothing to inspire trust. The man probably thought she was a junky, looking for a place to shoot up. Roles reversed, she would've thought the same thing.

"I'm not addicted to anything, by the way," she added, when she caught him studying her sunken and bloodshot eyes. "I smoked pot a couple of times in high school, but I never inhaled. I know that sounds like a line from a presidential deposition, but it's true. I thought that, if I inhaled, I would have these incredibly vivid hallucinations. I thought I'd wind up drowning myself in the school's lap pool. Ridiculous, huh?"

She hoped the humorous anecdote would humanize her and make her seem less like a joyriding, church-obsessed weirdo, but she missed her mark.

"No. It's not ridiculous at all," the officer said, working his thumbs under his belt. "My junior year in high school, a member of the football team ate some bad mushrooms, broke into the gym after hours, and decided to take a dip in the pool. The janitors found his body the next morning. He was so soggy, some of him broke off when the crime scene techs pulled him out. They had to drain the whole damned pool after that."

"Oh. I...uh...I had no idea," Lucia stuttered. She felt like she should apologize for something, but she wasn't sure *what*. It wasn't as if she'd supplied the mushrooms to the football player or helped him break into the gym.

"Anyways...the whole swim team was pretty bummed," the officer continued, as though it was perfectly normal for a person to turn up in a pool, the skin sloughing from said person's bones as if said person were wrapped in waterlogged newspaper rather than flesh. "It took our school's administration a week to get the pool up and running, and another week to air the place out. They had these big industrial fans blowing around the clock, if you can believe it."

"I can," Lucia said, imagining the scent of chlorine mixed with vomit and sautéed mushrooms. Then she cleared her throat and steered the conversation back to the church. She described the color and the shape, the crumbling bell tower and the weathered cross, and she asked if the officer could jot down some directions. She was confident that she could find it with or without his help, but she knew the additional information would expedite matters considerably.

To her chagrin, the officer still found her interest *unusual*.

"You're not one of those so-called *street artists*, are you?" he said, not-so-subtly inspecting the back seat of her car for cans of spray paint. "If you are, you should know that we take vandalism seriously around these parts. We don't take kindly to people marking up our property."

"Then you don't have anything to worry about," Lucia assured him. "I'm not a street artist, or whatever you want to call it. I'm a…" Her mind spun. She needed a plausible excuse to win his trust; to make her presence less suspicious.

She settled on the word "photographer."

"Really?" the officer said, cocking his hip and pushing his helmet up and away from his eyes. "You have credentials, or are you one of those artsy-fartsy hobby photographers?"

"Neither," Lucia said, detecting an opportunity to validate her story. "I'm an independent contractor. My portraits have been featured in *National Geographic* and *Rolling Stone*, but I specialize in architecture. Modern and classical. Right now I'm building up a portfolio for a big gallery in New York. I'm calling it *Rural America*. That sounds pertinent, doesn't it?"

"Maybe to a bunch of big-city snobs," the officer chuckled. "To me, it sounds like a clothing brand. Or a type of chewing tobacco.

But then…what do I know? I'm just a cop. They pay me to patrol the streets, not to comment on art."

"Then you'll point me in the right direction?" Lucia said hopefully. She wasn't trying to play the "helpless female" card—she hated it, in actuality; felt it was demeaning to her gender—but she must have batted her eyelashes in just the right way.

"Tell you what," the officer said, following a moment of introspection. "I don't have anything else going on tonight. Why don't you follow me to the church? I'll take you the backwoods way, so you won't have to park on the side of the highway—risk damaging that pretty little car of yours. Sound like a deal?"

"Sure. Yes. That sounds fine. Wonderful," Lucia said, in rapid-fire bursts. She was suddenly very aware of the man's height…of the scent of tobacco on his breath…of the way he leaned slightly closer when he spoke…but the deal was, effectively, done. There was no way she could turn the officer down without imperiling her mission.

*****

For a while, Lucia managed to hold her apprehension at bay. She managed to assure herself that the officer was just being friendly; that there was nothing sinister behind the perpetual smirk that curled his upper lip. But her apprehension turned to dread when the officer pulled away from the main thoroughfares, and led her down an isolated dirt road.

There was something off about the way he accelerated past the bevy of Do Not Enter road signs; about the way he continued to glance over his shoulder; about the way he repeatedly flashed a thumbs-up in her direction. It all seemed so *conducted*, as if she were the subject an elaborate television show prank.

Near the crest of a small hill, Lucia considered flipping a bitch, but common sense stopped her. If she turned around, the cop would inevitably run her down and prevent her from inspecting the church. To keep his trust, she had to stay cool and finish the game of *follow the leader*.

But what if—

No.

Lucia cut herself off. She couldn't allow her imagination to wander. Composure was her greatest ally, and to maintain it, she had to stay focused.

You got this, girl, she thought, directing her car around a washed-out section of road. *You've been in stickier situations. You can handle one small-town cop. He may be a foot taller and a hundred pounds heavier, but he's still a cop. He wouldn't dare try anything in this day and age.*

Telling herself that all police vehicles were fitted with video cameras and GPS trackers, she released a slow breath. Then she hit the brakes; slowed her Focus to a crawl.

The officer was still ahead—she could see his angry Cyclops brake light and his eggshell-white helmet—but he was no longer moving. He was parked off to the side of the track, his high-beam cutting through the darkness, revealing…

Nothing.

There were no markers ahead of the officer, to inform hikers of upcoming points of interest, and there were certainly no structures, roused by the artificial luminance. Lucia only saw dirt, weeds, trees, and hills.

Brows furrowed, Lucia pulled up next to the officer and lowered her window.

"Is something wrong?" she said, without shifting out of gear. "If we took the wrong road –"

"We didn't take the wrong road," the officer said, kicking his stand out and rubbing his gloved hands together. "We're here."

"Here?"

"Where you wanted to go," the officer said, making a vague gesture into the night. "This is what you wanted, isn't it?"

"I—" Lucia began. Then she stopped. She wasn't quite sure what the officer was talking about. The casual, borderline playful lilt in his voice was confusing. It reminded her of the way men talked to women at bars.

"I think I'd prefer to see the church from the highway," she concluded, when the officer dismounted his bike and stretched his arms. She made the phrase as subtext-free as she could, given the circumstances, but she must've let a glimmer of apprehension shine through.

"What? After we've come all this way?" the officer said, planting his fists on his hips. "You don't want to even give it a look?"

"No. I mean yes. I mean...tonight might not be the best time," Lucia said, flashing what she hoped could be construed as a "sorry for the inconvenience" smile. "In my line of work, lighting is everything. I doubt I'll be able to get a feel for the dimensions if I—"

Her voice faltered as soon as the officer flicked on his spotlight.

"This better?" the man said, playing the beam across a whitewashed façade.

Unsure how to respond, and unable to tear her gaze from the big arched doors, Lucia shifted her Focus into Park, killed the engine, and stepped outside. If not for the sobering gust of wind that swept across the valley, rustling the tops of the trees, she would've forgotten all about her cane.

"It's...um...it's beautiful," she said, partly to further the notion that it was her first time laying eyes upon it, and partly to prove to herself that she was not, in fact, in a dream.

"Yeah. It is a sight, isn't it?" the officer said, ejecting a wad of chew from his lower lip and burying the evidence with the toe of his boot. "Back in the early nineties, we used to give tours of the place. Then the bell tower started to collapse, and we had to board her up."

"So there's no way to get inside?" Lucia said, shocked that she'd overlooked the chains and padlocks that hung from the brass D-handles.

"No way?" The officer grinned. "I reckon there's always a way for troublemakers. Just two weeks ago, I chased this scrappy little thing from one of the rear windows. She must have broken a pane to get in. She—"

"What did she look like?"

"The girl?"

Lucia nodded breathlessly.

"Well...she was a youngster. Sixteen, maybe seventeen," the officer said, finger to his chin. "A little on the chubby side. Not fat, but not skinny, either. Red hair, green eyes...." He smirked. "Looked a little like you, actually."

Probably because we're related, Lucia thought.

She kept that bit of information to herself.

Extremities abuzz with nervous energy, she asked what the girl had been doing inside the church. She didn't want to appear too interested, but she figured she could get away with one or two follow-up questions.

Her assumption was correct.

"I don't know for sure," the officer said, "but I'd wager she was defacing city property. High school students these days, they don't have any respect for the past. They're so wrapped up in their cell phones and their videogames and their you-pad thingamajigs, they miss out on the important things. I have an eight-year-old daughter, and she already spends half the day on her devices.

"That's the real problem with the American youth," he continued, as if he were preaching to a room full of concerned single parents, rather than a near-desolate valley. "From birth, our children are taught to rely on technology. They learn how to work smart phones before they're potty trained. They grow up with this idea, this *conviction*, that the internet is the same as the real world. And it's not. The internet... it's a weird mirror. It lets you see the world the way you want to see it. So in many ways, it's dangerous. Know what I mean?"

Lucia did, and Lucia was, at least partially, in agreement with him, but she had other things on her mind. She couldn't stop picturing her sister inside the church, tiptoeing from one end to the other, sneakers crunching over shards of broken glass, eyes darting from corner to corner.

What did you see? she thought, seconds before she registered the look of concern on the officer's face.

"I...uh...I'm sorry," she stammered, rubbing at her cold-reddened nose. "I tend to do this thing where I line up my photographs in my head. It helps me to work out my angles, but it's not great in social situations. Do you mind if I...?" She waved a hand toward the church.

"No. Not at all," the officer said, making a "go right ahead" gesture of his own. "Just don't try to get inside. It's not safe in there. One of these days, that bell tower is going to go, and when it does, I hope to Heaven that no one's under it."

"Yeah. Me too," Lucia said, even though she was actively plotting her way in, out, and everything between. She wasn't exactly in Olympic gymnast shape, but she was fairly sure she could slip through an open window, case the joint, and sneak back out, in a matter of minutes.

Confident in her ability to execute her game plan, she started for the brooding structure. But she didn't get far. Halfway across the field, the officer cleared his voice and shouted: "Just a minute, Miss!"

It was precisely the kind of thing a detective would call to a suspect on a televised crime drama, and it immediately made Lucia cringe.

"Yes?" she said, knowing full well that she wouldn't stand a chance in a footrace.

The officer took a step toward her. It wasn't a threatening step, but it made her muscles tense, regardless. She couldn't tell, with the spotlight positioned directly behind his head, whether he was angry, confused, happy, or whether he was emotionally charged at all.

Her answer came a second later, in the form of a statement.

"I'm sorry," he said, hands once again on his hips, "but you've forgotten your camera."

"My camera? Oh. Yes. My camera," Lucia said, kicking herself for the oversight. "I actually prefer not to take any pictures until I've familiarized myself with the subject. It's not standard procedure, I know—it drove my professors crazy in art school—but I find that it brings me closer to the composition. You can't see everything through the lens of a camera, after all."

"No. I suppose you can't," the officer said. Then he encouraged her to carry on, and he retreated to his bike to answer a call from dispatch.

Chapter 17

Up close, the church was something from a surrealist art film. The paint was flaking, the front steps were warping, the doorposts were rotting, and those windows not boarded over were yellowed and smeared with fly excrement. There were a few patches on the exterior where the wood was exposed—where graffiti had been forcefully scrubbed clean—but she didn't linger in one place for long. She was certain that the next piece of the puzzle lay within the church's dusty confines.

Once she'd remained in the officer's direct line of sight for five minutes—an amount of time she deemed necessary to avoid misgivings—she moved around the church's southwest corner, keeping a weather eye for openings as she went. She couldn't hear much over the hiss of the cicadas and the roar of the officer's bike, so she didn't bother to regulate the sound of her footfalls. Not that she could have, if she'd wanted to. In the midst of the darkness and the knee-high grasses, it was damn near impossible to navigate quietly.

Failing to spot any viable entrances, she proceeded to the back of the church, where she immediately shrugged out of her jacket and stretched her cold-tightened muscles. It felt good to revisit some of her old swimming warm-ups, but her dopamine high was interrupted the second she turned her attention to the whitewashed wall.

While there *was* a window set into the boards, and while there were *no* panes separating Lucia from the obscure interior, the window itself was seven feet from the ground. Standing on her tiptoes, Lucia could barely reach the sill.

"Fuck," she hissed, trying unsuccessfully to leverage her body up and through the opening.

Twelve years earlier, she would have been able to complete the feat without difficulty. But then, twelve years earlier, she had possessed the physique and stamina of an athlete. She hadn't been tied to her Dirty Secret. Small bouts of activity hadn't tired her out; left her hating her physical limitations.

Something didn't add up, however.

The last time Lucia had seen Finley, the little runt hadn't stood taller than five-foot-four—a full inch shorter than Lucia. Unless the twerp had hit a major growth spurt, there was no way she could have reached the window. Which left one possible explanation.

Hopeful, but painfully aware of the time she was wasting, Lucia searched the nearby weeds. She kicked and prodded and poked and cursed until, by some minor miracle, she came across precisely what she needed.

There, half buried and camouflaged by uprooted brush, was a stump.

Thrilled by her concurrent strokes of good luck, Lucia clawed the hunk of wood out of its grave, rolled it to the church's foundation, righted it, and centered it beneath the broken window. The entire operation took nearly two minutes, from start to finish, and left her with a number of broken nails, cuts, and bruises, but it also left her with a distinct sense of accomplishment.

Watch out, world. Here I come! she thought as she clambered atop the stump; as she draped her jacket over the jagged windowsill; as she hauled herself into the rectangle of darkness.

She did experience a split second of regret as she perched between the two worlds, her arms trembling and her heart rebounding crazily off her ribcage, but it had nothing to do with the sounds or the scents that inhabited the church. Rather, she regretted her decision to lay her jacket on the lip. It was a cute jacket, after all. Not too heavy, and not too light. That rare jacket you could wear to a cocktail party after a night on the town. Or, in Lucia's case, after a matinee at a movie theater, accented by a large soda and a whole thing of gummy bears.

Re-resolving to beef up her workout regimen, Lucia pivoted and let herself down the other side of the wall. She should have used the light on her cell phone to inspect the floor beforehand, if only to clear her landing zone, but she didn't, and she experienced another stroke of luck. About five feet down, her toes struck a solid object, and she allowed herself a sigh of relief. Someone—possibly her sister—had placed a desk under the broken window.

Nostrils clogged with the odor of dust, mildew, and some unseen variety of organic rot, Lucia slipped from the desk and tested the reliability of the floorboards. Time was still at the forefront of her thoughts, but she couldn't afford to throw caution completely to the wind. If she happened to break even one of her ankles, she would be laid up for a week. If not longer. And that was unacceptable.

Reminding herself that she weighed 140 pounds, not 160 or—God forbid—180, Lucia ventured from the stage. She could see a little, here and there, thanks to the slivers of light that worried through the boarded and filmed windows, but the walls and the floors were mostly cloaked in gloom. She didn't realize that the center aisle, between the old-fashioned wooden pews, was coated in hymnal pages until she heard the individual sheets crackling under her flats.

"Looks like someone isn't a fan of worship music," she muttered, using her cell's screen to illuminate the shredded remains. She could tell words and pictures had been scrawled onto some of the sheets, but she couldn't make out much beyond smudged and faded four-letter words.

"Probably the work of a militant atheist who went off his meds," she concluded, following an encounter with a cartoonishly engorged phallus and a set of abnormally perky breasts.

Certain her answers lay elsewhere, she abandoned the hymnals and crossed, cautiously, to the southwest wall, where she uncovered another swath of—what some might have considered—artwork. There were several more penises and the obligatory vagina, of course, but her attention wasn't captured by the graphic sexual representations. She was drawn to the etchings—to the meticulous phrases, hash marks, and symbols.

"Thursday. Day of debauchery," she read, from one of the more articulate entries. "Day of Thor. God of trees. God of lightning. God of thunder. Protector of men? No. Prosecutor of men. Spiller of blood. Breaker of bones. Devourer of flesh. Collector of souls."

Was that a clue?

Lucia studied the symbols around the paragraph. She was familiar with the swastika, the doppelte Siegrune, the Celtic cross, and the broken sun cross, but the others were more esoteric. They may have been related to the Nazi imagery...or they may have been utterly meaningless.

Aware that she was killing too much time in one place, Lucia moved further north. And she discovered more of the same.

Literally everywhere she looked, she saw evidence of psychological torment. There were poems about dead school children on the floors, portraits of aborted fetuses on the walls, obscene images scratched into the pews.... There was even a pile of dead raccoons, birds, and squirrels next to the pulpit. And around the ode to biological frailty? A half dozen black candles, melted clean to the hardwood.

Back in the sixties and seventies, the church might have been a bright and welcoming place—a place where women in sundresses worshipped beside their suited husbands and fresh-faced children—but a change had occurred somewhere along the way. At one point or another, it had gone from bright and welcoming to bleak and dismal.

To Lucia's eyes, the place was still a house of worship, but it no longer worshipped a merciful and gracious Creator. It worshipped pain. It worshipped sickness. It worshipped disease. It was, quite frankly, a monument to human suffering, and the longer Lucia stood within it, the more she wanted to burn it down. To cleanse it with fire. To watch the embers crackle and pop. But then...even fire couldn't eliminate the ashes. No matter how hot the flames, something would remain. And that something would spread; take root elsewhere. Like a tumor.

Better to leave it in one piece, she thought as she walked the length of the structure, breathing through her mouth in a misguided attempt to keep the dust out of her lungs. *At least in one piece it's contained. At least it can't—*

The echo of a distant voice stopped her in her tracks. She couldn't tell, exactly, where the voice was originating, as each and every noise darted about the room, giving the impression of a hundred disembodied spirits, but she could tell *who* the voice was originating *from*. The authoritarian, macho-man undertones were impossible to mistake.

"I'm alright!" she called, once she'd scurried back atop the desk and thrust her head out the rear window. "I'll just be another minute! I have to finish…"

There, her mind went blank. She didn't have a camera on her, so she couldn't say she was taking pictures, and she didn't have any other valid excuses on standby. In that moment, she felt like a treed coon.

"You have to finish *what?*" the officer barked, sounding closer and more suspicious than before. "You're not trying to break into that church, are you?"

"No! Absolutely not," Lucia returned, mock indignant. "If you must know, I'm…"

Shit.

She needed to come up with a lie that would buy her several more minutes; something so diabolically simple that—

Bingo.

"It's my time of the month," she proclaimed, as loudly as she dared. She'd never used the mensies card before, in any circumstance, so she was simultaneously proud and ashamed.

At the very least, she didn't have to elaborate.

"Oh. Well then. Do continue," the officer grumbled, as if menstruation were a game to be won. "I apologize for…ah…for…"

When he didn't continue, Lucia scrambled from the desk and resumed her rounds. She assumed that, like most men, the officer was blissfully ignorant about the inner workings of the female anatomy, but not even ignorance would afford her infinite privacy.

Resetting her internal stopwatch, Lucia raced from wall to wall, snapping photos of this and taking video of that. She looked especially hard for recurring phrases and symbols, but virtually all of the content was, at the outset, disconnected drivel. There was nothing remotely sane about any of the etchings, any of the shit smears, or any of the aerosol atrocities. If there was a cohesive story unraveling amongst the madness, it was too abstract for Lucia to discern.

"Shit. Shit shit shit," she breathed, pivoting in the midst of the pews. She would have killed for a hint—for something to narrow her search. Because she was surrounded by bullshit.

I might as well be in an Egyptian tomb, she thought, running her fingertips over the remnants of a King James Bible. *I could spend days in here and still leave empty-handed.*

Experiencing a stab of frustration, she swept the Bible off the pew, and watched it spiral to the floor—watched the pages flutter and the jacket dance.

The sound that accompanied the action was less cathartic.

Certain the ceiling was collapsing, Lucia dashed toward the pulpit, her head low but her pupils raised. She knew the bell tower was located at the building's center, but she didn't have much faith in the structure's overall stability. Chances were good that, if the bell tower went, the rest of the roof would follow suit.

Dodging gouts of dust and insectile detritus, Lucia reached the stage…and abruptly fell on her face. It happened so fast that she didn't have an opportunity to scream or to protect her phone. When she opened her eyes, her chin was inches from a pile of yellowed syringes and her cell was propped against an overturned chair, the screen dirty but intact.

Thankful that the support beams were holding up, Lucia crawled to her phone, initiated the onboard light, aimed the beam upward, and—

Her jaw went slack.

"Fuck me," she whispered, taking in the design that spread, tentacle-like, above the pews. At first she thought someone had used black paint to create an ornate, concentric mandala—one that stretched ten feet, from corner to corner—but upon further review, she learned that wasn't the case.

The design wasn't a mandala, and it hadn't been created with *paint*. It was a giant QR code, which had been created with *fire*. Someone had literally *burned* the image onto the ceiling. How or why, Lucia couldn't say, but she was willing to go the extra yard to find out.

Mr. Sticks

Promising herself that the building was merely settling—that the roof would hold for at least the next five minutes—she opened her QR reader app, positioned herself directly beneath the scorch marks, and fought to hold her hands steady while the app extracted the necessary information.

Chapter 18

Cozzens Lake wasn't the same as Lucia remembered it. It was smaller, less blue, and the banks were filthy. There were soda bottles here, paper plates there, and sheets of slimy-slick algae everywhere in between. Even with the sun in her eyes, she couldn't help but notice the pockets of detritus; the dark suggestions of dead fish; the gnats and mosquitoes that swarmed in the shade.

The lake—not unlike the church in Drake—had undergone a metamorphosis in her absence. And it hadn't blossomed from caterpillar to butterfly. No. On the contrary, it had gone from butterfly to maggot. Or to something worse. To something utterly unrelated and unidentifiable.

No more was the fire pit, where countless stories had been told. No more was the tire swing, where countless kisses had been stolen. No more was the sandbar, where countless feels had been copped. And no more was the fallen oak, where countless bikinis and boardshorts had been hung.

During Lucia's tenure, the lake had been special. Unique. Set apart. It had been a place to decompress. From school work, from family, from friends, from social pressures, from responsibilities… from *everything*. There had been a magic about it, which had fulfilled every desire and answered every need.

Now that magic was gone.

Sitting with her toes in the water, Lucia didn't feel any lighter. She didn't feel like the weight on her shoulders was melting. If anything, the weight was *growing*. As if it was a sponge. As if it was absorbing all the toxins in the lake; filling her pores with soot and rot and *death*.

"Hey. Fancy meeting you here," Peter said, emerging from the tree line to the south. His appearance would've surprised her, under normal circumstances, but she'd heard his approach. She'd heard the purr of his hand-me-down Mustang, followed by the pitter-patter of his size eleven Chuck Taylors.

"Yeah. What a small world," Lucia deadpanned, without raising her gaze from the murky, more-brown-than-blue waters. Then she straightened and said: "How did you know I'd be out here, anyway? We didn't hang out much in high school. Not outside of class hours, at least."

"No. We didn't," Peter confirmed, shoving his hands in his pockets and stopping a dozen feet from the water's edge. "I was in chess club and math club and Japanese club, and you were…well…you were one of the jocks."

"As if," Lucia snorted. "I couldn't stand the jocks. I fit in with the jocks about as well as Henry Frasier."

"The kid with asthma?"

"And the forehead the size of Jupiter," Lucia said. "Whatever happened to him, anyway? Is he still around?"

"Sure. If by 'around' you mean…"

Peter jabbed an index finger toward his tennis shoes.

"Oh my gosh. Are you serious?" Lucia gushed. "When? Where? How?"

"Colonel Mustard, in the library, with the candlestick," Peter said. And in response to Lucia's flushed cheeks: "I'm just kidding around. Henry's fine. As far as I know, at least. He moved out east to go to college and he hasn't come back. Probably has a degree in quantum physics and a Victoria's Secret model as a wife. He better with a forehead that size, am I right?"

"Well, I don't know about 'right,' but you're definitely an asshole. No mystery there," Lucia said, feeling the heat in her face subside. "What kind of a person jokes about another person *dying*? That's mean."

"No. *Mean* is ignoring your friends and driving off in the middle of the night," Peter said, with an objectivity that only Peter could master. "That's mean."

"Granted. But you still haven't answered my question," Lucia reminded him. "How did you know I'd be out here? You didn't *spy on me*, back in the day, did you?"

"What? No. Of course not," Peter said. And then it was his turn to blush. "I knew you'd be out here because Brian *told me* you'd be out here. He called me on his way to work, and he said to check this spot in particular. He said this was your favorite place before the…ah…"

"The cataclysm?" Lucia said, with a sad smile. "You can call it what it is, you know. You don't have to pussyfoot around it. Everyone else in this town, they don't have the guts to face it. They pretend everything is okay—they say hello and goodbye and they yak about the weather—but I can see it in their faces. I can tell they're disgusted. To them, I'm a circus freak. I'm The Girl with the Crutches."

"Cane," Peter corrected. "And they do not. Some of them have a hard time making polite conversation, but they don't think you're a freak. I guarantee it. I *am* one of the normals, after all."

"Apart from the scoliosis," Lucia smirked.

She wanted to laugh at her joke—at the sour face Peter made in the aftermath—but she couldn't quite summon the energy. So she kicked her legs. She kicked her legs, and she reveled in the way the water felt between her toes; the way it slithered down her nails and beaded on her calves.

She wasn't ready for the magic to be gone. She needed the comfort—the sense that, no matter what went wrong, there was a place where she belonged. Because she didn't belong anywhere else.

"I found the church last night," she volunteered, when it became apparent that Peter had nowhere else to be. "I found the next clue, too, but…"

"But…?" Peter said, closing half the distance between them.

"It's a dead end."

"A dead end?"

"Yeah," Lucia said, fixing her gaze on the far bank without *seeing* the far bank. "The clue in the church…it led me to a blank website. Damn thing doesn't have a thing on it."

"You're sure?" Peter said, resembling a fashion-challenged stick figure in her peripheral vision. "Did you give it time to load? Did you refresh it? Did you try opening it on another browser?"

"Yes, yes, and yes," Lucia murmured. "I said the magic words, I turned around three times, I stroked a rabbit's foot, I broke a wishbone, and I crossed my fingers. Anything else I should've tried?"

"Well, you could've faced northeast and imagined a dragon in a tuxedo," Peter offered. "In certain Japanese regions, tuxedo-wearing dragons are thought to bring luck. It's a fact. I'm not suggesting that you should research it—some pretty weird things pop up if you type 'Japanese tuxedo dragon' into a search engine—but…you know…for future reference."

That said, Peter lowered himself onto the big rock beside her, awkwardly tucked his spiderish legs beneath him, and followed her gaze. He may not have been the most emotionally-attuned person on the face of the earth, but Lucia appreciated the show of solidarity. He was trying to communicate his support without overstepping his bounds.

"Do you mind if I take a look at it?" he said at last, swatting at an overly curious horsefly. "The website, I mean. Do you mind if I take a look at the website?"

"Sure. But you won't find anything," Lucia said, unlocking her phone and passing it sideways. She didn't even have to look at the screen to know that said website was cued and loaded. She'd been staring at it for the better part of the day.

If her indifference was disheartening, Peter didn't show it. He accepted the device with gusto and spent the next several minutes tapping here and swiping there. She could tell his internal cogs were turning by the way his eyes narrowed and his lips twitched, but she couldn't tell whether he was making any progress until he shifted suddenly and exclaimed: "Eureka!"

"What?" she said, shooting him a look that she usually reserved for disobedient toddlers and ownerless dogs. "Is there something there?"

"On the website? No. The website's a blank slate," Peter said. "But the *source code*…the source code is a different story. There's a message embedded in here. It says—"

Lucia didn't let him finish. She snatched the phone from his hands and, with an all-too-familiar throbbing in her chest, absorbed the newly-found words.

"Congratulations, dear Believer," she recited, as loudly as her lungs would allow. *"If you're reading this, it means you're halfway through your journey. Four more steps, and you'll discover what lies at the other end. Be warned, however. If you're not fully dedicated to The Search, you must stop immediately. There are trials ahead which require both faith and bravery. Those unable or unwilling to complete these trials will be punished severely. Travis St. John was a Believer, once, but he lost his faith, and for his lack of faith, his soul was required of him. Be careful not to make the same mistake."*

There, Lucia stopped, and willed herself to breathe. She was thrilled, on the one hand, that she was making progress, but she was troubled by the knowledge that she had half the game in front of her, and she was frightened by the implicit threats. Even if the author was blowing smoke and was unable to make good on his promises, he was still a psychologically twisted specimen. And she didn't want her sister near any psychologically twisted specimens.

Peter was on the same page.

"Sounds like we're dealing with a real nut job," he said, rubbing conspicuously at the nape of his neck. "You think we should call the police?"

"And tell them what?" Lucia inquired. "That Mr. Sticks is real? That we're working our way through his labyrinth? That he killed some guy six years ago—some guy whose death has already been ruled a suicide—and that he's likely to kill again? The dispatcher would laugh us off the line. They already think my whole family is crazy."

"Sure...but now we have proof," Peter pointed out. "We have—"

Lucia didn't let him get any further.

"We don't have *proof*," she sighed. "We have breadcrumbs. And right now, those breadcrumbs don't *lead* anywhere. Until we dig up some real, hard evidence, the cops won't give us the time of day. It's up to us to take the next step."

"Which is...?"

Lucia showed him the screen—the deep web URL beneath the block of text.

"We have to keep going," she said, in case the message went over his head. "We have to keep following the breadcrumbs. At least until we find something solid. Finley *needs* us."

"Agreed," Peter said. "But to maintain our group's structural integrity, we need to set up some ground rules. Specifically, there can be no more individual crusades. You, me, and Brian are a team, and we need to *act* like a team from here on out. Where one goes, the others follow. Simple enough?"

Lucia bit her lip. She understood the reasoning behind the imperative, and she agreed that a tribe of three was safer than a tribe of one, but she was hesitant to sign on the dotted line. She was hesitant because she knew—or rather, *sensed*—that she would have to, eventually, break the contract.

Peter must have read the misgivings in her eyes.

"Well?" he said, skipping a rock across the surface of the lake; creating ripples that spread and dissipated, spread and dissipated. "We are a team, aren't we?"

"Yes. We are. We're a team," she parroted, watching the lake return to its normal, dead self. "We're a unit."

"Good," Peter said. "Then let's get together tonight and look into this new website. Does seven o'clock sound good? My place?"

Chapter 19

A seven o'clock rendezvous at Peter's house did not sound good, in actuality—it sounded late as hell—but Lucia didn't share as much. To keep Peter on her side, she had to be somewhat accommodating. She had to prove that she could be a team player. She had to swallow her disagreements and put on a stiff upper lip. She didn't have to be as careful around Brian, since she was the only thing standing between him and a state penitentiary, but still, Brian was a human being. If she pushed him too far, he would retaliate, one way or another.

In an effort to continue the investigation without putting herself in undue jeopardy, Lucia returned to her mother's front door, where she knocked for five minutes before she noticed the note in the living room window.

"Gus, I'll be gone until eleven," the blue sticky read. "If you come by, the key is under the frog. There's sandwich makings in the refrigerator and a case of beer on the counter. Love, Caitlin."

Not sure who this "Gus" person was, but thankful for the insight about the key, Lucia let herself into the trailer and glanced about the living room. Not much had changed since her last visit, so she kicked aside a couple of empty soda bottles and wine boxes, and made her way down the hall.

As expected, her mother's room was a mess. The queen-size bed, which occupied three quarters of the space, was disheveled and covered in cigarette burns, the dresser was vomiting up a mixture of clean and dirty clothes, the carpet was discolored, the few pictures on the walls were crooked, and there were personal hygiene products scattered everywhere else. There were Q-tips and tampons on the windowsill, bottles of hairspray and deodorant on the bedside table, rolls of toothpaste on her shoe organizer.... There were even packets of toilet paper in her *closet*.

Disgusted, and more than a little relieved that she hadn't adopted her mother's cleaning habits, Lucia went across the hall. To her sister's room. She'd been inside a few times, on a few different occasions, but the stark lack of color still caught her off guard. The comforter on the twin bed was black, the pillowcase covers were black, the curtains were black, the décor was black, and the posters that plastered the walls, from floor to ceiling, trumpeting death metal bands and horror movie villains, were—primarily, at least—black.

Not sure what to make of the bleak and grisly imagery, Lucia proceeded to her sister's dresser. She felt strange as she went from drawer to drawer, moving socks and shirts, panties and bras, but she assured herself that her presence was validated. She assured herself that the breach of privacy was acceptable, given the circumstances, and that Finley would forgive her in the end. After all, she wasn't *snooping*. She was doing her damnedest to bring her sister home.

Regardless of her intentions, however, Lucia was sidetracked by the discovery of a pamphlet which bore the title: *Sexual Positions for Each Day of the Month*. The booklet was somewhat brief, and tastefully illustrated, but Lucia didn't see generic cartoon characters between the margins. She saw Finley and Brian. She saw their bodies, sweaty and bare, thrusting against one another. She saw their mouths gaping and their hands kneading. She saw their limbs twining and their chests heaving.

By page twenty, she could *smell* the tang of their animalistic lust. It was a heady odor—salty and sour: the scent of engorged glands and throbbing muscles—and it nearly caused her to lose her center of gravity.

Had Brian bought the pamphlet for Finley? Had he tucked it into the dresser, thinking—nay, *hoping*—it would result in sexual exploration? The mere thought sent shivers of rage directly to Lucia's core. If Brian had been in that room, in that moment, she would have given him more than a slap. She would have gone for his throat. She would have beaten him until the color of his skin matched the décor.

Then she would have tossed him out on his ass.

Aware that the edges of her vision were going soft, she stuffed the pamphlet back into the dresser and released a slow, steady breath. The stress was getting to her. She could feel it enveloping her, dancing through her veins and arteries. It wasn't anything more than a tickle, but she knew that would change. If she let the stress overtake her, the tickle would become a numbness, which would spread throughout her body and scramble her synapses.

Eager to avoid an attack, Lucia turned her attention on the closet. She glanced over the faded jeans, the denim vests, the paint-stained hoodies, and she prodded the mound of boots and high-tops. Her sister had never been a girly-girl, but the gothic aesthetic was something new. A result of her friendship with Destinee, no doubt.

Glad that she didn't have a daughter of her own, Lucia moved on from the closet. She wasn't sure what she was looking for, exactly, but she was certain she would recognize a lead if she found it. *When* she found it. Her sister might have been clever for her age, but she was no evil genius. In many areas, she was a typical teenager.

Remembering the backpack in her father's guest bedroom, Lucia lowered herself to her knees and peered under her sister's box spring. She only saw magazines and miscellaneous articles of clothing at first, but she became aware of more when her pupils adjusted to the dimness. In short order, she registered two packs of cigarettes, a baggie of weed, a couple of glass pipes, coated in resin, and—

Thar she blows.

Box of notebooks in hand, Lucia straightened, and took a seat on her sister's twin mattress. She'd asked to see the diaries before—several times before, in fact—but Finley had always denied her. Finley had maintained that the entries were personal, which made them "nobody else's fucking business."

How the tides have turned, Lucia thought, flipping from one notebook to the next.

While she knew she should limit her search to the notebook marked *2018,* she found herself drawn to the older compilations. There was an innocence in the cover sketches that was missing from the more recent editions. Instead of skeletons and skateboards and skulls, there were butterflies and horses and castles. There was a lightness to the script, as well, which transported Lucia to a happier time and place.

As a six-year-old, Finley had been a huge fan of her older sister. The two of them had spent hours at the park, running and jumping and hiding and seeking. Six-year-old Finley hadn't given a damn about their eleven-year age difference. Six-year-old Finley had just been happy to play.

When had things changed?

Disappointment churning in her guts, Lucia opened the notebook from 2015—Finley's last year in junior high—and surveyed the entries. Most of them were painfully short, and most of them were steeped in humdrum junior high drama, but she endured them anyway. It felt nice to get outside of her own head for a while; to lose herself in trivialities.

March four. Maggie is being a pain again, she read, basking in the loops of purple ink. *She called me fat in PE, and the teacher didn't hear, so I shoved her into the grass. I didn't shove her that hard, but her friends said I did. Her friends said I grabbed her hair and I tried to throw her into one of those hurdle things. I told the teacher the truth, but he didn't believe me. He sent me to the principal's office. Now Mom is angry at me. She says I need to start behaving.*

The next block of text wasn't much different.

March nine. I can't believe David. He's such an ass, it read. *I told him about my talk with Miss Perfect, and he told me to calm down. He said I was being stupid. As if. Sometimes I want to throw those dumb applesauce packets in his face. That would serve him right. He wouldn't walk around like such a cool kid after that. I bet his other friends would start calling him Apple Face.*

Hoping for a resolution to the conflict, Lucia sped through the next dozen pages and quickly became familiar with the cast of recurring characters. She got to know Maggie, the bitch; Susan, the science nerd; David, the football player-slash-love interest; Mr. Bartz, the principal...even Mr. Quail, the school janitor. But there was one character whose identity and motivations remained obscure.

Miss Perfect.

Lucia suspected that the alias belonged to her mother, since the two were usually mentioned in tandem, and since a majority of the other characters carried their own nicknames, but she couldn't say for sure. There were times that Miss Perfect said things and did things—allegedly—that were out-of-character for Lucia's mother. In virtually all the entries, Miss Perfect was this shadowy, ever-present figure, sewing dissent wherever she went. She seemed to take pleasure in Finley's shortcomings, not unlike a vindictive old crone.

Curiosity piqued, Lucia thumbed to the end of 2015, and started the next edition in the series. She expected Miss Perfect to appear less and less, since 2016 signaled Finley's first year at Eaton High, but that wasn't the case. Between the entries about boys, booze, marijuana, and school work, there were entries about the anonymous, titular figure.

I don't understand why she hangs around anymore, one of the excerpts read. *We're not friends. All she does is criticize me. She tells me I'm not studying hard enough. She tells me I'm not eating healthy enough. She tells me I'm not spending my free time with the right kind of people. I wish…I wish she would disappear.*

It was precisely the type of thing a hormone-imbalanced fourteen-year-old would write, following a day of disappointments, but Lucia could tell that the hurt and the anger was rooted deeper. Finley wasn't ranting because her skin was breaking out. She was ranting because, deep down, she harbored a very real hatred for Miss Perfect.

In the journal marked *2017*, Finley went as far as to call Miss Perfect a "home wrecker." Finley seemed to think that Miss Perfect had something to do with her parents' divorce. She never went into much detail, but the implication was clear enough.

Wondering whether Miss Perfect wasn't, directly or indirectly, to blame for Finley's disappearance, Lucia set the journals aside and massaged her temples. She needed rest. If she continued to push herself, without sleep, her body would rebel. The last time she'd pulled an all-nighter, she hadn't felt right for a week.

"Just fifteen minutes," she promised herself, leaning back and arranging the pillows under her head. A part of her was worried that Gus—whoever he was—might show up while she was sleeping, but that part was in the minority. Considering the rusted hinges on the front door, she doubted anyone could come or go without her knowledge. Not that she gave the possibility much thought. In a matter of minutes, she was out cold.

Chapter 20

Seven-year-old Finley was running. Her pale red hair was whipping around her cheeks, wild and free. She might have been screeching with delight, but Lucia couldn't rightly tell. The sounds in her world were muffled. Echoey. Distant. Eyes closed, she would have guessed that she was standing at the far end of a concrete tube. Time was running slow as well, but that particular disparity did not, for whatever reason, strike her as unusual. Perhaps the sight of her sister, young and happy and full of life, was more important to her than the mechanics of the dream world. Because she was dreaming. On some level, she realized it; she simply didn't care.

Don't go too far now, she thought as she followed the elementary-schooler through the cornstalks. She may have said those exact words, long ago, but if she had, they had since been devoured. Whether by time or by space or by an ancient race of subhuman deities, they had been devoured. The only noises that stood out to her were the crackles and thumps of footfalls; the drone of the wind through the dry and crusty stalks.

Had the stalks been dry and crusty back then? No. They couldn't have been. That particular day had taken place in August, well before harvest. The stalks had been tall and green; the tassels vibrant and yellow.

This revelation changed nothing about Lucia's environs, however. The further she went, the more sickly the stalks seemed to become, until they were little more than skeletal shoots—shoots which rattled and hissed at her passing. A few of them wavered in her peripheral vision, as if they were, in reality, the dried husks of snakes, revived by the late afternoon sun, but she paid them no mind. Her eyes were glued to her sister—to that hummingbird-print sundress and those slightly-too-big tennis shoes.

Lucia knew precisely what that little girl was going to encounter when she left those decaying cornstalks, but she was unable to imagine the course of events differently. She felt like a ghost or, perhaps more accurately, a balloon, attached to the seven-year-old's wrist. No matter how fast or slow the little girl ran, Lucia always remained a step and a half behind.

Sensing—rather than seeing—the field's perimeter, Lucia made one final effort to stop the girl. She reached out her hand and she willed the words "slow down" to reverberate from her lips. But she was too slow. In the blink of an eye, seven-year-old Finley was gone, and the repetitious *thud-crackle thud-crackle* thud of vulcanized soles was replaced by a long, lingering squeal. Not a human squeal, either. A—

Hinge! Lucia thought, jolting upright. She remembered right away that she was in her sister's bedroom, which meant that she was in her mother's trailer, but it took her an additional five seconds to realize that the sun was low on the horizon; that it was no longer one o'clock in the afternoon.

"Shit. Shit shit shit," she hissed, retrieving her cane and trundling to the doorway. Her left leg was a touch less responsive than normal, but she managed to cross the floor with minimal trouble, and she thrust her head into the hall, ignoring the wayward strands of hair that clung to her lips. Someone had tested her mother's front door, which led her to believe that she was no longer the only one on the premises.

"Mom?" she ventured, peering from one side of the living room to the other. She couldn't see the entirety of the north wall, due to the divider that separated the kitchenette from the rest of the trailer, so she was hesitant to approach. If the visitor wasn't her mother....

Lucia shook her head. She wasn't in some crime-addled *favela*. The likelihood of her encountering a masked maniac was ten thousand to one.

Still, her imagination whispered. *Think about the Wilson family. Think about what happened to them. Do you want to end up the same way? Do you want your picture on the front page of the* Herald?

Lucia didn't give herself an opportunity to answer. In any shape or form. Making sure she had a firm grip on her cane, she swept down the hall, her senses on high alert. Shivers jittered up her spine when, midway through the living room, she stepped on a foil wrapper, but she didn't let that stop her. She continued to the kitchenette, where she discovered—

Nothing.

The trailer was empty.

Aside from the numerous flies and roaches that occupied the sink, of course.

Pinching her nose against the spicy-sweet aroma of moldy food, Lucia returned to the living room and promptly took a seat on the couch. The nap had successfully reset a number of her internal gears, but it hadn't done a thing about her paranoia. She still felt like she was perched on the edge of a cliff. And beyond that cliff? Even she couldn't say. The space beyond and below was dark and caliginous. But it wasn't vacant. Like the stainless-steel trough in the kitchenette, it was crawling with life. Or a semblance of life, at least.

Assuring herself that she was alone—that the wind was responsible for the squealing noise, and nothing else—Lucia shut her lids and cleared her mind. She was determined to regain her center.

She shouldn't have let her guard down so soon.

As she sat and carefully deconstructed the little girl with the hummingbird-print dress and the slightly-too-big tennis shoes, something heavy hit the window behind her.

Lucia didn't scream in response to the clamor, but she did jump, and she did spin around faster than a dreidel on the last day of Hanukkah.

"Fuck, Brian," she gasped, once she was again in control of her vocal chords. "What are you trying to do? Give me a heart attack?"

"Well, I was trying to reach you on the phone, but the damn thing kept going to voicemail," Brian returned. He could tell she was angry—that much was painfully obvious—but he couldn't keep a mischievous smile from pulling at the corners of his lips. "What's going on, anyway? Peter and I have been looking for you for an hour."

"And a half," Peter amended, from elsewhere in the back yard. "Is this a functional hot tub, by the way? It looks nice. My parents used to have a hot tub. They got rid of it after my mom developed a yeast infection. Did you know that three out of four women—"

"I was asleep," Lucia said preemptively. She had no desire to discuss feminine health issues with two Y-chromosome-carrying members of the human race. Nor did she care to check the status of her own cell phone. If the thing was dead, she would feel compelled to relinquish some of her outrage. And she didn't want to do that. She wanted her anger to be justified.

For what it was worth, Brian didn't press the issue. He simply accepted her explanation and asked for her permission to enter the house.

A few minutes later, the three of them were gathered in the living room. There wasn't much sitting space, due to the exhaustive collection of fast food paraphernalia, but Brian and Peter made themselves at home, nonetheless. Brian took a seat atop a bucket of powdered laundry detergent while Peter cleared the fold-down countertop.

"Okay. Let's review," Peter said as he placed his laptop on the newly-polished surface and connected to a nearby wifi signal. "We know Finley's been gone for five days. We know she developed a weird fascination with Mr. Sticks' Labyrinth. We know she went to the church in Drake to find Mr. Sticks. But we don't know where she went after that. Is that accurate?"

"Up to this point. Yes," Lucia said. "I went through a couple of Finley's journals today and I found evidence of a feud with someone called 'Miss Perfect,' but I can't tell if that feud progressed to another level. It might be worth looking into."

"Yes. It might," Peter allowed. "But let's focus on the Labyrinth angle for now. If we run into a dead end, we can shift gears."

"Agreed," Brian said. "So far, the Labyrinth angle has been paying off. We shouldn't abandon it. Besides, we have no idea who Miss Perfect *is*. It could take weeks to track her down."

"In this town?" Lucia smirked. "It took my mom eight days to learn that my dad was cheating on her. I bet we could learn Miss

Perfect's name, address, age, and social security number in twenty-four hours."

"And I bet you're wrong," Brian scowled. "I was closer to Finley than just about anyone and she never once mentioned a 'Miss Perfect.' If this person was a real threat, she would've said something to me."

"Because you're oh so big and strong. Is that it?" Lucia snapped. "Or is it because you're such a nurturing individual?"

She was very tempted, in that instant, to confront him about the sex pamphlet—to wave it under his nose and to make her allegations terribly, irreversibly public—but she was waylaid by a sudden activity on Peter's laptop screen.

"Is that...?" she began.

Peter nodded his head. "It's the next piece in Mr. Sticks' puzzle," he confirmed, without averting his gaze. "Looks like a message board. But there's only one thread."

"And that's noteworthy because...?"

In lieu of reply, Peter clicked the thread; enlarged the text so everyone could read it.

Brian took the responsibility of narration upon himself.

"*Welcome, dear Believers,*" he recited, in a voice clearer and louder than the one Lucia would have summoned. "*The time for passivity is over. Now it is time for action. Now it is time to prove your unwavering dedication.*

"*To gain entrance to the site listed below, Mr. Sticks demands a tribute,*" Brian continued, in a more reserved tone. "*He demands that you write 'I Believe' on your forehead, on your chest, and on your palms, that you disrobe, and that you...*"

Brian swallowed and sucked in a shaky breath, as if the following words were solidifying and catching in his throat. Lucia half expected him to cough and to expel one of those multicolored alphabet magnets—the kind her parents had kept on the refrigerator during her kindergarten years.

To her relief, she didn't have to finish the sentence herself.

"Holy crap. That's messed up," Peter said, reaching the end of the paragraph. "What kind of a person would willingly strip naked, take a picture, and post that picture on a stranger's message board? That's crazy, isn't it?"

"Absolutely. That's borderline psycho," Brian said, standing and pacing as far as the heaps of trash would allow. "No rational person—male or female—would disseminate a nude picture of themselves for some faceless creep. How many submissions are there, anyway? Five?"

"Well...there are fifteen subthreads on the first page," Peter frowned.

"And how many pages?"

"Uh..."

"*Uh* isn't a number."

"Twenty-six."

"Come again?"

"Twenty-six," Peter repeated.

"Are you serious?" Brian said, using his fingers to tally up the numbers. "That's three hundred and ninety submissions."

"Give or take," Peter said. He went on to explain how message boards worked, on a computational level, but Lucia only caught a fraction of the lecture. Halfway through an analogy which—strangely—involved a puffer fish, a Chinese mystic, and an umbrella salesman, she stepped in and seized the spotlight.

"My sister," she said, visually dissecting the usernames on the first page. "We need to find out if she's submitted a photo. If she has..."

Lucia let herself trail off. She didn't want to think about that. Not yet. Not until she was *sure*.

"Try that thread there," she said, jabbing a broken fingernail at the screen.

"The one posted by RedHeadXxX?" Peter inquired.

Lucia nodded. She could tell that Brian wanted to object, for one reason or another, but he must have realized that, in the current situation, his opinion carried little to no weight.

Peter must have realized the same thing. Following a roll of his narrow shoulders, he clicked the link and silently waited for the new page to load.

The screen wasn't empty for long.

In the time it took for Lucia to curl her fingers into fists, she was no longer looking at a smattering of white text against a black background. She was looking at a photograph. It was a low-quality photograph, and it was badly composed, but it took her brain less than a second to process the image, regardless. Some of her classmates had taken similar pictures in high school.

Even though Lucia wanted to look away from the portrait of low self-esteem made flesh, she forced herself to focus. She forced herself to examine the pallid skin, the narrow arms, the bony hips, the underdeveloped breasts, and the butter-smooth cleft between the legs. Because she had to *know*.

Peter was less comfortable with the image.

"That's not…that's not *her*…is it?" he said, turning his face away from the screen and jerking a thumb over his shoulder.

Lucia shook her head. "No. It's not. But look at her," she muttered, more to herself than to either of her male companions. "That girl can't be more than fifteen. What would drive a fifteen-year-old to do something like that? To make those kinds of marks on her arms? Do you think—"

"I think it's useless to sit here and speculate," Brian interrupted. "I think we owe it to ourselves—and to Finley—to stay the course. We can't afford to get bogged down in the details."

"Yes, but this is more than a detail," Lucia said. "This is a human being. This is someone who has family and friends; hopes and dreams. This is someone who—"

"*Had*."

"Excuse me?"

"You're using the present tense," Brian pointed out.

"And…? Your point is…?"

"My point is, we don't know anything about this girl," Brian said. "We don't know her name, her address, her nationality…we don't even know if she's *alive*. It's not worth our time to chase after a loose thread."

Loose thread.

Details.

Both words echoed between Lucia's ears. She wanted, with all her heart, to throw them back in Brian's face, but she found herself unable. As much as she hated to admit it, the man was right. The three of them weren't police officers. They simply didn't have the resources to investigate any other missing persons. Therefore, it was in their best interest to limit their focus.

Giving the redhead in the photograph one last look, Lucia elbowed Peter aside and assumed command of the laptop. She had to power forward before she lost what little remained of her objectivity—before the thunderheads on her horizon broke and consigned her rudimentary fishing vessel to the depths.

For twenty minutes Lucia scrolled and clicked, scrolled and clicked, and for twenty minutes she encountered more of the same: unfamiliar males and females in front of bathroom mirrors, their bodies bare and their eyes hollow, the words "I Believe" scrawled across their chests, foreheads, and palms. Not all of the subjects were underage, but the teens and preteens vastly outnumbered the full-fledged adults.

"There's no rhyme or reason to any of this," she mumbled as she clicked away from the picture of a tawny teenage boy. "None of these subthreads are organized by date, gender, or alphabet. They're just *here*. Thrown together."

"Probably to discourage busybodies," Brian said from his makeshift stoop. He hadn't moved since Lucia had taken control of the laptop, but she could tell that he was losing patience. When he wasn't fiddling with his phone, he was glancing from window to window: scouring the oncoming dark.

Lucia wondered, briefly, if she wasn't mistaking boredom for fear—if he wasn't, in fact, afraid of something that lurked in the twilight, just beyond the realm of human comprehension—but the logical side of her brain rejected the possibility. Brian was neither a conspiracy theorist nor a believer in the supernatural. She'd never heard him belittle a religious person for his or her beliefs, but she'd never heard him take part in a philosophical discussion, either. Like most in the non-churchgoing crowd, he tended to distance himself from such subjects.

Forcing her eyes to remain on the strands of stark white text,

Lucia scrolled to the bottom of page sixteen—and abruptly stopped. Her spine must have straightened as well, because Peter crowded in and said: "What? What is it? A lead?"

"Maybe," Lucia said, maneuvering her cursor to a subthread authored by one LittleRed_16. "When my sister was a toddler, she had the reddest hair you've ever seen. Every time my mom took her out, someone would comment on it. Mrs. Todd called her Strawberry Shortcake, Mr. Lowe called her Baby Carrot, and Mrs. Smithfield called her Firecracker. But my mom liked Mrs. Marsh's nickname the most."

"Little Red," Peter said clairvoyantly.

Lucia inclined her head. She meant to say "That's the one," but she discovered that her lungs were damn near out of oxygen.

She hadn't been holding her breath for that long, had she?

Hoping Peter wasn't close enough to hear the rapid *tha-thunk* of her heartbeat, she accessed LittleRed_16's subthread, and anxiously watched the new page load. She wanted to believe Brian's initial assessment—that no rational person would stoop to such a level—but the weight in the pit of her stomach kept her on edge. She knew, very well, that people were complicated creatures. They couldn't be separated into two camps, like Xs and Os.

Maybe sanity, itself, exists on a scale, she thought, while the laptop struggled to process the incoming data. *Maybe there is no line that separates the rational from the irrational. Maybe the criminally insane are, in actuality, blessed with a different kind of survival instinct. A better kind. Maybe they're the next step in the evolutionary chain. Maybe—*

That was as far as Lucia got.

Before she could begin to consider the ramifications of a moral-free society, a picture materialized before her.

A picture of her *sister*.

In the photograph, Finley was posed in front of a full-length mirror, her hip cocked and her hair spilling over her shoulders. She was trying to look seductive, with her breasts pressed out and her lips oh-so-slightly parted, but she wasn't quite pulling off the sultry damsel shtick. Not to Lucia's eyes, at least. To Lucia, she looked like an uncomfortable tween, mimicking what she'd seen in the pages of

Vogue.

For what it was worth, both Brian and Peter looked away as soon as the picture appeared. They could sense how much the picture meant to Lucia—how much it hurt her.

"So. What now?" Brian said at long last. "Is this the end, or...?"

He let the question hang, unfinished.

Nothing more was necessary.

The three friends understood, all too well, what the picture signified; what one of them would have to do in order to continue the game. And none of the friends were prepared to do it.

Chapter 21

When Lucia finally dredged herself from the mire of sleep, at nine o'clock the next morning, she felt about as lively as a reanimated corpse. Given a choice, she would have gladly stayed in bed all day. Her head hurt, her neck ached, her left leg was next to incommunicado, and she couldn't shake the image of her sister's naked body. The fucking thing was burned to the underside of her eyelids.

Damn it, Finley, she thought, burying her face in her pillow. *Why on Earth did you have to take it this far? Why couldn't you let it go? You were supposed to be the smart one in the family. You were supposed to learn from your parents' mistakes—my mistakes. You were supposed to become a doctor or a lawyer or a damned ambassador to some damned third world country.*

In an effort to banish the pain from her skull, she set her knuckles against her temples and pressed until she could no longer differentiate the internal pressure from the external. She didn't blame herself, directly, for her sister's disappearance, but she didn't consider herself an innocent bystander, either. She was sure that, if she had played a more active role in her sister's life, she could have kept her from going off the deep end.

Her father wasn't nearly as conflicted.

"Well, good morning, Lucy Goosey," he said from the doorway. "Looks like you spent the night studying for a big test. What's the subject? Psychology?"

"In a way," Lucia croaked, rolling stiffly onto her back. When she'd gone to sleep, there had been six of Finley's journals on the mattress. Now, five hours later, there were three. She didn't move to retrieve the other three from the floor, though. She'd already pawed through the lot of them. She'd already flipped from cover to cover, reading and rereading; analyzing and reanalyzing. And her dedication had gotten her nowhere.

"You haven't heard from the police yet, have you?" she managed, following a massive yawn. She anticipated a simple yes or no, but the expression that crossed her father's face told an entirely different story.

"The police?" he said, as if he was struggling to comprehend some complex inside joke. "Why in the world would I hear from the police? You didn't do anything illegal last night, did you?" Then his eyebrows shot up and he said: "Oh! Because of Finley!"

"Yes. Because of Finley," Lucia deadpanned. "This is the sixth day. No one's seen her since last weekend. Aren't you worried?"

"Worried?" Her father scratched at his jaw. "I wouldn't say I'm worried, necessarily. Like I said before: Finley's a smart cookie. And not just book smart. Street smart. She's way more capable of taking care of herself than I was at her age. She's probably at the California coast as we speak, sipping champagne and soaking up that prime West Coast sun."

"And if she's not?"

"If she's not?" The man crossed his arms. "My money would be on Texas. Their waves aren't as nice, but they have some decent beaches. Either way, she'll come back as soon as she's nice and ready. In the meantime, would you care to get some breakfast with me? There's this new diner over in Galeton. I'm sure it's not as fancy as those places you have down in Denver, but it's quaint, and the food is to die for. They have these things called *brenchiladas*, and they—"

"Thanks, but I'm not hungry," Lucia said as she maneuvered herself upright. She wasn't lying, exactly, but she wasn't telling the whole truth, either. At the moment, she just wanted her father to leave. She wanted him to take his dimpled chin, his tastefully-disheveled hair, his fly-by-the-seat-of-his-pants attitude, and she wanted the whole package to disappear.

He must have missed that memo.

"Are you positive?" he said, leaning against the doorframe. "When you were on the swim team, you used to eat six meals a day. And on Pancake Fridays...heck...you were a monster. You used to down more than your mom and I *combined.*"

And then your cute little athlete got sick and became the grotesque aberration you see before you. Is that what you're getting at? Lucia thought.

She kept those words inside.

Instead, she shuffled around until her legs dropped over the side of the mattress and said: "Honestly. I'm fine. Today I have some things to do. Some errands to run."

"Then let's run them together!" her father exclaimed. "I've got nothing to do until two. We can jump in my truck and make a morning of it. Sound like a deal?"

Thankfully, Lucia didn't have to come up with a response. As she sat and contemplated the most effective way to turn her father down, her phone chimed.

It was her mother.

Seeing the name on the caller ID, her father took a step back and mouthed: "I'll leave you two alone." Then he eased the door shut and tiptoed down the hall.

Any other morning, Lucia would have let the call go straight to voicemail, but she supposed that she owed the woman, since the call had liberated her from an extremely awkward conversation.

"Hello?" she said, pressing the device to her ear. "Mom?" She was tempted to add the phrase "I'm surprised you're up this early," but, for the sake of her own sanity, she decided not to. She'd have plenty of opportunities to test the tensile strength of that already-strained relationship in the future.

As expected, Caitlin McBride was less than alert.

"Lucia? Is that you?" the woman managed, sounding about as enthusiastic as a tracheotomy patient under a cocktail of semi-legal sedatives. "You can hear me, can't you?"

Lucia rolled her eyes. "Yes. I can hear you," she said. "And yes. It's Lucia. At the moment, I'm the only one who should be calling you 'Mom.' Unless you have some more daughters running around that I don't know about."

Her mother didn't respond to the not-so-subtle jab. Rather, she cleared her throat and said: "Lucia. I need you to do something for me. I need you to run down to the hardware store. I need you to run down to the hardware store, and I need you to get something for me."

"You need me to *get something* for you?"

"I would go myself, but my Jeep…it's not exactly *together*," her mother continued, undaunted, as if Lucia hadn't uttered a thing. "I let Gus take it off-roading one weekend, and he…well…. Long story short, two of the tires are gone. They're gone, and I can't get to the hardware store without them."

"Okay. That much I understand," Lucia said. "What I don't understand is—"

"It's not very far," her mother interjected, in a pleading, singsong tenor. "It's just down on 1st Street. You can get there in five minutes if you go the speed limit. Three, if you don't." There, she chuckled dryly and said: "You are at your father's house, aren't you?"

"Yes. I am," Lucia said. "But I'm not running any errands for you."

"You're not?"

"No."

"Why?"

"Because you won't tell me what you *need*," Lucia growled. She could've easily hung up then and there, and sent all her mother's subsequent calls straight to voicemail, but something stopped her. Maybe it was curiosity. Or maybe it was the helplessness in the woman's voice. Whatever the case, she stayed on the line.

It was a move she immediately regretted.

"Don't take that tone with me, young lady!" her mother demanded. "You have no idea how hard your father and I worked to raise you. You have no idea how many extra shifts I picked up at the bar so that you could do your sports. Your *swimming*."

That last word cut through the phone line like a poisoned barb—it was simultaneously damning and sad and remorseful—but Lucia resisted the urge to respond in kind. She knew that any type of retaliation would, ultimately, strengthen her mother's hand.

For once, her mother rewarded her self-restraint.

"I'm sorry, baby," the woman slurred, at last. "It's just…someone broke into my house last night…and I need a new lock for my front door. I think…I think they used my spare key to get in. This morning—"

"Someone *did* use the spare key to get in," Lucia interrupted. "It was me. I needed to look through Finley's room. I was hoping…" Lucia paused; took in the composition notebooks that lay around her. "I was hoping to find some details."

"Details?"

"Passwords," Lucia clarified. "Login information."

"Oh." A beat passed. Then: "Have you checked her tablet?"

"Her what now?"

"Her tablet," the woman repeated. "The one she uses for school. That's where she keeps her notes and her schedule and…well…everything like that."

"No. I haven't," Lucia said, sitting up straight. There was a good chance her mother was talking out of her ass, since she'd clearly spent the night with a variety of bottom-shelf liquors, but the prospect of a semi-secret tablet gave Lucia a case of the electric chills, nonetheless.

"Do you have any idea where that tablet might be?" she inquired, when her initial surprise and excitement began to wear off. "It's not somewhere around here, is it?"

"In your father's house?" Caitlin McBride made a sound that might have been a laugh. But the laugh didn't resolve into any kind of meaningful dialogue. It merely tapered to a wheezing, reedy hiss, before vanishing entirely.

With no more patience left to expend, Lucia terminated the call and immediately dialed Brian's number.

Brian answered on the second ring. He sounded somewhat exhausted as well, but Lucia didn't give a shit. She was on a mission.

"Finley's tablet," she said, in lieu of *hello*. "Where is it?"

"Why?" Brian mumbled.

"Just answer the question."

"Does this have something to do with last night?"

"Maybe."

"Maybe?"

"Yes. It does," she conceded. "If we can track down that tablet, we may be able to find Finley's password to the dark net site; skip further into the game. But *we need that tablet.*"

"Okay, okay. I get it," Brian said. "Give me a minute to think."

"You don't have a minute."

"Thirty seconds?"

"I'll give you fifteen."

"Fair enough," Brian murmured. Then he went quiet.

When he spoke again, his voice was focused. Optimistic.

"It's in her locker," he said. "I texted her last Friday night—the night before she disappeared—and asked about one of her upcoming tests. She said she was a little shaky on the terminology, but said she couldn't study because she'd left both the textbook and her tablet in her locker."

"You're sure?"

"Positive," Brian confirmed. "I have the text messages right here. But we can't exactly waltz into the high school and pry her locker open."

"We can't?"

"Nope. No way. Things have changed since you and I were in school," Brian said. "They don't have metal detectors set up yet, but they do have security guards inside the front doors, and they always have a police officer on the premises. No one except students and faculty are allowed inside. And by 'no one' I mean *no one*. Even if we bum-rushed the place, we'd be in handcuffs inside of five minutes."

"Then we'll have to figure out some other way," Lucia said, before hanging up and reaching for her cane.

Chapter 22

By eight o'clock that evening, Lucia was showered, made up, and dressed. She'd spent the afternoon running from one store to the next, buying hip clothes and hip makeup supplies and hip hair products, but, standing in front of her father's bathroom mirror, she found that she didn't feel any younger. The overly-tight threads and the overly-bold beauty products...they didn't make her look like a free spirited, neo-hippy party girl. They made her look like a fashion-backwards almost-thirty-something with an extremely loose grasp on her own body image.

The fitted tank top was especially troubling.

"Do girls these days actually *wear* these things?" she said, turning a hundred and eighty degrees and inspecting the horrified woman who mimicked her movements in the mirror. She wanted, more than anything, to don a conservative skirt, heels, and a blouse that didn't accentuate the shape of her lower back and stomach, but then, a skirt, heels, and a blouse were the clothes of a consummate professional. Where she was heading, young and reckless was the name of the game.

Promising the horrified woman in the mirror that she'd look better under lower lighting, she shuffled to the bed, adjusted the knee-high boots that the seventeen-year-old sales associate had called "fierce," and stuffed her keys and cell phone into her pockets. Or...she *attempted* to stuff her keys and cell phone into her pockets. Following a two-minute fight with the taut denim, she gave up and tucked both items into her bra. It wasn't the most comfortable arrangement, but the padded cups seemed to disguise them well enough, so she decided to roll with it. After all, she wasn't dressing for comfort.

Just relax, she told herself as she stepped into the hall. *You look fine. No one will give you a hard time. They'll accept you as one of their own, no questions asked.*

Wouldn't they?

Catching a reflection of her butt in a framed picture, Lucia jolted to a halt. But her father didn't give her a chance to retreat back to her room.

"Hey there, Lucy Goosey" he said, emerging from the living room not unlike a villain from a black-and-white motion picture. "What's the rush? Do you have a hot date or something?"

"Or something," Lucia mumbled. She proceeded to tug discreetly at the low-cut top, but each time she pulled the fabric one direction, it revealed a patch of skin on the other, so she ultimately gave up and resolved to change the subject.

"What about you?" she said, using an imaginary itch as an excuse to avoid eye contact. "Do you have a hot date tonight?"

"Little old me?" her father grinned. "No. Not tonight. On Fridays, I hit the bowling alley with a group of guys. We play a couple games, pound a couple drinks, then we go home. We used to close the place down, but we're not really spring chickens anymore."

"No. You're not," Lucia confirmed. It was a simple rejoinder, and it wasn't delivered with any particular flair, but it got the both of them chuckling, regardless.

"You better be careful there, girlie," her father cautioned, with a wag of his finger. "I may not be a twenty-year-old track star anymore, but I can hold my own in a bar fight. The last time I visited Mike's Place, I ended up breaking a stool over the bartender's head, clubbing a guy with a billiard ball, and choking a bouncer with a pool cue."

"Yeah?" Lucia smiled, despite herself. "That sounds exciting. For you *and* Jackie Chan."

"Jackie who?"

"Jackie Chan. The martial arts superstar," Lucia said. "That fight you just described? It's from the movie *Rush Hour*. Jackie Chan fights a bunch of scumbags in a pool hall."

"No."

"Yes. The clip is on Youtube and everything."

"Then someone has some serious explaining to do," her father glowered. And in response to her raised eyebrow: "Isn't it obvious? Some Hollywood hack has been following me around; mining my exploits for personal gain. If I'm not careful, they'll make a movie about a couple of hotshot fighter pilots who play volleyball and practice taking off their aviators all day!"

"Whatever you say, Dad," Lucia smirked. Then she gave him a hug and made for the front door.

Even though the man frustrated her, she appreciated his ability to put her at ease. It was his gift. His superpower. Did he occasionally abuse that superpower, in order to sleep with vulnerable women? Sure. But Lucia was learning to forgive his shortcomings.

Nobody's perfect, she thought as she ducked into her Focus and accelerated through the encroaching dark.

*****

Half a block from the old community baseball field, Lucia brought her car to a stop and rolled down the window. She could hear a distant pulsing—the sound of subwoofers competing for dominance in a limited space—but she couldn't *see* anything. Aside from a couple of cars, staggered at the parking lot's northern end, the place looked dead. But then, that wasn't unusual.

Ever since the opening of Eaton Commons Park, the old community baseball field had been deteriorating. Lucia knew there was a proposal on the table to transform the place into an outdoor concert venue, but she also knew that proposal would fail. None of the town leaders were interested in renovating—what had once been—a landfill. They considered the place to be an eyesore at best, and a waste of taxpayer money at worst.

Assuring herself that Deborah Hollinger was trustworthy—that she would discover a gaggle of shitfaced teenyboppers when she reached the top of the bleachers and gazed into the oval-shaped bowl—Lucia doused her headlights and eased her car into the lot. She was hesitant to kill the engine completely, since she was alone and since she wasn't entirely sure how a gaggle of shitfaced teenyboppers would react to the appearance of a stranger in a Sassy Bitch tank top, but the thought of her sister in a dingy, windowless room helped her to overcome her reservations.

Bass-heavy music throbbing in her ears, she powered the Focus down and stepped into the night. There were more than a few crushed beer cans, shattered forties, flattened cigarette butts, spent lighters, and crumpled fast-food wrappers in the vicinity, but that wasn't, in and of itself, evidence of a party. That was merely evidence of humanity's continued existence.

Taking in the spray-paint-laden cement walls and the beat-to-shit garbage cans, Lucia wound her way toward the guest team's dugout. In a matter of seconds, the entire field would be laid out before her. She would be able to see—what remained of—the pitching mound, the dugouts, the chain link backdrop, and the—

"Hey. You. Girl. Who are you?"

The inquiry came from Lucia's left, where the bleachers gave way to sloping, weed-clotted earth, and caused Lucia to jump.

"Oh. Hi. I'm...um...I'm here for the party," Lucia said, trying—and probably failing—to hide her cane. She could make out a feminine form in the midst of the blackness, but not much else. Which gave her a measure of hope. If *she* couldn't see enough to identify *the girl*, there was a good chance *the girl* couldn't see enough to identify *her*.

Play it cool, she reminded herself. *Confidence is key. Convince this girl that you're the genuine article, and you're in.*

"It's nice that you—" she began.

The girl wasn't interested in hearing the rest of her monologue.

"You know what? I don't care. Just get over here and hold my hair," the girl said, placing her hands on her knees and sucking in her stomach. "You know how to do *that*, right?"

"Yeah. Yes. I do," Lucia said, hurrying to the girl's side.

Up close, Lucia could tell the girl was wearing a button-laden denim vest, threadbare jeans, and two-sizes-too-big work boots, but she didn't mention the girl's particular style. She merely gathered up the clumps of ratty black hair, leaned back, and held her breath while the girl heaved.

Once the buttons stopped clacking together, the girl ran a hand over her lips, swallowed, and muttered: "Damn it. That's the last time I mix rum and champagne." Then she straightened and offered the same hand as a gesture of appreciation. "Hi. My name's Blake," she said, smelling of Sailor Jerry-infused bile. "I'm a friend of Marissa's; go to school up in Ault. What about you?"

"Denver," Lucia said, shaking the hand, but wincing at the sliminess of it. "Highlands Ranch. I'm a friend of—" She scoured her memory for a name. "—Destinee's," she concluded.

She should have gone with something else.

Anything else.

"Oh. Shit. Destinee *Cutler*?" the girl said, eyes flashing in the moonlight. "What are you doing up here, then? All the booze is *down there*. Unless…." Her eyebrows lowered. "You don't have *the stuff*, do you?"

"The stuff?"

"Yeah. The *E*," the girl said, looking Lucia up and down with the voracity of a wild hog. "Destinee said one of her friends was on the way with ecstasy. Is that you, or…?"

The girl let the question linger between them. And the longer the question lingered, the more suspicious it became.

"Yes. It is me. Duh," Lucia said at last, adding a laugh for good measure. "I'm afraid I have a confession to make, though. My…ah…my *dealer*…he didn't have the goods. He was clean out. Some guy came in before me and bought it all. He—"

"Motherfucker."

"Hmm?" Lucia said. She wanted to believe that the expletive was directed toward her fictional drug dealer or at her fictional drug dealer's fictional clientele, but in the low light she couldn't say one way or another.

Apparently, the *who* wasn't important.

"Come on. Let's get you something to drink," the girl said, snagging Lucia's wrist.

The next thing Lucia knew, she was at the foot of the bleachers and her newfound friend was tugging her toward the field—toward the strobe lights and the speakers and the pockets of twirling, shimmying bodies. She tried to get a rough count of the occupants as she rounded the guest team's dugout, but the rapid-fire lighting was less than amenable. It made her feel like she was a character in a stop-motion television show. She half expected the cartoon mouse to materialize in the midst of the group and to beckon to her with its long, boneless fingers.

If Blake noticed her discomfort, she didn't show it.

"Booze or beer?" the girl shouted, as soon as the two of them reached the infield. She proceeded to shout something else, but Lucia only caught a few syllables over the pulsating music. That didn't stop Lucia from saying "Beer" or from following her host to the opposite dugout, however.

With bees in her stomach, Lucia watched her host pull a red Solo cup from a bag, size up the array of mini-kegs that dotted the bench, and fill the cup with a foamy golden liquid.

"PBR," the girl explained as she handed the handed the cup over. "It's the only good option tonight. Eddie was supposed to bring some Oskar Blues, but he pussed out. You don't mind PBR, do you?"

"No. Not at all. It's my drink of choice," Lucia lied, before tipping the cup to her lips.

Thankfully, the beer was eighty-percent head.

Using the substance as an excuse to remain silent, Lucia turned and surveyed the party once more. There appeared to be a dozen people at the pitcher's mound, a handful at home plate, and another dozen spread in between. Not all of them were dancing, but she could tell that most of them were drunk.

"What happened over there?" she inquired, tilting her cup toward a pile of lacy undergarments that lay around first base. "Did a group of girls decide to go streaking or something?"

"In this weather?" Blake smirked. "Nah. That stuff belongs to Gus."

"Gus?"

"Yeah. Gus Stansky," the girl said. "He's this local creeper. Likes to buy and wear lingerie from secondhand stores. Marissa and her boyfriend came out here one night and caught him masturbating on the mound. He was wearing a purple bra and leopard-print panties."

"Are you serious?"

"Dead serious. Ask anyone here. Gus is kind of a legend."

"He sounds dangerous," Lucia said, thinking back to the note on her mother's living room window. "Hasn't anyone called the cops on him?"

"For what?" Blake said. "It isn't a crime for a man to dress in women's lingerie."

"No. But it *is* a crime to masturbate in public," Lucia pointed out.

Her concern was lost on the teenager.

"*Ahhh*. Gus is harmless," the girl said, with a "forget I said anything about it" hand motion. "He's a big ol' teddy bear. He's never done anything bad to anyone."

That you know of, Lucia contributed mentally.

At the same moment, the music came to a stop and someone filled the newfound silence with the phrase: "What the fuck are *you* doing here?" It was the kind of thing a person rarely heard outside of reality television show finales, so it didn't go without notice. From second base to home plate, heads turned and conversations tapered.

Thinking she was about to witness a spat between two former lovers, Lucia stepped away from the dugout...and quickly discovered that *she* was the focus of the outburst.

"Don't you dare play stupid," Destinee said, emerging from the crowd like a pit bull on steroids. "I want to know why you're here, and I want to know *now*. Are you here to spy on us? Are you here because you want to report all of us to the cops?"

"No. I'm not. That's...that's not my intention," Lucia returned, as evenly as possible. She didn't like the way the partygoers were forming a half circle around the Cutler girl—it reminded her of an old-fashioned lynch mob—but she couldn't afford to beat a hasty retreat. Not yet.

"For those of you who don't know me, my name is Lucia Corvi. I'm Finley Corvi's older sister," she announced to the crowd at large. "Some of you may not like my family, for one reason or another, but I'm not here on behalf of my family. I'm here for *Finley*. I'm here for *your classmate*. I'm here because I think one of you can help bring her home."

"From where?" one of the drunken blondes inquired.

"That's exactly what I'm trying to determine," Lucia said, before Destinee could barge in and steal the spotlight. "Finley's been missing for almost a week, and I have reason to believe that she's in danger. I also have reason to believe that there's a valuable clue in her locker."

"Then you want one of us to…what? Break in and steal it?" said a bleary-eyed boy in a backwards visor. "That's…well…"

"That's dumb. That's what that is," Destinee intervened, as if she didn't trust Backwards Visor to come to the correct conclusion on his own. And to Lucia: "You seriously think one of us is going to buy into your little fantasy? For the last time: Mr. Sticks *doesn't exist*. He's a fucking *urban legend*. Why can't you get that through your fruity little brain? Is it the MS…or are you just naturally stupid?"

That final jab scored a round of throaty laughter from Destinee's fellow high school students, but Lucia forced herself to take the insult in stride. She knew that a brawl would solve nothing. Best-case-scenario, it would give her a momentary release—purge some of the heat from her core. Worst-case-scenario, it would alienate the whole high school community and make it impossible for her to recover the tablet.

"You know what?" she said, when she was finally able to work the glue out of her jaw muscles. "You're absolutely right. I am stupid. It was stupid of me to buy these clothes, it was stupid of me to drive out here, and it was stupid of me to think that any of you would help me, for any amount of money. I can see that now."

"Good. Then go on and hit the road," Destinee said, with a dismissive wave. "It's past your bedtime, anyway. If you hurry, you might catch the end of *Sixty Minutes*. Am I right, guys?"

Judging by the smug expression on the girl's face, she anticipated a wall of laughter, followed by a flurry of jeers and taunts. But she wasn't rewarded with either.

Following a drizzle of guffaws, a slender boy with black nails and Sid Vicious hair stepped forward and said: "Money?" Lucia recognized him as Battle Jacket, from Destinee's personal entourage, but she wasn't in a position to be discriminatory.

"Fifty dollars," she confirmed, to Destinee's clear displeasure. "Twenty-five dollars up front, and twenty-five when the job is finished."

"Okay. How soon?" Battle Jacket inquired. "Monday?"

"No. I need it done by tomorrow night," Lucia said. She fully expected the declaration to garner an eye roll and a series of garden-variety insults, culminating in dismissal, so she was pleasantly surprised by the boy's reaction.

"You do realize that tomorrow's Saturday, don't you?" he said, scrutinizing her the way a frog might scrutinize a juicy, two-legged cricket. "That means less classes and less students. Less cover."

"And…?" Lucia said. "Your point is…?"

In response, Battle Jacket rubbed at his neck; considered.

When he finally spoke, his voice was louder—more confident.

"A hundred dollars. Up front. In cash," he said. "That's my price. We have a deal?"

Yeah. We have a deal. In your dreams, Lucia said inwardly.

Outwardly, she said: "How about this? Fifty dollars up front and fifty upon completion, with a twenty-dollar bonus if you can have the job done by three o'clock."

It was a more-than-generous offer, in her estimation, for five to ten minutes of actual work, but Battle Jacket was a harder sell. He stood there, *hmm*ing and *haw*ing, until Blake stepped into the picture and said: "Help the chick out, Eddie. It's a good deal."

That validation was what, ultimately, won the boy's allegiance.

Chapter 23

From the top of the Great Western sugar plant, Lucia could see the whole town. She could see north to Hawkstone Park, east to Mr. Potter's farm, south to the Dry Creek Inn, and west to Benjamin Eaton Elementary. The town looked quaint, clean, and organized from that height, but she couldn't quite bring herself to become lost in the scenery—in the brilliant greens and yellows. No matter how many times she cleared her mind, her thoughts returned to the boy with the black nails and the Sid Vicious hair.

Lucia didn't trust the kid. There was something about him that gave her pause. Maybe it was his attitude...maybe it was his style...or maybe it was the way he looked at the girls in his class when he thought no one was watching. The guy didn't strike her as a drug addict or an experienced con man, but she sure as hell wouldn't have entrusted him with a copy of her car key.

Wondering how she would progress if Eddie "Battle Jacket" Tate failed to fulfill his end of the bargain, Lucia stretched her legs and accidentally kicked a chunk of brick off the building's edge; listened as it skipped once...twice...and settled into the dirt below. As a teenager, she had thrown lots of things off the roof—computer monitors, televisions, bottles, videotapes—but she'd since lost her appetite for destruction. She'd since learned to appreciate the silence and the wind and the barn swallows that swooped in and out of the sugar plant's empty windows.

Hearing a moan rise from the bowels of the structure, she shifted and glanced from one end of the roof to the other. She shouldn't have been up there in the first place—the building had been abandoned for forty years—but she had a measure of faith in the thing's stability.

Besides, she didn't have anywhere else to go. Her lake was no more, her mother's trailer was a pit, her father's house was a tomb, and the Feed and Tack...? The Feed and Tack was a vault of mixed memories.

Wishing her sister would return and end the ridiculous game of hide-and-seek, Lucia lay back and closed her eyes. The bright morning sun felt good on her skin, so she rolled her shirt to the underside of her bra and spread her arms; willed the heat to cleanse the anxiety and the frustration from her pores. If she concentrated hard enough, she could almost feel Cozzens Lake beneath her—around her. She could almost hear the *plop!* of the current against the shores. She could almost smell the richness of the—

"Catching some rays, are we?"

"What? No. I mean yes. I mean...shouldn't you be at work?" Lucia said, working feverishly to cover up her abdomen while she sat upright.

Brian laughed from the access hatch. "Actually, I talked my boss into a half day," he said. "I told him that I have a mentally-unstable family member in town, and he let me off, no questions asked." Then he tilted his head and said: "Mind if I join you?"

"Not at all. Make yourself at home," Lucia returned, with a sniff. She shouldn't have felt self-conscious, since she hadn't been doing anything socially unacceptable, but she did. She felt like she'd been caught skinny-dipping in a motel pool. By a family of four, no less.

In an effort to make the situation less awkward, she cleared her throat and said: "Remember the first time we came up here? Deborah was a nervous wreck. She barely made it up that fourth set of stairs. I thought she was going to faint when she saw the ladder."

"Yeah. If not for Jared Nelson, she probably would've stopped right there," Brian said, lowering himself to the concrete beside her and crossing his legs. "She had the biggest crush on that guy."

"Because he was tall. And he was the only one, freshman year, who could grow any kind of facial hair," Lucia said. "It had nothing to do with his looks. The minute he shaved that goatee, she lost interest."

"For a while," Brian corrected. "During prom, senior year, she had too much to drink, and she kissed him on the mouth. In front of his date."

"Really?" Lucia chuckled. "I wasn't aware of that. Did it happen in the parking lot or something?"

"Nope. The whole thing played out in the middle of the gymnasium," Brian said, skipping a pebble off the roof's edge and dusting his palms on his jeans. "Mrs. Walsh—the chaperone—tried to break the group up, but she wasn't really successful. She ended up on the floor when Jared's date gave Deborah a shove. Deborah retaliated with a shove of her own, which knocked over the dessert table, and everything went downhill from there. It was bad."

"*Haha* bad?"

"No. *Cops* bad," Brian said. "I don't think anyone was arrested, but the janitors had one hell of a mess to clean up the next morning. There was frosting everywhere."

"Yeah. Okay," Lucia grunted.

Brian must have detected the sarcasm in her voice.

"You don't believe me?" he said, eyebrow arched and lips turned down.

For what it was worth, his poker face was very good.

"Of course not," Lucia said, searching his façade for signs of insincerity. "If something that crazy had happened, I would've heard about it. Deborah would've told me or—"

"Not necessarily," Brian interrupted, in a tone that suggested she should stop and listen. "From the start of senior year to the end, you were…well…you *weren't there*. We saw you a couple times a week, sure, but you were checked out. Mentally, I mean. You'd show up, go to class, and leave. You wouldn't talk to anyone."

"Anyone?" Lucia smirked. But inside, she was conflicted. Had she really been emotionally detached during her senior year? Had she really ignored her friends? She didn't think she had, but then, senior year was a blur. She couldn't recall much from that entire period.

"Okay. *If* I was absent, I'm sure it was for good reason," she said at last. "At the time, I was juggling school work, physical therapy, and college applications. That's a lot for a teenage girl."

Brian didn't argue. He merely shrugged, spat, and stared off into the distance. She couldn't tell whether he was looking at anything in particular, but she got the feeling that he wasn't. She got the feeling that he was stalling—that he was working through some complex problem in his head.

She decided not to hassle him. Drawing a deep breath into her lungs, she lay back and focused on the clouds that drifted across the placid blue sky. She watched them merge, separate, condense, and lengthen. And, before long, she found herself thinking about her life outside of Eaton. She found herself thinking about her apartment and her bills and her job. She was fairly sure her boss would approve an extra week of leave, but anything beyond that was—in her mother's words—up in the air.

Up in the air.

Lucia let that phrase marinate in her synapses.

A month earlier, her job would have taken precedence over everything else in her life, but now...now it didn't seem so important. In a way, it didn't seem *real*. Both it and her existence in the city seemed *apparitional*, as if they were the products of a long, incredibly detailed dream.

Was Lucia losing her marbles or was her hometown sucking her back in?

Promising herself that it was impossible for a *place* to influence the decisions of an intelligent, biological creature, Lucia sat up; discovered that Brian was staring at her.

"What is it?" she said, massaging the kinks from her neck.

Brian didn't answer immediately. He opened his mouth once...twice...three times...but each effort had the same result. Each effort ended in silence.

"I...um...I think I'm still in love with you," he managed, on the fourth attempt. And in response to Lucia's abject lack of reaction: "I know it's stupid and I know we burned that bridge a long time ago...but seeing you again...hanging out with you... it's got me...well...it's got me all turned around. It's got me wondering *what if*, you know?"

"No. I don't know," Lucia said, again searching for cracks in his façade. She couldn't tell whether he was joking or whether he was legitimately baring his soul, so she opted to play it safe. She pivoted until her body was facing him head-on and she said: "Are you being serious right now?"

Brian's expression was answer enough.

It told her that he *was* serious.

His words followed suit.

"Of course I am!" he exclaimed, squeezing his hands together until his fingertips were white. "Ever since you showed up in my store, I've been a *wreck*. I haven't been able to eat…I haven't been able to sleep…. Hell…I haven't been able to stop *thinking* about you. I realize that's fucked-up since…well…since Finley is missing…but my heart doesn't give a shit. It won't let go. Is there any way—"

There, Brian cut himself off, as if unsure what to say. Lucia suspected that he was waiting for validation—for her to express her enduring affection for him, in spite of their predicament—but she had no desire to venture down that road. While she did appreciate his attention, she didn't know how she felt about *him*. As a *person*.

Did she resent the man for taking advantage of her baby sister? Yes. Did she occasionally want to kick him square in the balls? Without a doubt. But she couldn't bring herself to outright *loathe* him. He possessed certain qualities that she, even now, found *endearing*.

Reminding herself of the condoms and the sex pamphlet, to shore up her emotional defenses, she released a breath and said: "Look. Things have changed. The two of us…we're not the same people. We may have had something, once, but it's long gone. Our lives and our personalities…they just aren't compatible anymore. Your future is with the Feed and Tack and mine is—"

"In the big city. I know," Brian interjected. "But here's the thing: it doesn't *have to be*. There are half a dozen companies *here* that would hire you, no questions asked. You could take a sales position at Plains Automotive; a managerial role at the Paint and Body. Hell, Mrs. Tibbs would hire you if you so much as *glanced* at the general store. She's been asking about you ever since you left. You were her favorite customer."

"Because I was free labor," Lucia pointed out. "Because I helped her stock the top shelves whenever she misplaced her stool. Which was a lot."

"True," Brian allowed. "But that's not the point. The point is... you *belong* here. The people...they know you. *I* know you. Wouldn't it make sense—"

"No," Lucia said, before Brian could lay any more verbal track. "These people don't know me. And you don't know me, either. I'm not the girl you went to high school with. You said so yourself. You said—"

"That modern-day Lucia is different than sixteen-year-old Lucia. Yes," Brian confirmed. "But these past few days have proven that there's still some of the old Lucia left in you. I mean, look where we are. Do you have any idea how many sunsets we watched up here?"

Lucia considered the question in silence. She supposed that they had spent an inordinate amount of time atop the sugar plant, talking and exploring and lounging around, but again, she had no desire to disclose that information. She was happy leaving the past in the past. It was easier that way. In her experience, resurrecting the past was tantamount to resurrecting a waterlogged corpse—it was awkward, messy, and it often led to unforeseen problems down the road.

Thankfully, Lucia didn't have to come up with a response. As she sat and digested Brian's proposal, her cell phone chirped and gave her an excuse to break eye contact.

"It's Eddie Tate," she said, once she'd read the text message in its entirety. "He wants to meet in fifteen minutes. Behind the Factory Road gas station."

"For what?" Brian inquired. "You're not *buying drugs*, are you?"

"What? No. Of course not," Lucia said with a scowl. "Last night, the two of us struck a bargain?"

"A bargain?"

"For Finley's tablet," Lucia confirmed.

Apparently, that was all the information Brian needed.

"You paid a *high school student* to steal the tablet?" Brian said. "That's not just reckless. That's..."

"Unethical?" Lucia guessed.

"No. *Stupid*," Brian said, even as he helped her to her feet. "If the cops find out, you'll be looking at more than a slap on the wrist. You'll be looking at a hefty fine. Or worse. The DA—"

"The DA won't find out about shit," Lucia promised him. "I covered my tracks. Besides, Mr. Ogilbee and I are on good terms. We go way back."

"Maybe so," Brian countered, "but Mr. Ogilbee isn't the district attorney anymore. He retired in 2016. The current district attorney is Samuel Tate. Which means—"

"I made a deal with the DA's son," Lucia concluded.

"And if you don't make the DA's son happy…well…"

Brian let his sentence end there.

Chapter 24

From the street, the gas station on Factory Road looked like any other mom-and-pop shop. It had cracked-and-duct-taped windows, sun-bleached advertisements, rusted display racks, and fly-excrement-yellowed fluorescent lights, which buzzed above stripped-and-stained linoleum floors. But Lucia wasn't fooled by the down-home aesthetic. She knew that it was, at its core, a carnivore.

During her time in high school, the gas station had chewed up and spit out three separate owners. The last one, a Pakistani man named Tariq, had put up one hell of a fight, but he, too, had ultimately succumbed to the structure's appetite—to the sentient tendrils that some mistook as roots.

Wondering how many other entrepreneurs had fallen in the interim, Lucia pulled into the lot and parked as far away as possible. She was anxious, but she still planned to undertake the transaction by herself. She figured it would be easier that way.

Brian was of a different opinion.

"I should come with you, you know," he said, as soon as she pulled the key from the ignition. "I've spent some time around Destinee's friends. I know what makes them tick."

"And you think I don't?" Lucia said, a tinge of resentment in her voice. "In case you've forgotten, we were teenagers at the same time."

"Yes, but Eddie isn't *some teen*," Brian pointed out. "He has connections and he knows it. He's going to try and use his position to bully you."

"And…?"

Brian spread his hands. "Don't you think it would be wise to bring backup?"

Lucia considered his argument while she groped for her cane. As a twenty-first-century feminist, she wanted to tell him to go to Hell, but her paranoia stopped her. At the end of the day, he was bigger and stronger. If things went south, he would have a negotiatory advantage—if only because of his size.

"Okay," she said at last. "You can come. But leave the talking to me."

Expectation communicated, she stepped out of the car and made a beeline for the building's southwest corner.

Eddie Tate was already there when she arrived. And he was looking about as relaxed as a raccoon in a garbage can.

"Well, well. Look who showed up," the teenager said, lifting a wad of chew from a can and tucking it into his cheek. "It's Brian and his new squeeze That *is* what you two are, right? Lovers? Forgive me if I'm wrong, but Brian *does* have a thing for Corvi women. Just a week ago—"

"Friends," Lucia interrupted, faster and louder than she intended. She understood, on a rational level, that the boy was trying to upset her, but that didn't stop his words from resonating with her emotions. Given an alleyway and a cover of darkness, she would have laid her cane upside his head.

"We're old friends," she amended, when she felt more in control of her vocal chords. "But we're not here to make conversation. We're here for the tablet."

"Then I hope you brought your wallets," the boy said, extracting the device from his battle jacket and turning it over in his tobacco-stained fingertips. "This thing here? Well, it was a real bitch to get a hold of. Harder than I expected. Considering the circumstances, I think a finder's fee is in order."

"A *finder's fee?*"

The question was posed, simultaneously, by both Lucia and Brian.

"Yeah. A finder's fee," the boy repeated, depositing a glob of brown saliva between his boots. "Ten percent is boilerplate, but I'll have to ask for thirty. *Plus* the bonus you promised."

"And if I refuse?" Lucia ventured.

The boy shrugged. "You can refuse if you want. No skin off my back. On the street, I can probably get seventy…eighty bucks off this thing. Maybe a hundred if I'm patient. Or—" His eyes took on a mischievous sparkle. "—if there are nudie pics on here."

There, he stopped, and let his words sink in.

"What do you think?" he mused, when his counterparts failed to reply. "If I turn this thing on, will I find some goodies in the gallery? I'm tempted to give it a look right now. I mean, there's got to be *something* special about you Corvi girls." And then, directly to Brian: "Am I right?"

In response, Lucia set her teeth and silently counted to ten. She was proud of Brian for keeping his cool, but she wasn't sure how much longer she could match his composure. Already, her cheeks were burning and the muscles in her neck were tightening.

"We had a deal," she managed, between clenched incisors. "Fifty up front and seventy upon completion. That's more than fair."

"As of last night," Eddie smirked. "Since then, demand has gone up. It's simple economics. When the quantity of a particular good drops and the demand goes up, the price will—"

"We both understand how supply and demand works," Brian interrupted. "Now, cut the shit and hand the thing over. We're done negotiating."

"No. I don't think we are," Eddie said, slipping the device back into his jacket and using one of his index fingers to reorient the wad of chew in his lip. "I don't think we've agreed on anything. In fact, the finder's fee just went up. I'll need an extra *fifty* dollars on top of the bonus. You can either fork it over or you can walk. What'll it be?"

The question may have been posed to Brian and Lucia, as a unit, but Brian opted to answer on his own, without any kind of prior consultation.

"No deal," he said, crossing his arms and spreading his feet. "Seventy—*total*—is our final offer. You can take it or you can leave it. Either way, we'll be leaving with the tablet."

"No. You won't," Eddie retaliated, angry for the first time. "I'm the one calling the shots. If I tell you to jump, you two better ask how high. I'm not fucking around here."

"Neither are we," Lucia said, taking a step toward the irate young man and extending her hand, palm-up. "We're here for the tablet and we're going to get it. One way or another."

It was the type of thing one movie gangster would say to another movie gangster over a bowl of cold spaghetti, and it didn't sound the least bit intimidating to Lucia's ears, but it must have worked its way beneath the rapscallion's veneer of masculinity.

"You know what?" the boy said, after a fleeting indecision. "I'm done. This whole thing is whack."

He then made a move toward his bicycle, but Brian was ready for him.

"Whoa there. Where do you think you're going?" Brian said, shifting between the boy and his bike and giving the boy a cautionary shove in the opposite direction. "You haven't given the tablet to my friend."

"No. I haven't. And I'm not going to," Eddie spat. "Both you and your friend are fucking *crazy*. Do you have any idea who my dad is?"

"Actually, yes. We do," Brian said, keeping his arm outstretched, in case the boy made another lunge for his mode of transportation. "But we're not worried about him. We know you'll keep him out of it."

"Like hell I will," the boy fired back. "If you touch me one more time, I'll have both your asses thrown in jail so *fucking* fast that you won't have time to *fucking* apologize. Get me, *fucker*?"

That said, he made a second move toward his bike, but Brian didn't budge. With the ease and ambivalence of a slumbering steer, Brian arrested the boy's momentum and returned him to his previous position.

To Lucia's surprise, the action was not met with unrepentant fury. If anything, the boy seemed *confused*. He seemed genuinely flummoxed by his inability to reach his bike, as if he had never before encountered such a level of resistance.

Brian took advantage of that confusion.

"Let me explain myself," he said, in a tone of voice that suggested he was addressing a troublesome toddler rather than a spoiled teen. "I happen to know that your grades at Eaton High are less than stellar, and that, as a result, your father is considering military school. I also happen to know that your father and my boss are extremely close friends. If my boss—who's an Army veteran, by the way—was to endorse that military school…well…that might just convince your father to pull the trigger. And you don't want your father to pull the trigger, do you?"

In response, Eddie bristled and wiped the creases from his white tee. Lucia could tell he wanted to curse Brian out and stalk off into the sunset, but Brian had him pinned between a rock and a hard place. Without a father to fall back on, the boy was left with one of two choices: relinquish the tablet or fight.

For a split second, Lucia actually thought the teen was going to throw a wild hook—she saw his fingers curling and his nostrils flaring—but in the end, his tough guy act was exactly that: an act.

With a sniff and a faux "I don't really give a shit" eye roll, he pulled the tablet from his jacket and said: "Here. Take it. The damn thing's pretty much useless to me, anyway. Even if there are naked pictures on there, I'm sure they're hideous. I, personally, wouldn't pay a dime to see Finley's tits. I hear they're saggy as hell. And her pussy—"

Brian didn't let him get any further. The moment Lucia had the tablet in her hands, he rocketed forward and planted his fist upside the boy's nose. It wasn't a blow worthy of a golden belt, but it was solid, and it was more than enough to lay the boy on his ass.

"What…what are you doing?" the teenager croaked, when he was finally able to stop his eyeballs from spinning. "That's not…that's not fair. You shouldn't…you can't…"

"What? Put a little snot in his place?" Brian fumed. "If you talk like a man, you better be ready to fight like one. Now. Are you going to stand up and defend yourself or are you going to keep pissing yourself on the ground?"

It wasn't a rhetorical question, but, based on the fear on the kid's face, it might as well have been. Lucia could tell that he was down for the count. Nothing short of a bona fide miracle could have convinced him to get off his ass. And that filled Lucia with joy.

She shouldn't have derived happiness from the kid's suffering—he was still a teen, after all—but she couldn't help herself. The sound of his sniveling was music to her ears, and the sight of his blood-and-tobacco-stained chin was as visually pleasing as a renaissance painting.

Satisfied by the conversation's conclusion, she bent down as low as she could, thanked the boy for his cooperation, then hooked her arm through Brian's and nodded toward the car.

It was time to hit the road.

Chapter 25

"Holy shit. Did that just happen?" Lucia said, as soon as she brought her car to a stop across from her father's house. "Did you *actually* punch that punk for me?"

She didn't mean to sound overly giddy, but she was. She felt like an eight-year-old on a sugar high. She couldn't stop thinking about the confrontation—about the way Brian had quickly and effectively shut the kid up. She wished she'd captured it all on her smart phone.

Brian wasn't so flip.

"For you?" he said, keeping his bruised knuckles elevated and flexing his fingers. "Yeah. I guess it was for you. But in my defense, the kid was asking for it. He should've stopped while he was ahead."

"Yeah. I don't think there's any argument there," Lucia laughed. Then she noticed the grimace on her compatriot's face and she reprimanded herself internally. She needed to get her head back in the game. She may have won a battle, but winning a battle was far different than winning a war.

"Come on. Let's get you inside," she said. "We can take a look at that hand in the bathroom."

*****

Following a brief examination, Lucia tracked down a package of paper towels and a roll of duct tape, and went to work on the injured extremity. She would've preferred to wrap the hand with gauze and medical tape, but her father's restroom wasn't exactly overflowing with first aid supplies. Aside from a box of butterfly bandages and a bottle of expired hydrogen peroxide, the cupboards were empty.

"Okay. Is this too tight?" she inquired, once the last strip of silver tape was in place. "You can still move your fingers, can't you?"

Mr. Sticks

"Yeah. I think so," Brian said, examining the mitt the way a dog might examine a cone of shame. "I mean, it's hard to concentrate with the lightning bolts of pain shooting through my fingertips, but otherwise…. Hey. Where are you going?"

"To the guest bedroom. To see what's on the tablet," Lucia said as she stood and sauntered down the hall. "I'm officially done feeling sorry for you."

"Really? Because it doesn't seem like it," Brian said, hurrying after her. "It seems like you want to say 'Thank you.' Or 'Sorry.' Or 'Brian, that was incredibly masculine of you. Will you please hit someone else so I can bask in your manliness once more?'"

Coming from anyone else, that last sentiment would have sounded hateful and narrow-minded, but from Brian? From Brian it sounded aloof and playful. It reminded Lucia of the times they'd sat at the center of the Greeley mall and made fun of the passers-by.

Knowing she wouldn't be able to keep a straight face if she looked him in the eye, Lucia continued to the guest bedroom, where she sat and said: "Actually, I was going to ask how you've survived so long with such brittle bones. You must have a bird in your family history, because your hands are weak."

"You think so?" Brian said from the doorway. "I do dream about flying quite a bit. And I am strangely attracted to magnets…." He pursed his lips, as if deep in thought. Then he shook his head and concluded: "Nope. Definitely not related to any birds. My great-great-grandmother was a lemur, and lemurs can't stand birds."

"Are you sure?" Lucia said, to keep herself from laughing while she worked the tablet from her tote. "I watched a documentary about lemurs once; they're very accepting."

"When the cameras are on, sure," Brian returned. "But behind closed doors? They're hostile as shit. My grandmother was racist until the day she died. She refused to speak to a single person of Eastern European descent, which—and this might surprise you—made family reunions extremely awkward."

"For you or for the Eastern European slaves your family kept in the basement?" Lucia returned, with a grin. She was proud of herself for coming up with the repartee on the spot, but she was immediately sidetracked when the machine responded to her touch.

"It still has some battery left," she said excitedly. "And it's not password protected. I shouldn't have any trouble accessing any of Finley's files."

"Then what are you waiting for?" Brian said, sliding onto the mattress beside her. "Let's go digging!"

"Yeah. Okay," Lucia stammered, fumbling from one screen to the next. She was more than a little distracted by the closeness of his body—by the heat that radiated through her jeans and T-shirt—but she wasn't about to point that out. If she did, there was a chance he would notice the gooseflesh on her forearms or—worse—the rapid *thumpa-thumpa* of her heart.

"Do you...ah...do you happen to know where Finley keeps her login information?" she managed as she scrolled through the list of Word documents. "None of these filenames make sense. What is 'purple_hippo' supposed to mean, anyway?"

"No idea," Brian murmured, before leaning forward and placing his elbows on his knees; before brushing Lucia's thigh ever-so-slightly with his injured paw; before inadvertently sucking the wind from Lucia's lungs. "It might be best to focus on the recently-modified documents. You can bring them to the top by—"

"I know how to sort by date, thank you very much," Lucia said, using mock indignation as an excuse to straighten and to put some space between the two of them. "I might not be a tech wizard like Peter, but I'm no idiot. At the office—"

The *office*, she heard, in some distant part of her brain. *Not my office.*

"—I solve all the day-to-day tech issues. *I'm* the only one who can clear the printer when it jams, *I'm* the only one who can change the toner, and *I'm* the only one who can reset the wireless network."

"Well then, I apologize for doubting you," Brian said, with a flourish. "Next time the credit card machines go down at the Feed and Tack, I won't bother calling tech services. I'll just get in touch with my local Lucia Corvi!"

"Or you can use the old hammer-and-baseball-bat method and save yourself a lot of time," Lucia smirked. She would have felt somewhat better if she had been repulsed by the thought of his number on her work phone's caller ID, but she hadn't been repulsed at all. In actuality, the thought had sent a warm jolt down her spine.

Determined to regain control of her physiological reactions, Lucia began working through the list of recently-modified Word documents. She opened, scrolled, and closed—opened, scrolled, and closed—as fast as she could. Until she reached a document with two dozen neat, individual entries. Then she stopped, and she jabbed a finger at the very last line of text.

"That's it. That's the password," she whispered.

To prove her hunch, she unlocked her cell phone, accessed her encrypted web browser, brought up the archive of naked Believers, and followed the link on the main page. She was somewhat afraid she would encounter an Error: Website Not Found message when her cell phone finished processing her request, but that fear was quickly put to rest.

In a matter of seconds, a dialogue box appeared and she dutifully filled the text field with Finley's information. Then she hit Enter on her virtual keyboard and waited.

Under normal circumstances, Brian would have filled the silence with an off-color joke or with an equally offensive observation, but he must have felt the tension in the air. He remained perfectly still while her cell phone worked—while it traded data with some distant server. And when the security protocols finally cleared…? He didn't react then, either.

To be fair, the gallery of milky-eyed and ashen-faced figures was equal parts confounding and disturbing.

"What…ah…what is this?" Lucia mumbled, as one image dissolved into the next. She thought she recognized a few of the subjects from the previous web page, but she couldn't say for sure. Most of the pictures were blurry and most of the models were lying at strange angles. They seemed to be staring at something just out of frame. Or…maybe…they weren't staring at anything at all.

Dread bubbling in the pit of her stomach, Lucia scrolled down and encountered a block of sterile, white text.

According to the text, the people in the photographs were the *Transformed*: true Believers who had reached the end of the maze, and been freed from their material bonds—their fears and pains and sorrows and cares. And the text didn't stop there.

"If any Believer wishes to become one of the Transformed," Lucia recited inwardly, "he must go to a payphone at 3:00 a.m., turn around six times, and say these words: *'Sein ist die Hand die schafft. Sein ist die Hand die verletzt. Sein ist die Hand die heilt.'* Once this incantation has been spoken, contact will be made."

Imagination spinning, Lucia lowered her phone and pressed her fingertips to her temples. She couldn't believe that she was actually taking the instructions seriously. A week earlier, she would have dismissed the whole paragraph as semi-coherent nonsense. After all, Mr. Sticks didn't exist.

Right?

Hoping to banish some of the more outlandish thoughts from her head, she looked up and asked for Brian's opinion. If anyone could inject some rationale into the situation, it was him.

Brian didn't disappoint.

"Are you serious?" he said, glancing between her face and her phone. "The whole thing is crazy. Everything from the payphone to the magic ritual. You're not *actually* thinking about going out tonight, are you?"

"No. I mean…not on my own," Lucia amended. And to pacify his look of mystification: "I just…I feel like we've come too far to quit *now*. This may turn out to be a dead end, but I'd rather reach a dead end than *no* end. You know what I mean?"

Brian sighed. She could tell that he was tired of the games and the riddles and the virtual puzzle boxes, but she could also tell that he wasn't ready to give up the search. He was still determined to locate her sister, no matter the cost.

"Yeah. I guess you're right," he said, scratching absentmindedly at his injured hand. "We might as well give this thing a shot. It's not like we're drowning in leads, after all."

"But...?" Lucia said, in anticipation of the conjunction.

Brian's mouth formed a half smile. "*But*," he said, "if I end up getting pneumonia from this little excursion, *you're* going to pay my medical bills."

Chapter 26

"So. This is it?" Lucia said, from the back of Peter's hand-me-down Mustang. "This is the last payphone in town?"

"If we're being technical," Peter said, from the driver's seat. "There's another one outside the general store, but that one's no longer in order."

"A couple of bums came through last summer and masturbated all over it," Brian said, from the passenger side. "The city sent some people to clean it up, but those people decided it would be simpler to disconnect the damn thing. The handset itself—"

"Nuh-uh. I'm not interested in the details," Lucia said, placing her hands over her ears and squeezing her eyes shut. The latter was a useless precaution since the inside of the cab was black as pitch and since the only source of light, externally, was the old U-Fill It gas station across the road, but she played it up, regardless. She had to keep her mind occupied. If she started staring across the street, toward the squat cinderblock structure with the paint-blackened windows and the chattering fluorescent bulbs, she would inevitably begin to *see* things. Things that could not—or *should not*—exist. Things that preferred to prowl just outside the station's sulfurous glow. Things with knobby fingertips and sallow, hunger-distended bellies.

Glimpsing something large and white in the rearview mirror—something that her brain failed to categorize before it disappeared back into the preternatural gloom—Lucia straightened and asked what time it was.

Peter responded by turning his key in the ignition.

"It's currently 2:50," he announced, once the dashboard sprung to life. "Ten minutes until the witching hour." Then he turned and, face washed in ghostly blue light, said: "You know why it's called *the witching hour*, don't you?"

"Because it's the only time that witches can safely ride their broomsticks around the moon," Lucia shrugged.

Apparently, that wasn't the right answer.

"It's called *the witching hour* because, from three o'clock to four o'clock, there are no scheduled church services or prayers taking place," Peter said. "You see, the Catholic Church has been following *canonical hours* for hundreds and hundreds of years. Around 484 A.D., a Greek monk named Sabbas took it upon himself to—"

Brian didn't care to hear the rest of Sabbas's story.

"Oh my gosh. What a great history lesson," he said, while staring emptily into the blackness. "So rich and full of texture. I can't wait to find out how it ends. In the meantime, can we please turn on the radio? I need some kind of stimulation to keep me awake."

"Me too," Lucia chimed in. But that wasn't entirely the truth.

While Lucia *was* tired, she wasn't in danger of falling asleep. Ever since she'd clambered into the back of the Mustang, she'd felt vulnerable and alone.

Is this how Travis St. John felt before the end? she wondered as the sounds of avant-garde jazz filled the speakers. *Did he become so paranoid that he actually started seeing things? Things that he couldn't explain?*

It wasn't a concept that would ever register on the Scale of Cheery Thoughts, but Lucia managed to derive a degree of comfort from it, regardless. If extreme mental stress was to blame for the Shapes in the Margins, then the Shapes in the Margins could not—truly—exist. And if the Shapes in the Margins did not exist, they couldn't actually hurt her. They couldn't wrap their cold, devoid-of-life tendrils around her, or drag her into a place between places—into a darkness not borne from an absence of light, but from an absence of *substance*.

Unable to lose herself in Peter's music, Lucia poked Brian in the back of the head and asked him to move his seat. She didn't particularly *want* to get out of the car, but she needed to acclimate herself to the darkness. She needed to breathe and stretch—to work the anxiety from her ligaments.

It didn't take her long to regret the decision.

Outside the car, the night was abnormally thick. It called out to her when her back was turned and it shifted gleefully in her peripheral vision, beckoning her toward some unseen maw; some immaterial gateway between dimensions.

Brian wasn't nearly as intimidated.

"Hey. You okay?" he inquired, while settling back into the passenger seat. "You look about as nervous as a puppy on the first day of obedience school. Do you need—"

"No," Lucia said, louder than she intended. And then, at a more controlled volume: "I'm fine. It's…. I thought I saw something. That's all. Not a big deal."

"Really?" Brian returned. "Because I think that's a fucking *huge* deal. If there's someone out there—"

"There's not," Lucia interrupted, for a second time. "Trust me. If I see anything *remotely* suspicious, I'll let you guys know. Until then…" Lucia swallowed. She wanted to end the conversation with something witty and humorous to lighten the mood, but, at the moment, her well of witty remarks was dry.

She ended up settling for the phrase: "Keep the car warm for me."

Brian wasn't convinced by her made-to-order mettle.

"If you're having second thoughts, we can reschedule," he offered, on the heels of a rapid-fire bass solo. "Or one of us can take your place. I'm sure Peter would be more than happy to complete that silly little ritual for you."

"Yes. *More* than happy," Peter confirmed.

It was a touching gesture, but Lucia couldn't bring herself to pass the proverbial mantle. Since she had set up the excursion, she felt that it was her responsibility to lead the charge. Besides, if there *was* something or someone out there…and that something or someone chose to lash out….

"Thanks," she said, before the creatures in her imagination could claim what remained of her composure, "but I can do this on my own. I'm a big girl." Then she patted the Mustang's roof and started across the road.

Halfway to the opposite curb, she detected a low rumble—not unlike the purr of an expensive automobile—but a succinct visual search revealed little. If there *was* a vehicle nearby, it was proceeding slowly, and it was navigating without its headlights.

Unsettled by the phenomenon, Lucia hurried the rest of the way across the street and took refuge behind one of the U-Fill It's two gasoline pumps. From there she could see the Mustang's outline, but she couldn't see anything *within*. Hell, she couldn't tell where one window ended and another began.

Assuring herself that Brian and Peter were watching her every move, she abandoned the pump and completed the ten-yard jog to the payphone—to the squat cinderblock structure, surrounded by the halo of flickering light.

On the one hand, she was thankful for the bank of fluorescents, but on the other? On the other, she wished they would disappear. Beneath the lights, she felt terribly exposed, as if everything and everyone were watching her. As if the eyes of the world were upon her.

Reminding herself that her sister's life was in the balance, she took a breath and fished her cell phone from her pocket.

Three o'clock, on the dot.

"Showtime," she muttered, to no one in particular.

A second later, she cued up the magic words, recited them to the best of her ability, and turned around six times. The last revolution nearly caused her to lose her balance, but she was able to steady herself against the payphone's steel enclosure, and she straightened, feeling accomplished. Except...nothing happened. No bulbs went out, no dogs barked, and no people appeared.

Afraid that she'd done something wrong, or that she'd overlooked some important detail, Lucia pivoted; glanced toward the Mustang.

There was no reaction.

Shit, she thought, scouring one vortex of darkness after another. *Should I try it again or should I wait?*

She was tempted to give the recitation another stab since she was sure she'd butchered the initial effort, but she didn't want to jump the gun.

"Um... hello?" she ventured, shuffling toward the building's southeast corner. "Is anyone there? Can anyone hear me? My name's Lucia and I'm...well...I'm looking for my sister. If you can help..."

Lucia chose not to finish her sentence. As she peered down the length of the south-facing wall, the darkness seemed to swell and intensify, as if it were pressing back against the light—as if it meant to swallow the ratty fluorescents whole and claim everything within the halo of luminescence. The effect may have taken place entirely within her head, but it was disturbing nonetheless.

Grip tightening on her cane, Lucia retreated to the payphone, where she closed her eyes and counted to three. She usually counted to ten when she was frustrated or angry or otherwise emotionally volatile—her physical therapist had taught her to count to ten—but ten seconds suddenly felt like an eternity. In the span of ten seconds, a thousand things could happen.

Unable to tell whether the weight on her chest was real or imaginary, Lucia unlocked her phone and brought up her contacts list. She intended to call Brian and to ask how she should proceed, but, as she scrolled through her saved numbers, the payphone behind her rang. And caused the device to slip from her fingers.

Skin prickled and heart pounding, Lucia turned toward the payphone. Any other night, she would have left the damned thing alone, but she suspected that the call was meant for her. She suspected that the person—or *being*—on the other end was distinctly aware of her presence.

Muscles abuzz with nervous energy, Lucia reached out, lifted the handset from the cradle, and said cautiously: "Hello?"

Her inquiry was not immediately acknowledged.

Following several seconds of white noise, interrupted intermittently by—what may or may not have been—muted dial tones, she heard a reverb-laden and indistinct "Hello." It wasn't much of a response, but it was encouraging nonetheless.

"Do you know who I am?" Lucia returned, as soon as she could summon the words from her vocal chords.

The being on the other end of the line said "Yes."

"Okay. Then you must know why I'm here," Lucia said, hoping to conjure more than a single-word reply. "You must know what I'm looking for."

Again, the being said "Yes."

Either he—or she; Lucia couldn't distinguish her counterpart's sex from the one- and- two-syllable answers—had nothing else to add, or he was determined to maintain complete anonymity.

Torn on what to say next—on how to keep the conversation going—Lucia swallowed and said: "Is she…is my *sister*…okay?" She wanted to go one step further and ask where her sister was, but she was afraid that such a question might alienate her counterpart.

Her restraint was rewarded.

"Yes," the being said, after a brief pause. But it didn't provide any more detail. It let its voice receded into the white noise, as if it was an alligator, stalking its prey from a muddy swamp.

Of course, Lucia didn't have any reason to trust the being—she knew it might be lying to her, to keep her happy and to make her easier to manipulate—but she was relieved by its proclamation anyway. At the moment, hope was the only thing keeping her together.

Seeing her sister's bruised and gagged face in the advancing dark, Lucia squeezed the handset a little tighter and said: "Can I see her? Can I see Finley?" And then, as the seconds lengthened: "I won't cause any problems. I promise. I just want to see her again. If you can do that, I…well…it would mean the world to me."

There she went quiet, and she waited for a response. She was aware of her cell phone buzzing at her feet—she could make out Brian's number on her caller ID—but she couldn't bring herself to bend down. Thanks to the cold and the adrenaline pulsing through her veins, she felt about as flexible as a rigor mortis-stricken corpse.

"Um…hello?" she said, when she could no longer stand the hum of the fluorescent lights above her. "You can hear me, can't you? If you can, please say something. My sister…she's just a girl. She doesn't deserve this. She doesn't deserve whatever she's gotten herself into. I don't have much money…but if you're after a ransom…I'll find a way to pay it. I'll—"

Detecting the loss of composure in her voice, Lucia stopped herself. She was starting to babble. If she didn't get a grip, she was liable to go off the deep end—to start promising things she couldn't supply. And that wouldn't do anyone any favors.

"Look," she resumed, in a steadier tone. "I don't know what Finley's heard or seen or *done*, but I guarantee you that, if you let her go, she won't talk to the police. Neither of us will. We'll pretend like nothing ever happened. We'll walk away and you'll never hear from us again."

Was she telling the truth? To be honest, she wasn't sure. She wanted Finley's kidnappers—or *kidnapper*—to pay for what they'd done. She wanted to look them in the eyes, and she wanted to tell them how sad and disgusting they were. But she didn't want her anger to put any of her friends or family at risk.

Mentally running through the possible forces at play, Lucia transferred the phone from one hand to the other and willed a positive response from her soft-spoken counterpart.

She didn't get one.

Instead, she was treated to a sudden stab of sound—a high-pitched whistle that penetrated her eardrums and vibrated ever deeper. She made an effort to mute the noise by dropping the handset and by flattening her palms over her ears, but the reaction didn't do much.

The noise had already worried into her psyche.

Seeing flies at the edges of her vision, Lucia stumbled away from the payphone. She was tempted to grab her cell and to make a dash for the Mustang, but she knew her sense of balance was teetering. She could feel the pavement shifting beneath her feet; could hear the murmur of subterranean waves. And within those waves…?

A voice.

No.

Not *a* voice.

Multiple voices.

The longer Lucia listened, the more she detected. And the more she detected, the more she wanted to crumple into a ball and cry.

She couldn't understand the majority of the voices since they were relegated to whispers and since none of them paused for more than a second between tirades, but what she *did* understand...it was bad enough.

In a matter of minutes—what she believed to be minutes, at least—her head was filled with horrific vitriol. Stories of abduction; stories of imprisonment; stories of rape; stories of emotional and physical defilement.... All of them followed a different narrative path, but none of them came to a different conclusion.

All of them ended with death.

Unsure where the voices were coming *from*—or *why*—Lucia returned the handset to the cradle and groped feverishly for her cell phone. But the device was able to impart little comfort.

The moment her fingers closed around the glossy polka dot case, she sensed a presence on the road and she jolted in the opposite direction.

"Who...ah...who is it?" she said, straining to make out any kind of physical attributes. She thought she caught a glimpse of broad shoulders, a stumpy neck, and an ovoid skull when one of the fluorescent lamps briefly flared, but she couldn't be positive. Without a moon in the sky, the presence was less of a man and more of a disparity—a merging of shadows, sexless and nameless.

But it wasn't nameless.

As Lucia worked up the courage to utter a follow-up question, she became aware of the stillness in her head. The voices were still there, but they were no longer babbling incoherently, like a bunch of toddlers on Adderall. They were muttering the same two words, over and over.

"*Mr. Sticks*," they were saying. "*Mr. Sticks.*"

Lucia didn't wait for them to say anything else.

Jaw set and fists clenched, she bolted into the darkness. She was certain that one of her two companions would come to her aid as she approached the road, since she was clearly unsettled, but she was mistaken.

A quarter of the way to the Mustang, the blackness constricted around her; caused her to spiral uncontrollably to the pavement. And from that blackness came a new voice. A deeper voice. A voice that promised to open her mind both to unmolested wonders and to unfathomable terrors.

Chapter 27

When Lucia awoke the next morning, she felt about as cohesive as Humpty Dumpty, post tumble. Her head was throbbing, her muscles were sore, and her entire left side was buzzing, as if a colony of bees had inhabited her skin during the night. She was so disoriented, in fact, that it took her a full minute to realize that she was lying in Peter's bed.

Unable to remember how she'd ended up in the room, she—with more than a little difficulty—leveraged her legs to the edge of the mattress and began the search for her cane. The latter shouldn't have taken more than ten seconds, from start to finish, but her eyes were on the filmy side, so it did. It took her a full minute to locate the damned thing and another full minute to retrieve it.

Once on her feet, she shuffled to the door and, hearing the telltale clatter of silverware against china, gingerly picked her way across the basement. She expected her memory to clear as she navigated the staircase, but the ascent had little effect on her cobwebbed synapses. She couldn't say, with certainty, what had occurred. Or in what order.

Cursing her inability to walk in a straight line, she crested the stairs and found both her compatriots at the kitchen table. Along with Mrs. Janowski.

"Oh! Good morning, dear!" the old woman said, as soon as she became aware of Lucia's presence. "We didn't wake you up with our gossiping, did we?"

"No. You didn't. My…ah…my cell phone woke me up," Lucia said.

It wasn't a perfect lie, but it probably would have flown if Peter hadn't immediately lifted her phone from the table, given it a shake, and said: "You mean *this*?"

"Yes. That," Lucia replied, between her teeth. And then, in an effort to camouflage her hostility: "Where did you find it?"

"In the Mustang," Peter smiled, as if he anticipated a cash reward for his honesty. "It was lying on the floor, behind the passenger seat. You must've dropped it last night."

"After you left the bar," Mrs. Janowski said. And in response to Lucia's raised eyebrow: "Oh. Don't worry. I wasn't stalking you. Peter and Brian told me all about your little shenanigans. Sounds like you three had a pretty busy evening!"

"Yes. We did," Lucia said, glancing from Brian to Peter and receiving "play along" winks and hand gestures from the both of them. "I guess I shouldn't have ordered that last shot. I feel like—"

"Your head is in a vise?" Mrs. Janowski grinned. "Yeah. I know the feeling. Believe it or not, I used to be quite a party animal. Used to wake up all over the place. But that's old news."

That said, she stood; beckoned for Lucia to take a seat at the table.

"Come on over, dear," she fussed. "We have eggs and bacon and cereal, and more than enough coffee. We even have some Baileys if you need some hair of the dog."

"Or," Peter said, between slugs of orange juice, "maybe you can make Lucia your special hangover cure."

"Hangover cure?" Lucia inquired. But she was too late. By the time the first syllable left her lips, Mrs. Janowski was completely onboard.

"Yes!" the woman exclaimed, causing her white bob to bounce about her jawline and her sterling silver necklace to jump from breast to breast. "That's a wonderful idea! I can't believe I didn't think of it myself! I may have to get some of the ingredients straight from the garden, but...." Her pupils centered on Lucia; became suddenly solemn. "You're not allergic to dandelion root, ginger, clove oil, kale, cabbage, milk thistle, artichoke, wolfberries, kudzu root, turmeric, amla, chicory, or date palms, are you, dear?" she inquired.

Lucia bit her lower lip. In all honesty, she wasn't familiar with half the ingredients, but she wasn't about to admit as much. She could tell, based on the excitement in the woman's voice, that "No" was the only acceptable answer. So she obeyed her gut.

Mrs. Janowski's reaction was priceless.

With the charisma and agility of someone half her age, the woman clapped her hands, squealed "Excellent!" and rushed from one end of the kitchen to the other, before disappearing out the back door, gardening implements in tow.

Peter was the first to speak in her absence.

"Well," he said, swirling his orange juice as though it was, in reality, a fine cognac. "That ought to keep her busy for a while."

"Long enough for us to get to the bottom of things," Brian agreed. Then he swiveled toward Lucia and said: "Speaking of...what the hell happened last night? Do you even remember?"

"I remember talking to someone on the payphone," Lucia said, taking a seat between the two of them and pouring herself a tall cup of coffee. "After that...well...." She shrugged; watched the muddy liquid ripple outward from the center. The substance itself sharpened her memory of the preternatural darkness—she could picture her breath curling upward; being consumed as soon as it breached the fluorescents' hazy perimeter—but she saw a completely different image in the concentric waves.

In those miniature tides, she saw the *disparity*.

Heart skipping a beat, she looked up and said: "The stranger. On the road. You didn't find out who he was, did you?"

It was a simple question, but it wasn't met by a simple answer.

Following a series of glances, Brian cleared his throat and said: "What are you talking about? There wasn't a stranger on the road."

"Yes. There was," Lucia maintained. "I tried to run from him, but he knocked me over and pinned me down. Then...." She narrowed her eyes. "Then he told me how to do it."

"How to do *what*?" Peter inquired.

"How to summon Mr. Sticks," Lucia said, in a considerably lower voice. "He told me to fast for three days...to wait until midnight... then to go half a mile northwest of Collins' Crossing...to turn around three times...and to give the ground a taste of my blood. He said the blood would purify the earth, so I should proceed barefoot. He said the ceremony would—"

Lucia cut herself off. Her companions were exchanging glances again—eyeing her the way two specimens in a zoo might eye a new addition to an artificial habitat.

"What is it?" she said, when it became clear that neither one of them was ready—or willing—to offer up an explanation. "You saw him knock me over, didn't you?"

"No. We didn't. We didn't see any of that," Brian said, as diplomatically as possible. "We saw you drop your cell phone, but after that…." He swallowed. "After that, you didn't budge. You stood there, with the handset to your ear, for *fifteen minutes straight*. Peter and I tried to get your attention, but you kept staring at the wall. It was like…" He pushed his tongue against the side of his mouth, as if he couldn't come up with an apt analogy.

"It was like you were in a trance," Peter extrapolated. "You seemed to be oblivious to everything. And when we crossed the street to check on you—"

"You pushed us away. You told us to leave you alone," Brian said. "You treated us like we were strangers. Heck, you gave me *this*."

Brian lifted his shirt; revealed a yellow-and-purple welt on his rib cage.

In response, Lucia frowned and took a swig of her coffee. She was tempted to call his story poppycock, but she was inhibited by his sincerity; by Peter's corroboration.

"Okay. Assuming that's the truth…what happened next?" she said, unable to find refuge in the liquid's acerbic bite. "Did you two leave me alone?"

"For a while. Yeah," Brian said, taking a sip from his own mug. "Then you started muttering things—things that didn't make any sense—and we got worried. We thought you might be having a seizure, so we tried to take the phone away and lay you down. Except…" He looked to Peter for support.

"You called both of us *pedophiles* and threatened to stuff pins in our eyes. Then you collapsed," Peter said, dabbing the corners of his mouth with a napkin.

Lucia half expected the both of them to break down in the

aftermath—to admit that the whole version of events was bullshit—but they didn't. They remained stiff-lipped and somber-eyed, which led her to wonder—

Had she suffered from a flare-up?

She supposed an attack was the most sensible answer, based upon her perception of the night's events, and upon her current physiological state, but she wasn't entirely convinced. Normally, her attacks happened in stages. They weren't like the bombs left over from the Second Indochina War. They didn't go off without some kind of warning.

Feeling the screws behind her eyes tighten, Lucia leaned back and counted to ten, while massaging her temples.

"You're sure there was nobody else out there, huh?" she said, once her ritual was complete. "I mean…there's no way somebody could've poisoned me, right?"

"Not while we were watching," Brian muttered. "You were alone the whole time. If we'd seen anything, we would've told you." Then he pushed his coffee mug aside—to make room for his elbows—and said: "Maybe we should take a break for now; let everything digest. We're all tired. Chances are, our thinking will be clearer later on."

"Agreed," Peter volunteered. "The brain's a tricky organ. It can do some crazy things."

"Especially if it's not properly hydrated," Mrs. Janowski said, emerging from the back doorway with a variety of herbs. Most socially-conscious people would have paused then and there and allowed the conversation to continue, but Mrs. Janowski was not "most socially-conscious people." With a smile on her face, she proceeded to the sink, where she washed the fruits of her labor and explained the finer workings of the human body.

Lucia made several attempts to excuse herself while the woman rambled on about gluten—"the Devil's protein"—but none of her interjections managed to penetrate the woman's monologue. Mrs. Janowski kept talking and working, talking and working, until her juicer was filled with a greasy green-and-brown liquid. And by then, it was too late to escape.

Chapter 28

With Mrs. Janowski's hangover cure roiling in her stomach, Lucia drove to the local mail and copy. She'd spent an hour in the Janowskis' kitchen, digesting the wretched concoction, and another two hours in her father's guest bedroom, mulling over the events of the previous night, but she hadn't made much progress on either front. The taste of the remedy remained on her tongue, while the disparity clung to the forefront of her thoughts.

The things she'd experienced outside the gas station...they'd seemed so *real*. She hadn't doubted their authenticity for a moment. The cacophony of voices had been rich and clear, and the disparity...? The disparity had filled her with dread. True, bone-chilling *dread*. His voice alone had sucked the oxygen from her lungs; left her dizzy and weak. And the things he'd told her...the directions he'd given her...?

Unable to reconcile her memories with her friends' accounts, Lucia parked beside the old brick structure, checked her appearance in the vanity mirror, decided she didn't care what she looked like, anyway, and hustled through the glass double doors.

Inside, she was greeted by a middle-aged man in overalls, wire-frame spectacles, and a hairstyle that would've given James Dean a run for his money. She thought he might have worked for Eaton High, once upon a time, but she didn't bother to inquire. She wanted to keep the interaction professional.

Not that it mattered.

The second Lucia went to the counter, produced a picture of her sister, and asked how much it would cost to format and print fifty posters on white cover stock, the questions started rolling in.

First, the man asked whether Lucia was related to John Corvi.

Then he asked whether the girl in the picture was Finley Corvi. Then he asked whether everything was okay. He seemed aware that Lucia was tired and conflicted, but she did her best to put his curiosity to bed. She told him that everything was fine; that Finley had been missing for a few days; that a road trip with a boyfriend was the likely culprit. Then she thanked him for his concern and steered him toward the beluga-sized copy machines.

She didn't mention anything about Mr. Sticks, the labyrinth, or the eerie photographs she'd found on the dark net.

She didn't mention any of that because, deep down, she was afraid she might transfer her curse.

She was afraid that the innocent mail and copy clerk with the toner-stained fingertips might wake up one night and see the disparity at the foot of his bed.

*****

Once her business in the mail and copy was finished, Lucia walked from Elm Avenue to Park Avenue—from Collins Street to 2nd Street—and left a swath of "missing" posters in her wake. She secured the posters to telephone poles, tucked them under windshield wipers, and taped them to vacant storefronts. But the excursion failed to accomplish its intended goal.

Outside of Monarch Music Supply—or the building that had once housed Monarch Music Supply—she stopped, and realized that she didn't feel any less *lost*. She didn't feel like she was doing anything productive; anything of value. Looking back, the direction she'd come, she felt distinctly underwhelmed.

Did she really believe the posters would assist in Finley's recovery? No. She didn't. She'd lost faith in the community. She was sure that plenty of folks would see the posters and shake their heads, but she didn't think anyone would lift a finger otherwise.

Frustration and exhaustion mingling in her chest, she watched two elderly women dodder from the Old World Café; watched them pluck the posters from their respective cars; watched them chatter, shrug, and drive away. Neither appeared particularly troubled by the posters or particularly surprised.

Releasing a strangled sigh, Lucia turned to the Monarch Music Supply building and tore herself a fresh strip of duct tape. But she didn't get a chance to use it. As she centered a poster in one of the two picture windows, she heard a cringe-inducing *bla-loop!* followed by the crackle of all-season tires on old pavement.

It was the police.

"Can I help you?" she said, turning on the squad car with the enthusiasm of an eighty-year-old ex-convict. She expected to see Officer Gonzalez behind the wheel, eyes narrowed and nostrils flared, so she was more than a little surprised when Officer Dan emerged.

"Mighty nice day, isn't it?" the man beamed, while he circled the car. "Back where I'm from, we'd call this a 'fishin' day.'" Then he hesitated, stretched his impossibly-tanned arms, and said: "Lucia, isn't it? Lucia Corvi?"

"Yeah. That's right," Lucia said, tucking the tape under her arm so she could brush a stray hair from her forehead. She did notice that she was standing straighter than before—that she was pushing her chest out and ever-so-slightly angling her body so that the sun caught more of her good side—but she assured herself that the posture was inconsequential.

The guy's a foot taller than me, she mused. *Of course I'm going to stand up straighter.*

Fortunately, the officer wasn't privy to her internal monologue.

"Lucia," he repeated, as if her name was a wine and he was sampling it for depth and richness. "That's pretty unique. What is it? Spanish?"

"Italian," Lucia said. "My parents named me after Saint Lucia, of Syracuse. She was a Christian who was blinded and killed during the Diocletianic Persecution." And in case that was a little too dark: "I guess the Catholic Church considers it an honor to sit in Heaven and to listen to people bitch. Personally, I'd rather lounge on a cloud and strum a harp."

"Same here," the officer chuckled. Then he smoothed the creases from his button-down, gestured vaguely toward the street behind Lucia, and said: "I appreciate what you've done with the place, by the way. It's very *art noir*. Reminds me of those pictures they used to print on the side of milk cartons. You know what I'm talking about, don't you?"

"Yeah. Of course," Lucia said, adjusting her grip on the remaining posters. "When I was little, I used to look at those missing kids and wonder where the hell they were—what had happened to them."

"Same here," Dan said, in a wistful tone. "Nowadays, kids don't even *drink* milk. Not the real stuff, at least. They drink almond milk and coconut milk and soy milk and rice milk and cashew milk.... Shit. I think there's even *hemp milk* out there. Isn't that crazy?" He shook his head. "If Thomas Jefferson were alive today, he'd be mortified. And *he* grew hemp on an industrial scale!"

"Yeah. Things sure have changed a lot since the 1800s," Lucia said, trying and failing to determine where the conversation was headed. She wanted to believe that the officer was being friendly, plain and simple, but his interest struck her as professional rather than personal. The way he was leaning against his car; the way he was appraising her; the way he was talking about everything and nothing? It was all extremely calculated. She got the feeling that he was biding his time; searching for a way to breach a delicate subject.

Perhaps incentivized by her waning smile, he took a tentative step forward and said: "I'm going to be honest with you, Lucia. I think that what you're doing here—for your family, for your sister—is great. I wish that everyone had a streak of Lucia in them. But I'm not the only person in this town. As the community service officer, it's my job to act as a liaison. In other words, it's my duty to consider the bigger picture. If something goes wrong with the ship, I'm not only the one who has to patch the holes; I'm also the one who has to chart a course to land. Do you follow?"

"Yes. But what does any of that have to do with me?" Lucia inquired. "I'm not under arrest, am I?"

"What? No. Of course not," the officer said, with a laugh that couldn't have sounded more artificial. "I just need you to understand that this community...it's bigger than you and me. It's filled with different people who come from different backgrounds and who share different values."

"Which means…what?" Lucia said. She was growing tired of his "this is the way the world works, little lady" tone of voice, but she knew nothing good would happen if she unleashed her Irish temper.

Her irritation must have shown through, nonetheless.

With a sigh, the officer advanced one more step and said: "Simply put, there are some in our community who feel that this—" He made another vague gesture toward the posters down the street; toward the duct tape pinned to her side, "—is unnecessary. They feel that it'll give our town a negative image; that it'll encourage an atmosphere of fear and distrust."

"So you're telling me to take these posters down?" Lucia said. "You're telling me to stop looking for my sister and…what? Leave town?"

"No. By no means am I suggesting any of that," the officer said quickly. "You're more than welcome to stay for as long as you want. It's just…the people around these parts expect the *police* to take care of *police business*. They're not used to this type of…well…vigilantism. It makes them nervous."

"Then they should hold their police department to a higher standard," Lucia retaliated. "If their officers actually *did* what they're *supposed to do*, there would be no need for *vigilantism*."

Displeasure communicated, Lucia turned and started for her car. Her well of verbiage wasn't dry—not by a long shot—but she no longer possessed the patience to dredge the bottom for the few civilized words that remained.

Chapter 29

Lucia was perched on her father's back porch when Brian arrived, toting a pizza and a two-liter bottle of soda. She considered telling him to get lost as he sidled up beside her, smelling of new leather and old hay—two scents she would forever associate with the Feed and Tack—but the truth of the matter was, she was thankful for the companionship. She'd been sitting there—alone—for the majority of the evening, mulling over the officer's words; over her sister's continued absence. The prospect of a conversation, no matter how shallow, made her feel less like a death row inmate.

"Nice out here, isn't it?" Brian said as he sat; as he swung his legs over the side of the wooden structure. "End-of-summer sunsets are my favorite. There's something different about them. Maybe it's the time of year—the knowing that autumn is just around the corner."

"Yeah. They sure are something," Lucia said, without raising her eyes from the threadbare lawn. It was, quite possibly, the most non-committal phrase in her directory of non-committal phrases, but Brian wasn't deterred.

"Remember that semester when we took that photography class together?" he said, giving her a playful nudge with his elbow. "We thought we were so cool, but we couldn't even figure out how to switch out the lenses. We had to ask the teacher."

"Mr. Garrett. Yeah. I remember," Lucia said, favoring him with a ghost of a smile. "I also remember that we filled a memory card with pictures, and every single one of them was overexposed."

"Because *you* told *me* not to fiddle with the shutter speed," Brian returned, mock indignant. "You said the shutter speed was supposed to be slow, and the ISO was supposed to be high."

"To let more light into the camera. Yeah. It makes sense on paper," Lucia shrugged. Then she chuckled.

"Those pictures we submitted for our final assignment?" she said. "I'll bet Mr. Garrett still has them posted in his office. He probably uses them as examples in his classes."

"And he should!" Brian exclaimed. "Those were some good ass pictures! I mean, sure, we didn't *take* them, but we should get credit for downloading them and printing them, right?"

"Yeah. Without a doubt," Lucia smirked. "Although, I think there's a technical term for that. Several, actually. Copyright infringement and plagiarism come to mind."

"True. But those are the negative ones," Brian pointed out. "I prefer to look on the bright side."

"Which is?"

"We were disseminating the works of lesser-known photographers," Brian said matter-of-factly. "We were showcasing their talents; giving them a wider platform."

"By taking credit for their hard work," Lucia contributed. "That's literally the definition of plagiarism."

"But we did it for free," Brian offered. "That's worth something, isn't it?"

In response, Lucia rolled her eyes and laughed. She hadn't laughed since her experience at the payphone, sixteen hours before, so the noise was somewhat foreign to her ears. But it—like Brian—was a welcome surprise. It warmed her chest and temporarily raised the weights from her shoulders.

"Anyways…I'm glad you're doing okay," Brian said, once her laughter tapered off. "I was *really* worried about you last night. The way you were acting…it was bizarre. It was like…." He swallowed. "It was like you stopped being *you* for a while—like something else took over. And when you collapsed…?"

Brian shook his head; flicked a wayward ant back into the grass.

"Just promise never to do that again," he concluded in an "I've never been more serious in my life" tone of voice. "Peter and me, we were scared out of our minds. The only reason we didn't call an ambulance was…well….." He paused; scratched at the back of his neck. "To be honest, we were afraid of how you'd react. We were afraid you'd hurt yourself. Or the responders."

"So you brought me to Mrs. Homeopathic Remedy 3000's house and encouraged me to drink a godawful hangover cure," Lucia deadpanned. "Makes perfect sense."

"Yes. It does," Brian grinned. "And since we're in agreement, let's celebrate. You haven't become a conscientious objector to sausage-and-pepperoni pizza, have you?"

"No. Except…." Lucia bit her lip; looked down at her hands.

"Except *what*?" Brian prodded. "Don't tell me you're taking that wacky voodoo shit seriously. It's—"

"Crazy. Yeah. I know," Lucia interjected. "But you didn't *see what I saw*. You didn't *hear the voices*. The stranger on the road…he was more than an illusion. He was *there*. I could *feel him*. And the things he said to me…?" Lucia shuddered. "He wasn't leading me on, Brian."

"So…what? You're going to starve yourself?" Brian inquired. "All because a phantasm told you to? Are you also going to drive to Mr. Potter's cornfield at midnight, turn around three times, and cut yourself with a ceremonial dagger?"

He chuckled to himself, then, as if he expected someone to pop out of the bushes and to yell "Gotcha!" while dancing a merry jig, but his humor ebbed when he saw the look of solemnity on Lucia's face; when Lucia straightened and said: "If that's what it takes to get Finley back. Yes. I'm willing to do that and more."

Lucia's bravado didn't last, however.

Following ten seconds of indeterminate silence, she released a deep breath and admitted that she was confused—that she no longer knew what to think. She felt stupid in doing so, but it was the honest-to-god truth. Ever since the stranger—the *disparity*—had materialized before her, she'd been an emotional and psychological mess. She'd pulled over twice, on her way back to her father's house, because she'd convinced herself that something was *following* her. That something was *stalking* her. That something was waiting for the right moment to *pounce*; to drag her into an ephemeral lake of darkness.

Were those fears ridiculous and unfounded? One Week Ago Lucia would have said yes, but Present Day Lucia wasn't so sure. Present Day Lucia saw strange shapes in her peripheral vision when she turned her head too quickly. Present Day Lucia heard whispers in the murmur of distant traffic. Present Day Lucia experienced stabbing headaches when she tried to visualize the disparity's face—when she tried to assemble those obscure proportions into a comprehensive mass.

Cheeks hot, Lucia turned toward the horizon and took in the smattering of oranges and pinks and reds. A master painter couldn't have created a more picturesque scene, but she was unable to appreciate the majesty of it all. There was a small piece of One Week Ago Lucia yet inside her, and that piece was mocking her.

Brian wasn't so callous. In fact, he was downright gentlemanly.

Recognizing her internal conflict, he reached out, placed a hand on her knee, and said: "It's okay. I get it. You and me...? We're in one hell of a situation. We're trying to win a board game, even though we don't understand the rules or who we're competing against. But here's the thing: *we are going to win*. Do you know why?"

Wearily, Lucia shook her head.

"We're going to win because we're not living *in* the past. We're living *with* the past," he said. "We're acting out. We're dealing with the consequences of our actions. We're fighting to make things right; to turn things around. Besides..." Brian paused; waited for her to look away from the horizon. When she did, he offered a sympathetic smile and said: "We have each other."

It was a corny declaration, even by made-for-television standards, but Lucia found herself unable to laugh. There was an authenticity to the words that belied the melodramatic clumsiness; that caused Lucia's pulse to quicken. She tried to regain her composure by mentally tallying his offenses—by reminding herself that she was in an emotionally vulnerable state—but none of those thoughts did the trick. None of those thoughts were enough to slow her heartbeat or to eliminate the electric jitters that were spreading outward from her spine.

Unsure what to say or how to say it, Lucia redirected her gaze; muttered something about the two of them making a sad version of the Dynamic Duo. A part of her hoped the whole conversation would end then and there, but the rest of her…? The rest was thrilled by the proximity of their bodies; by the heat that radiated from Brian's palm.

That part of her didn't object when Brian moved closer, when he wrapped his arms around her stomach, or when he buried his chin in the crook of her neck.

Chapter 30

Lucia was groggy as hell when she awoke the next morning, but her lust for coffee was short-lived. The instant she opened her bedroom door, she was assaulted by the scent of twice-burnt Folgers, and the instant she stepped into the living room, she was assaulted by the sight of her father's boxer-clad nether regions.

Upon glimpsing that plaid-print fabric, she made an effort to disappear, but her father was three steps ahead of her.

"Ho there, Lucy Goosey!" he called, from his favorite recliner. "I was beginning to think that you were going to sleep all day!" And then, following a slug of over-percolated goop: "Did you have a late night or something? You look about as lively as Mr. Bojangles...and it took Animal Control *three days* to scrape *him* off those railroad tracks."

"Yes. I remember," Lucia murmured, while trying unsuccessfully to ignore her father's sparsely-adorned lower half. "I was the one who found him. And the one who called Animal Control. And the one who broke the news to Mr. Billings."

"Really?" her father frowned. "I could've sworn that the little Cutler girl was involved. You know who I'm talking about, don't you?"

"Yeah. I do. But she didn't. And she's not so little anymore," Lucia grunted. "She's seventeen. And she's become one heck of a—"

Lucia stopped herself. Her father didn't need to hear about all her petty conflicts.

Following a protracted breath, she said: "You know what? Never mind. It's a...well.... It's a long story."

"Then let's hash it out over breakfast!" her father beamed. "Remember that place I was telling you about? That place over in Galeton? They have these new cinnamon rolls that are *to die for*. Bigger than a bull elk's brain, and twice as tasty." And in case that wasn't tempting enough: "They also have the best coffee this side of the Mississippi. They grind it fresh every morning *and* they only use triple-filtered Rocky Mountain water."

"I'm sure they do," Lucia returned, "but I really shouldn't. I have things that I need to do around here."

"Such as…?" her father inquired.

Lucia didn't believe he was intentionally trying to call her bluff, but he *was* calling her bluff, regardless. At the moment, she couldn't come up with a single thing on her to-do list. She'd already consulted with Finley's closest friends, spoken with the police, driven from one end of the town to the other, scoured Finley's notebooks, and dispersed more than a few "missing" posters.

Her father must have seen the conflict in her eyes.

"Come on," he said, inadvertently spilling some coffee in his hurry to stand. "Let's have us a father-daughter breakfast. We can talk about boys…cars…jobs…life…or nothing at all. I promise I won't pry or comment on your choice of entrée. Hell, I'll pay for the whole damned thing. What do you say? Is it a date?"

Lucia pursed her lips in response. She'd turned her father down plenty of times in the past, but this time? This time, the word "no" was harder to conjure. She didn't have a valid reason to stay at the house and, to be honest, she was more than a little hungry. The thought of a giant cinnamon roll made her stomach groan and her mouth water.

"Tell you what?" she said, at long last. "I'll go to breakfast with you, but you have to agree to two non-negotiable conditions. First off, you have to promise that the coffee at the diner is a hundred times better than whatever you have in your mug."

"And the second?" her father grinned.

Lucia reigned in a deep breath.

"The second is that you'll put on pants," she said, not allowing her pupils to stray below his waist. "And I don't mean right before we leave. I mean now. This minute. The way the light's reflecting off your legs? It's giving me a headache."

*****

Distracted by the prospect of a proper breakfast, Lucia followed her father through the diner's front doors and took a seat at the long,

L-shaped bar. She was a fan of the kitschy posters that hung here and there and the old-timey napkin dispensers that dotted the booths, but she wasn't such a fan of the color scheme. The tables and counters were topped with robin's-egg-blue Formica, the walls were painted daffodil yellow, and the floors were covered with seafoam-green laminate.

Wondering who had designed the monstrosity, and whether that individual was still on the loose, Lucia set her cane aside and smoothed her skirt around her legs; waited for the three-hundred-pound waitress to notice them from the kitchen.

Her father wasn't so patient.

"Hey! Rosemary! Two cups of your Brazilian blend! With cream!" he shouted, in the woman's general direction.

Lucia expected the outburst to draw glares from the two old men who sat at the other end of the bar and who nursed mugs of coffee over grease-smudged newspapers, but neither of the men took notice. Either it was common practice to shout at the wait staff or the regulars were used to her father's antics.

Judging by the woman's reaction, it was the latter.

"Well, well, well. Look who the cat dragged in," the woman said as she waddled—leisurely—from the kitchen. "I didn't think I'd see you again for some time, considering what happened last month."

"Then you must not have much faith in the resiliency of the human spirit," Lucia's father returned, in an aristocratic lilt. "Besides, that thing that happened last month…it was just a big misunderstanding."

"Really?" the woman—Rosemary O'Keefe, according to her nametag—smirked. "The way I remember it, there was no misunderstanding at all. The way I remember it, Mr. Dyer caught you having breakfast with his wife. And when he called you on it—"

"When he called me on it, the two of us had a perfectly civilized conversation about boundaries and the consequences of crossing those boundaries," Lucia's father interjected, with a "that's the way things are" hand gesture. But Lucia could tell that he wasn't telling the truth. Not the whole truth, at least.

"The guy threatened to kick your ass, didn't he?" she volunteered, before her father could change the topic of conversation.

That drew a bark of laughter from the waitress.

"Mr. Dyer did, indeed," she said as her laughter reverberated through the kitchen; reflected from one stainless steel appliance to the next. "If my memory serves me—and it hasn't failed me yet, praise Jesus—Mr. Dyer promised to break both this poor man's legs. If'n Mr. Dyer caught him back in this town, of course."

Story finished, Rosemary released a long, happy sigh, set her meaty forearms on the bar in front of Lucia, and said: "What's your name, darlin'? I don't usually bother to get to know the women John brings in here, on account of their short shelf life, but you…? I like you. You've got *cojones*."

"That's because she's related to yours truly," Lucia's father smiled.

Lucia decided not to give him any more runway.

"Lucia," she said, offering a hand in greeting. "Lucia Corvi. But you can call me Lucy."

"Well then, it's good to meet you, Lucy," Rosemary said, gripping the proffered hand and giving it a hearty shake. "You live around these parts or are you just visiting?"

"Just visiting," Lucia said. "I have an apartment down in Denver. And a job."

"Where at?" Rosemary inquired, pulling two hefty mugs from beneath the bar.

It was a question Lucia had fielded a thousand times before, but she suddenly found herself at a loss for words. She couldn't recall what the firm was called. Or even what the company logo *looked like*. She tried to visualize the letterhead that she kept in her desk's bottom drawer, but she was unable to conjure any pertinent details.

Fortunately, her father was on the ball.

"It's an advertising firm," her father said, while Rosemary filled the mugs with a dark, rich liquid. "They're called Walsh International. They have contracts with some pretty heavy hitters, too."

"Yeah. We do," Lucia confirmed. "We've worked with Pepsi and Ford, along with a bunch of local upstarts. You've probably heard our work on the radio."

"Not the television?" Rosemary said, sliding the mugs across the Formica and fishing a couple of laminated menus from her apron. "No offense, but isn't the radio kind of *old fashioned*?"

"Yes. But in rural areas like this—" Lucia began.

Her dissertation ended there.

From the kitchen came an explosive clatter, followed by a string of semi-coherent curses and the sound of agitated footsteps. The noise wasn't enough to disturb any of the regulars, but it was more than enough to capture Rosemary's undivided attention.

"What in tarnation is going on back there?" the big waitress exclaimed. "If that's you again, Rodney, you better pray for a divine intervention, because I'm done playing games!" Then she was gone, and the kitchen door slammed in her wake.

A muted argument was next on the docket, but Lucia's father wasn't concerned by any of it. He merely shrugged, took a sip from his mug, and said: "Don't worry about them. They'll work everything out. This sort of thing happens every other day."

"Really?" Lucia muttered, amidst an expletive-laden cacophony. "Because they don't sound like they're 'working everything out.' Are they—"

"Married?" her father guessed. "No. They're fraternal twins. Born a couple of hours apart. In two different counties. But that's a story for another time.

"To be honest, I didn't ask you out this morning to shoot the breeze," he continued, in a significantly more solemn tone. "I asked you out because…well…I want to make sure you're okay."

"Okay?" Lucia repeated, over the lip of her mug. "Okay with what?"

"With the way everything turned out," her father said. "Between me and your mom, I mean. I realize I'm turning over old stones here, but I don't think we've ever really talked about it. And I think that's wrong. I think I owe you an apology."

Just one? Lucia's mind blurted. But she didn't allow those particular words to travel to her vocal chords. Instead, she took a long draft from her mug, swallowed, and said: "For what? For the divorce?"

"No. Not for the divorce. At least, not directly," her father said, while rotating his own mug on the blue Formica. "More for…well… for the way everything was handled. Your mother and me, we should've done things differently. We shouldn't have aired our dirty laundry, the way we did. We should've kept you out of it. And we should've been up-front with you when the time was right. We should've kept the lines of communication open."

Yes. You should, Lucia thought. But again, she kept those sentiments inside. She didn't want her father to know that his actions—that her mother's actions—were a continuing source of pain and resentment. She wasn't sure why it mattered to her, but it did. It mattered a lot.

"I…uh…I appreciate that," she said, once she had some of her more volatile emotions containerized. "But I'm not the only one who was affected. Finley was affected, too. You should really be apologizing to her. She may have been a little thing when it happened, but I guarantee that she has her questions."

"Yes. She probably does," her father admitted. "But you're first on my list. You're my flesh-and-blood. I need you to understand—*really understand*—that what happened…it wasn't your fault. Not in any way, shape, or form. Your mother and me, we just weren't right for each other. Our decision to separate had nothing to do with you or your sister. The day you were born—"

"You lit a cigar, ran around the house twice, and nearly broke your neck when you tripped over a rake. Yeah. I've heard the story," Lucia interrupted. "What's the point?"

"The point is, you're the best thing that ever happened to me," her father said, sliding his coffee mug to the side so he could brace his elbows on the countertop. "I may not act like it all the time, but it's the truth. You're everything I hoped you would be, and more. When I look at you, I see the best parts of myself. And the best parts of your mother."

It was a surprisingly touching—and candid—confession, but Lucia didn't have much time to react. As she struggled to maintain her indifferent façade, she saw the front doors open, and she saw a familiar person enter.

She saw her *sister*.

Finley didn't approach the bar when their eyes locked, however. On the contrary…she tugged her baseball cap down so that the bill covered her face and made a beeline for the women's bathroom.

Equal parts confounded and exhilarated, Lucia grabbed her cane, excused herself, and followed in her sister's footsteps. Ten years earlier, she could have reached the bathroom in five seconds flat, but she tried not to focus on her physical limitations.

Heart jackhammering, she pressed through the restroom door and frantically inspected the length of the room. She took in the twin sinks, the twin mirrors, the twin paper towel machines, and the twin wastebaskets, but she didn't notice any signs of life until her gaze swept across the twin toilet stalls. There, she noticed a pair of dirty Converse tennis shoes.

Unsure how, exactly, to proceed, she approached the partitions, wet her lips, realized she wouldn't be able to speak until the golf ball-sized lump in her throat dissipated, then rapped her knuckles against the occupied stall. She wasn't sure why her sister was playing hard to get, but, at the moment, the "why" wasn't particularly important. She just wanted to embrace the bitch. Explanations could come later.

Or so she told herself.

The second the stall door opened, her excitement tapered.

The person standing before her was not her sister. It was a middle-aged woman with short blond hair, a full face, and breasts the size of cantaloupes, which were currently stuffed into a two-sizes-too-small polo.

"Can I help you?" the woman inquired, one eyebrow notched higher than the other. Her tone wasn't outright combative, but there was definitely an edge of suspicion to it.

"Oh…uh…I'm sorry," Lucia stammered, as soon as she was able. "I thought you were someone else. I'm…ah…I'm looking for my sister."

"And you expect to find her in a public restroom?" the woman said. "That's a strange place to look, isn't it?"

"Yes. I guess it is," Lucia said, with a halfhearted smirk. "It's just…I thought I saw her come in here. You haven't seen anyone else, have you?"

"No. Can't say I have," the woman said, while she made her way to the nearest sink. "Not since I started my dump, at least. Kind of hard to see from the inside of those stalls." Then she toweled her hands dry and returned to the diner proper. She wasn't the least bit interested in furthering the conversation. And Lucia didn't blame her.

I'd probably act the same way if some head case ran into the bathroom and pounded on my toilet stall, she thought as she considered her reflection in the mirror. But then, *she* wasn't a head case. She *had* seen her sister. Hadn't she?

In retrospect, she'd been fighting back tears when the diner door had opened, so her vision hadn't been entirely clear. There was a small chance that she'd misidentified the girl in the baseball cap from the get-go. But even if she *had* misidentified the girl, then where had the girl gone? Had she clambered through one of the narrow, frosted windows that skirted the ceiling? If so, *why?* Had something frightened her?

Feeling a dull pain behind her eyes, Lucia gripped the edges of the sink and let her head hang between her shoulders. If she didn't lie down soon, the pain would intensify and throb outward; claim one neural network after another; leave her half-blind, half-crippled, and half-coherent.

So much for that father-daughter breakfast, she thought as she shuffled for the bathroom door.

Chapter 31

By the time Lucia's headache finally passed, the sun was low on the horizon and her father was long gone. She was tempted to stay in the house for the remainder of the evening—to watch television and to gorge on whatever he had in the refrigerator—but the emptiness ultimately got to her.

Determined to keep her imagination caged—to prevent it from painting ghouls in the shadows and cartoon mice in the wallpaper—she donned a light jacket and started down the sidewalk. She didn't have a particular destination in mind, so she continued south until she reached 1st Street. Then she hung a left and plotted a course east—past Eaton High.

She noticed a handful of cars in the high school parking lot as she approached Park Avenue, but they were all tucked into the faculty spaces—proof the students had gone home for the day; that the town was beginning to shutter its collective windows; that it was only a matter of time before Eaton's few stoplights started to blink.

Aware of the darkness within the houses to the south, Lucia crossed Cheyenne Avenue and continued past the Eaton Police Department. She half expected Dan to jog from the front doors as she neared the Old World Café, but the pristine panels of glass remained immobile. There might have been someone inside, monitoring her movements with the concentration of a hungry hawk, but she didn't care to find out. She wasn't on a warpath. Her goal was simply to *walk*; to take in the fresh country air.

Across from Mrs. Tibbs' general store, her thoughts strayed toward her experience at the diner, but she wasn't able to come to any real conclusions. She wanted to believe that she'd seen her sister, in the flesh, but she couldn't fathom why her sister might have run away. *She* wasn't one of the bad guys, after all. *She* was the one who was fighting tooth-and-nail to bring her sister home.

Experiencing a sudden loss of energy, she took a seat on a rusted old bench and ran her hands through her hair. The latter was greasy and in need of a thorough washing, but it wasn't that realization that made her breath catch in her throat. It was the sensation of something striking her lower calf.

Fortunately, the thing on her leg was not a hand or some variety of otherworldly appendage. It was a sheet of paper. A sheet of white cover stock. And it was emblazoned with her sister's smiling face. Or...what had once been her sister's smiling face. Some enterprising artist had added sharp teeth, horns, and a dialogue bubble that read: "I'm the Devil's bitch. Eat my cunt."

Disgusted by the modifications, Lucia crumpled the sheet into a ball and made for the nearest garbage can. But something else caught her eye en route.

Six feet past the garbage can, she spotted another altered poster. It had been taped to a telephone pole upside-down, and the photograph of Finley had—again—been ravaged. The artist had colored Finley's eyes black and had splashed red paint beneath her nostrils.

Teeth clenched, Lucia tore the poster from the pole. Then she spun in a circle; looked up and down the street. She could feel her headache returning, but she no longer gave a damn about that. She had a new problem on her hands.

As quickly as possible, she walked from Maple to Oak, followed Oak north to 2nd and took 2nd back to Maple. The whole loop only took her fifteen minutes, from start to finish, but, in that time, she managed to round up twenty-five defaced posters. A few were simply coated in red paint or covered with the word "slut," but she didn't find those any less insulting.

With her nostrils flared and her jaw aching, she marched straight to the police department, threw open the impeccably-polished doors, crossed the cavernous lobby, and dropped the whole stack of posters on the front desk.

Officer Gonzalez was not amused.

"Can I help you?" the woman said, looking up from her computer with all the eagerness of a ketamine-flush middle schooler.

Lucia didn't react in kind.

"Actually, yes. You can help me," she said, with a patronizing smile. "You can tell me who the fuck did *this*."

"And what, exactly, is *this*?" Officer Gonzalez said, using her pen to lift one of the sheets. "Looks like some kind of art project."

"Well…it's not," Lucia snapped. "It's vandalism. And I want to know who did it."

"Just like that?"

"Just like that," Lucia confirmed. "See, I put these posters up yesterday, at about noon. That means they were vandalized between now and then. Most probably, between 9:00 p.m. and 4:00 a.m. Even if none of your co-workers saw the vandalism taking place, which I find hard to believe, I happen to know that you have security cameras on top of your building. It should only take a few minutes to look through the footage and to find out who's responsible."

Admittedly, it was a brash thing to say, but Lucia was tired of playing games. One way or another, she was going to get to the bottom of the bullshit and she was going to get her answers.

In response, Officer Gonzalez released a small sigh.

"Ma'am, I appreciate your concern…and your desire to assist in this particular situation…but you have to understand that these things…they take time," she said, slowly and carefully. "We can't just burn our security footage onto a disc and hand it over to you."

"No. But you can review the footage yourself," Lucia returned. "Or you can get on the horn and you can ask your co-workers if they saw anything last night."

"Yes. I *can*. But I *won't*," the officer said, with a patronizing smile of her own. "You see, that would be a flagrant waste of police resources. Considering that no crime has been committed, I'm under no obligation to comply with your requests. If you'd like—"

"Hold up. *No crime?*" Lucia interrupted. "These posters are *vandalized*. Most of them are covered with *obscenities*."

"Yes, but you were instructed not to post those in the first place," Officer Dan said, emerging from the hall with a cup of coffee in his hand. "Therefore, *you're* the original vandal. Whoever did this…?" He swept the Styrofoam container over the lump of papers. "He deserves a smack on the wrist, at worst. Maybe a class in penmanship, if we decide to really lower the hammer."

"Or the soap treatment," Officer Gonzalez volunteered. "My parents used to make my brothers suck on soap when they cursed."

"But not you?" Dan wondered.

The woman shook her head. "Nope. I was the youngest," she said. "I learned from their mistakes. I—"

Lucia didn't give her an opportunity to extrapolate.

"In other words, neither of you are going to help me," she deadpanned. "No one in this fucking department is going to do a damned thing about my sister."

"Well..." Dan intoned.

Lucia didn't appreciate the tone of his voice.

"Don't 'well' me," she hissed. "No one in this place has done anything for me or my family. You may think that we're a fucked-up bunch...and we *are*...but we're *human beings*. We care about each other. We want what's best for each other. And right now, one of us is in trouble.

"All I'm asking for is a little cooperation," she continued, in a less confrontational tone. "I'm not asking you to move the moon. I realize that these things take time, but my sister's been missing for almost ten days. That's ten days too long for a sixteen-year-old girl. Even if this whole thing started as a weekend road trip, something may have gone wrong. She may have gotten picked up by a predatory truck driver. She may have run out of money in some town, a hundred miles away. She may have—"

Lucia bit her upper lip; willed her mind not go down any darker paths. The left side of her body was already buzzing—radiating a familiar numbness.

With some difficulty, she placed her forearms on the top of the desk and said gently: "Look. My sister is my number one priority. She may seem invincible on the outside, but she's not. She's...well...she's *disturbed*. If I've learned anything this past week and a half, it's that she's a twelve-year-old in a sixteen-year-old body. Her whole life, she's been a pawn in my parents' fucked-up head games. I don't think she understands what happened between them or why things are the way they are. And I think that's a cause for concern. Wherever she is, she's vulnerable. Emotionally and physically."

There, she stopped, and dropped her eyes to the floor. She didn't have anything else to say. She'd burnt through her reserves of anger and righteous indignation.

Feeling equal parts drained and defeated, she scooped the stack of posters off the desk and trudged toward the exit. She heard Dan clear his throat several times as she crossed the lobby—her footsteps echoing between the rafters and the colorful marble floor—but he never muttered an actual phrase. Either he no longer cared about Finley's plight or he no longer possessed the courage to speak his mind.

Lucia didn't linger long enough to find out.

Outside the station, she dumped the posters in a garbage can, drew in a shaky breath, and set a course for her father's house.

Chapter 32

Lucia anticipated a slow and uneventful trek back to 325 Cedar Avenue, since she was all out of fight, and since the streets were nigh desolate—bathed in an oppressive blue light—but her expectations were quickly uprooted.

Between the police department and the First Baptist Church, which occupied a small plot of land down from the larger—and more ornate—United Methodist Church, her skin began to prickle.

In order to keep her imagination in check, she promised herself that the dropping temperature was to blame for her discomfort, but she was only able to deceive herself for a few blocks. Across from the Eaton High football field, her muscles seized and her heart stuttered.

Suddenly sure that she was being watched—that her body was reacting to a nearby presence—Lucia pivoted on her heel; scrutinized the houses on the north side of the road. A silhouette in a doorway or a sashaying set of blinds would have put her mind at ease, but she didn't notice any activity whatsoever. Both the houses and the streets beyond were empty. Desolate.

She did spot a hooded figure at the far end of the football field, but he didn't appear the least bit interested in his surroundings. He lumbered along with his head down and his hands thrust into his pockets; a backpack dangling precariously from one shoulder.

When the hooded man failed to look up or to otherwise demonstrate a shred of spatial awareness, Lucia adjusted her grip on her cane and pressed forward. She didn't want to be out on the street anymore. She wanted to be back in her father's house. She wanted to be behind locked doors. She wanted a bottle of wine and a box of chocolates.

She wanted safety and comfort, in equal measures.

Across from the middle school soccer field, she slipped her phone from her pocket and restlessly thumbed through her contacts list. She resisted the urge to place any outgoing calls, however. She knew that Brian and Peter were at work, and she knew her father was otherwise occupied. Besides, she didn't have any proof that she was *actually* being followed. She hadn't seen or heard anything.

Yet.

Unable to shake the sentiment that she could turn around at any given moment and discover a hulking shape, she increased her pace. She nearly ran past Mr. Fischer's house—the first and only pink bungalow in the history of the entire town—and she didn't let up until she was mere steps from her father's porch. Only then did she arrest her momentum and give the street another look.

Of course, there was nothing perched in the waning twilight, beckoning with oily, scythe-like fingers, but that gave her limited comfort. She still locked the door in her wake and hurried from window to window, bolting this and shuttering that. She was sure her father would ask about the fortifications when he returned, since he rarely locked anything, but she didn't let that knowledge slow her down.

Once she was certain that the whole place was secured—to the best of her ability, anyway—she lapsed onto the couch and released a long, slow breath. Her sides were aching from her excursion and her stomach was cramping, calling out for nourishment, but her attention was quickly pulled to the rear door.

Was it just her imagination or was there someone *out there?*

Hoping her ears were playing tricks on her—that the *swish!* of fabric against fabric was no more real than the cartoon mouse from the video—she slunk to the kitchen and pulled a hammer from the utility shelf. There was a knife block set next to the refrigerator, but the numbness in her extremities kept her from the eight-inch *Santoku*. At the moment, she didn't trust herself with anything sharp. If she lost her balance or if something knocked her down...? The risks simply weren't worth the rewards.

"Hello?" she ventured as she peered through the rear door's

window; as the fence-encased yard crept into view. There was a chance her father was back there, fiddling with a lawn mower or a leaf blower, but that chance was slim. Once the sun went down, her father did precious little tinkering. He preferred to romance a six pack of tall boys while watching some variety of sports program.

Second-guessing her decision to keep her fears to herself, she crept to the sink-adjacent window and used the hammer's claw to part the blinds. From there she could see the entire back yard, but the source of the noise was no longer *in* the back yard.

Hearing a rustle outside the master bedroom, she abandoned her post and scurried east. She very nearly took a tumble over her father's recliner in the process, but her cane—and her cane alone—kept her upright. Not that it mattered.

By the time Lucia reached her father's bedroom, the author of the noise was gone. He—or *she* or *it*—seemed to be circling the house; stealthily searching for vulnerabilities.

Giving the hammer an exploratory shake, Lucia returned to the living room. She was pretty sure the culprit was out front, based upon one or two muted footfalls, but she didn't make a move for the picture window. Instead, she listened for another disturbance, then bolted for the back.

Her play paid off.

Moments after she arrived at the rear door, a shape flitted into view. It was a humanoid shape, with two arms and two legs, and it wove gradually in her direction, inspecting each window that it passed.

Wondering whether the Wilson family hadn't experienced something similar in 1996, Lucia pressed her spine to the door's frame and gave her hammer another shake. She didn't *want* to use the thing—her muscles were tense, her palms were slick, and her vision was blurry—but she was prepared to, regardless. Because her sister needed her.

With Finley in mind, Lucia propped her cane against the wall and felt for the bank of light switches. She planned to surprise the visitor with seventy-five watts of naked, incandescent radiance…but there was a problem.

All three of the exterior bulbs were dead.

Cursing her father's proclivity for procrastination, Lucia glanced over the utility shelf—over the threadbare pairs of work boots, the dusty holiday decorations, and the oxidized gardening implements. She hoped to locate a flashlight amidst the mess, but her search was interrupted by the sound of metal striking metal.

The visitor was no longer at the house's northeast corner.

He was right behind her.

And he was trying to get *in*.

Bile burning in the back of her throat, Lucia spun away from the door, flipped on the kitchen lights, and—

"Deborah?"

"Oh. Hi, Lucia," the bottle-blond said, following a moment of stunned silence. "I...uh...I didn't realize you were here. I'm...um... I'm looking for John."

"*John?*" Lucia repeated, as loudly as her lungs would allow.

"Yeah. John. Your dad," Deborah clarified. "Is he around, by chance? I need his help."

"At this time of night?" Lucia inquired.

Her old schoolmate nodded; said her problem was extremely time-sensitive.

"It's the coffee shop," the woman explained. "The front doors won't lock. We need someone to take a look at them."

"And you didn't think to call a locksmith?" Lucia frowned. She didn't mean to sound cold, but she wasn't sold by Deborah's story. Both the logic and the presentation left much to be desired.

Deborah must have realized as much.

"No. I did. I called three. None of them answered," the woman said quickly. "Must have something to do with Monday night."

"Yes. It must," Lucia said, vacant a trace of humor. She wanted, more than anything, to tell her former friend to drop the act and to get on with the bean-spilling, but she knew such a demand would scare the woman off, so she took a less heavy-handed approach.

With a wooden smile on her face, she returned the hammer to the utility shelf, opened the door, and invited the woman inside. She mentioned that her father wasn't home at the moment, but she assured Deborah that she was welcome to wait in the living room. And she watched Deborah's expression falter.

"I...uh...I appreciate the offer...but I really shouldn't stay," the woman stammered, while casting small glances over her shoulders. "My mom's the only one at the shop right now and I promised I wouldn't be gone longer than fifteen minutes."

"Then we're in luck!" Lucia exclaimed, snagging the woman's elbow and pulling her into the kitchen. "We have a whole five minutes to talk! Seven, if you push the speed limit on your way back!"

"Yes. I...um...I guess we do," Deborah said, with an agonizingly forced and fleeting grin. It was, quite possibly, the least convincing grin Lucia had ever seen, but Lucia pretended to overlook it. She had a cemetery-worth of skeletons to unearth and a limited amount of time to do the digging.

"So. How long has my dad been doing odd jobs for the coffee shop?" she inquired, right out of the gate. "Usually he tells me all about new accounts, but he hasn't mentioned anything about you guys."

"No?" Deborah said, using her new environs as an excuse to avoid eye contact. "He probably forgot. I mean, he *has* been preoccupied by this whole Finley business." Then: "How is the search going, by the way? Have the police found any leads?"

"Yeah. A few," Lucia lied. "They're following up as we speak. They expect to have a perp in custody by the end of the week. Possibly sooner. Assuming..."

"Assuming *what?*" Deborah prodded.

Lucia shrugged her shoulders. "Assuming the perp doesn't run, I guess," she concluded. Then she took a miniscule step closer to Deborah and said: "Please don't let that information get out, though. The police asked me not to talk about the case because...well...you know..."

In response, Deborah shook her head.

Apparently, Lucia was being too vague.

"The police believe the perp is *from here*," Lucia said, in a conspiratorial whisper. "They believe he—or *she*—might be a *lifelong resident."*

"Are you serious?" Deborah returned, in a similar tone. She seemed genuinely shocked and disturbed by the allegation, but then again, the two women hadn't been on the same wavelength in some time. Lucia couldn't tell—definitively—whether the bottle-blond was unnerved by the concept of a hometown perpetrator or whether she was alarmed by the revelation that the police were closing in.

To be honest, Lucia hoped her childhood friend was not, in any way, involved in her sister's disappearance, but she couldn't discount the possibility. Deborah *had* been acting strangely, after all, and she *did* possess a violent temper.

Remembering the incident in the Eaton High locker room, freshman year—the incident that had resulted in the school-wide evacuation, the visit from the fire department, and the series of tongue-lashings from the school's administration—Lucia bobbed her head. Then she changed the subject.

"At any rate, you look gorgeous tonight," she said, thinking the sudden shift might loosen the woman's tongue. "Is it a special occasion or something?"

"No. Not really," Deborah muttered, as if the blue cocktail dress, the dangly earrings, the designer clutch, the six-inch heels, and the sapphire necklace were all petty afterthoughts. "I just like to try new designs. Don't you?"

Lucia said she did while she contemplated an alternate approach. It was clear that the woman was hiding something, but the bigger question was *what?*

Deborah didn't give her an opportunity to exhume that particular coffin.

"You know what?" the woman said, feigning a look at her watch. "It's past time for me to go. I do wish I could stay and chat, but I'm afraid those doors won't fix themselves."

"No. I'm afraid they won't," Lucia said. Then she turned—however reluctantly—and accompanied Deborah to the front door. There, the two exchanged pleasantries, tittered at a joke that Lucia promptly forgot, and parted ways. As Lucia watched Deborah's pickup accelerate down the road, however, she came to a startling realization.

She realized that, even with Deborah out of the house, she still didn't feel *alone*.

Chapter 33

That night, Lucia's subconscious played a single dream over and over. And it was no more pleasant than her trek from the police station.

In the dream, she was walking through a *void*—through a cavernous space which pulsed with a palpable red light. She could see her sister ahead of her, suspended within a web of sticky, roiling blackness, but her sister was always well out of reach.

In each itineration, Lucia made an attempt to speak out—to get Finley's attention—but she was never successful. Each dream cycle ended with her sister spreading her arms and falling back into the ebony cloud.

When Lucia finally awoke, her body was coated in a sheen of sweat and her sheets were piled on the floor—bathed in early morning sunlight. She found the state of her bed strange, in and of itself, since she was a stationary sleeper, but that wasn't the strangest thing she discovered. The strangest thing was the antler-handled knife, which was perched at the foot of her mattress. Beneath her open window.

Equal parts confused and afraid, she scrambled upright and retreated to the far side of the room. She wanted to believe that she'd simply forgotten to secure the window, but she knew that wasn't the case. She'd double- and triple-checked the latches, right before she'd locked her bedroom door. There was absolutely no way anyone could have gained access to the room. Unless…

Seeing the disparity in her mind's eye, she shivered; snatched her cell phone from the bedside table. She needed to talk to someone. If she didn't get some perspective, she was liable to go off the deep end.

Assuring herself that the voices in her head were not—in any way—*real*, she dialed Brian's number and anxiously waited for him to pick up. Except…he didn't. After eight rings, the call abruptly terminated. So she tried Peter's number. And she got the exact same result.

Is something wrong? she wondered, while Peter's voicemail message droned in her ear. *Did something happen while I was asleep? Are both of my friends okay? Are* either *of them okay?*

With no answers in sight, she hurriedly pulled on a pair of jeans, slipped a T-shirt over her head, and dug her keys from her purse. She was tempted to fling the antler-handled knife out the window as she searched for a pair of flats, but she couldn't bring herself to *touch* the damned thing. Deep down, she was afraid that it would infect her—that she would regain consciousness in a pool of blood. And not *her* blood.

*****

Unsure where else to go, Lucia drove to the Feed and Tack and parked in the rear lot, beside a rusted flatbed. She looked for Brian's truck as she advanced on the loading dock, but she didn't see it, so she pressed through a door marked Employees Only and purposefully cleared her throat. She could have easily found her way through the warehouse and through the storefront proper, but she didn't have the time or the patience for that. She needed answers and she needed them *fast*.

Fortunately, the stock boy was on the ball.

"How can I help you, miss?" he said, emerging from a mound of plastic containers with a ball-and-socket joint in one hand and a rag in the other. Lucia probably could have identified him on the street, without the trucker cap and the overalls and the grease-smeared face, but, in the moment, she only saw a dirty seventeen-year-old.

"Actually, I'm looking for someone," she said, sounding more breathless than she cared to admit. "It's your boss. Brian Van Pelt. Have you seen him around? I need to talk to him."

"Then you should probably head to the police station," the stock boy said, without batting an eye. "I don't know what's going on, exactly, but a couple officers showed up this morning and escorted him out of here. They said he was wanted for something."

"They did?" Lucia said, trying and failing to keep her eyebrows from knitting.

The stock boy nodded. "Yes, ma'am. They said it was in his best interest to come quietly. Then they took off. I tried to ask when he'd be back, since he's my manager and all, but they didn't answer. Do you think…"

There, the stock boy hesitated and glanced about, as if he expected a spy camera to drop from the ceiling.

"Do you think he *killed* somebody?" he continued, in a significantly quieter voice.

It was a silly question and it was posed in a ridiculously overdramatic manner, but Lucia found herself unable to laugh.

"I…uh…I'm sure it's nothing that serious," she said, as soon as she regained her ability to speak. "He was probably a witness to a crime and the police want his testimony on the record."

"For real?" the stock boy said, while absentmindedly polishing the ball-and-socket joint. "Last year, my dad witnessed a hit-and-run and the cops didn't bring *him* down to the station. They questioned him right there, outside his car. After they were done, they—"

Lucia didn't wait for the rest of his story to unfold. As calmly and as quickly as she could, she turned around, pushed through the door, and marched back to her car. She knew her behavior would turn heads as soon as it reached the grapevine—and it *would* reach the grapevine—but that was a minor concern.

With the stock boy's voice echoing in her ears—imploring her to wait another second; inviting her to peruse their "end of summer sale"—she ducked into her Focus, stabbed the key into the ignition, threw the transmission into gear, and peeled out of the parking lot. And she didn't slow down until she was half a block from the police station.

Chapter 34

Fire in her chest, Lucia shouldered through the Eaton Police Department's front doors and marched straight to the desk, where Officer Gonzalez sat, shuffling papers. She realized that she probably looked like a crazy person, what with her just-out-of-bed hair, her lack of makeup, her crumpled T-shirt, and her unwashed jeans, but she didn't give a damn. The time for polite appeals was over.

"Brian Van Pelt. Where is he?" she demanded, before the officer could say good morning. "I need to talk to him. Right now."

"And what, may I ask, is this regarding?" Officer Gonzalez said, in an infuriatingly calm and collected manner. "If you're still concerned about those posters, you're more than welcome to—"

"It's not about the posters," Lucia interrupted. "It's a personal matter. Therefore, it's none of your damned business. Are we clear?"

In response, Officer Gonzalez set the papers down, pressed her lips together until they were little more than a bloodless white line, and said: "Ma'am? I really don't appreciate your tone of voice. I'm going to have to ask you to leave."

"And if I refuse?" Lucia retaliated. "Are you going to lock me up? Are you going to throw me in a cell for disturbing the peace? Or are you going to come up with some other bullshit charge? Personally, I think the chief would prefer a disorderly conduct citation. I'll bet that one comes with the highest fines."

"Maybe. And maybe not," Officer Gonzalez said. "Either way, I'm not going to book you. Booking requires paperwork and I have more than enough paperwork on my plate as it is. Now, if you don't mind?"

The officer made a "run along" motion with four of her expertly-manicured fingertips.

Lucia ignored it.

"No," she said simply. "I'm not leaving until I get to talk to Brian. It's urgent."

"More urgent than a criminal investigation?" a large, balding man said from the hallway. If not for the lanyard that hung around his neck, she would have taken him for a stray inmate or a frumpy, past-his-prime lawyer. His gray suit was cut one size too loose, his wingtips were scuffed, and his tie...? His tie looked like the seventies had thrown up all over it.

"For your information, this is Detective Sergeant Trotter," Officer Gonzalez said, without turning to properly acknowledge the new arrival. "He's in charge of your sister's case. You can direct all your future inquiries toward him."

"Great. But there *is no case*," Lucia returned, in an equally saccharin tone. "You've been saying that for a week. Last night—"

"Last night, we didn't have any evidence of foul play," Officer Gonzalez interjected. "Now we do."

"This morning, at 0600 hours, we received a particularly troubling tip," Detective Trotter concurred, maneuvering his considerable bulk around the desk. "We learned that Mr. Van Pelt was sexually active with your sister the night before she disappeared. We also learned that he's been spending an inordinate amount of time around your sister's classmates."

"Which means...?" Lucia said.

She had wanted to blurt "You have no idea what you're talking about," followed by, "Brian is a good guy," and "He wouldn't hurt a fly," but common sense had held her back.

The detective rewarded her restraint with an overly-loud sneeze.

"Well," he said, using a white handkerchief to evacuate his nostrils, then to dab at his sweat-beaded forehead, "at the moment, it means Mr. Van Pelt is Suspect Number One. Even if he's not involved in your sister's disappearance, he'll still face jail time for statutory rape."

"Or worse," Officer Gonzalez added. "Considering your sister's age, a number of serious charges may come into play."

"Possibly," the detective allowed. "Regardless, Mr. Van Pelt will not be allowed to speak to anyone—aside from his lawyer—for some time. We still have a lot of questions to ask him."

"Yes. I'm sure you do," Lucia muttered. It was, admittedly, a weak response, but it was the only thing she could really *say*. If she started flapping her gums, there was a good chance she would wind up in the next cell over. She'd known about Brian and Finley's relationship, after all, and she hadn't said a thing.

In a way, the whole situation was *funny*. She'd spent her first few days in town hating Brian's guts—fantasizing about this very moment—but now? Now she wanted everything to *change*. She wanted the charges against Brian to vanish and she wanted the police to release him, no questions asked.

Feeling more helpless than angry, Lucia bit the inside of her lip and started for the exit. Even though her thoughts were a mess, one thing was exceedingly clear: she could do no more good at the police station. To help Brian, she had to think—and *work*—outside of the box. She had to—

"Oh, and ma'am?"

"Yes?" Lucia said, hesitating a yard from the polished double doors and glancing back toward the desk—toward Officer Gonzalez and her glossy, zebra-striped nails. She anticipated a frosty farewell or a directive to keep her nose out of police business, going forward, but she was treated to neither. Rather, she was treated to a smile and a good-natured "You're welcome."

"For what?" Lucia inquired, as the smile gradually morphed into a self-indulgent smirk.

"For catching the person responsible for your sister's disappearance, of course," Officer Gonzalez concluded. And then, when Lucia failed to respond: "If you'd like to show your gratitude, you're more than welcome to make a donation to the Donald A. Sutton Scholarship Fund. You can find details over there, on that bulletin board."

*****

Outside the station, Lucia rolled her hands into fists and gritted her teeth until her jaw ached. There was a scream building in her chest—a scream energized by the fumes of fury, frustration, confusion, and despondency—but she refused to let it out. It was up to her to channel those emotions into something positive.

It was up to her to find out how the police had gotten their information.

To that end, she whipped her phone from her pocket and began scrolling through her contacts list. She planned to ring her mother, first of all, since the woman had known about the Brian-Finley relationship from the get-go and since her mother was the most bipolar person in town, but she was waylaid by an incoming call. From an unknown number.

Afraid of who might be on the other end, but too curious to let the call go to voicemail, Lucia hit Accept and said "Hello?" as loudly as she dared.

"Hello? Lucia?" Peter responded, sounding both tinny and out-of-breath. "Is that you?"

"Yeah," Lucia said tentatively.

Apparently, that was all the verification Peter needed.

"Thank the Lord!" he gushed, before she could compose any kind of a follow-up question. "I've been trying to get a hold of you all morning!"

"Then you should try answering your stupid phone!" Lucia retaliated. "I called you twice, and both times you ignored me!" Then she collected herself, took a breath, and said: "Is your phone even *on*?"

"To be honest, I have no idea," Peter confessed. "The cops took it earlier, when they came by my house. They said it was evidence."

"Evidence?" Lucia parroted. "Evidence of *what*?"

"They didn't say. They just bagged it and tossed it into one of their cruisers," Peter said. "But that's not why I'm calling. I'm calling because Brian—"

"Is in jail. Yeah. I know," Lucia grunted. "I just got the rundown from Detective Trotter. He said that someone called in a tip; told them all about Brian and Finley. Do you—"

"Eddie Tate," Peter said, before the full question could fall from Lucia's lips. "I overheard a couple of the cops talking outside my back door. They said Eddie told his father and his father called the police chief. That's why everything's happening so fast. The orders are coming from the top."

"Shit."

"Shit is right," Peter confirmed. "But the cops may be the least of our worries."

"How so?"

"Well...I did some more research last night—into Mr. Sticks' Labyrinth, I mean—and I...uh...I put two and two together," Peter fumbled. "I'm not positive about anything, you understand—not that anyone *anywhere* can be positive about anything; gravity itself is merely a *theory*—but I'm fairly certain that...well...." He swallowed audibly. "I'm fairly certain that the whole Labyrinth is a charade."

"A charade?"

"Yeah. A charade," Peter repeated, in a slightly lower voice. "Those pictures we found on the dark net? Those teenagers with 'I Believe' written all over them? Well...I managed to dig up a few of their names."

"And...?"

"All of them are listed as missing."

"All of them?"

"Yes. Except for one," Peter amended. "Jenny Holtzmann, age sixteen, was found in a ditch, just outside Sioux City, Iowa, in 2010. She'd been missing for one year, one month, and three days."

"Which means...?"

"In my opinion?" Peter said, making a smacking noise with his lips. "We're not dealing with some internet weirdos. Or even a criminal organization with ties to the dark net. I think we're dealing with one highly sophisticated *serial killer*. I think some psychopath has been using Mr. Sticks' Labyrinth to lure at-risk teens into his web. And I think that psychopath currently has his eyes set on *you*."

"I wish I could tell you that I'm joking around, but I can't," he continued, while Lucia struggled to digest that first bit of information. "Any engineer worth his salt can set up servers, hide messages in source code, and design basic videogames. If you don't believe me—"

"I do believe you," Lucia interrupted angrily. "It's just...what about the payphone? If some fucked-up techie is behind everything, how did he know which phone to call at three o'clock in the morning? How did he know I'd go to *that particular one*? Was he, personally, hiding in the bushes?"

"*Personally?*" Peter said. "No. But I'm sure he was there *digitally.*"

"As in—"

"Your phone. Yeah," Peter confirmed. "You might be invisible while using Tor or Orbot...since those browsers are encrypted and since they utilize proxies...but outside of those browsers?" He hesitated. "Outside of those browsers, you're vulnerable. Run-of-the-mill search engines like Chrome, Safari, and Internet Explorer? They're about as secure as your mother's trailer. No offense."

"But I never used any of those search engines," Lucia protested. "In the Labyrinth, I only used Orbot."

"You're sure?"

"Yes. I'm positive."

"Even when you scanned that QR code?"

"What QR code?" Lucia started to say. Then she stopped.

The church.

Between the tablet-in-the-locker operation, the payphone fiasco, and Brian's legal troubles, she'd forgotten all about the creepy, abandoned chapel.

"Okay. Say I *did* use one of those unencrypted browsers," she said, in a considerably more somber tone. "What would that *mean*, exactly? How much could a hacker *steal?*"

"Steal?" Peter clucked. "It's not a question of stealing. It's a question of *access*. With the right tools, a hacker could literally take over your phone. He could see all your text messages, listen to all your phone calls, extract all your contacts, read all your emails, go through your calendar, track your movements based on your GPS coordinates.... Heck, he could even activate your cameras and *see you*. In real time."

"Yeah. Okay. Sure," Lucia fumbled. "But wouldn't I notice? Wouldn't my phone start acting...I don't know...*weird?*"

"No. Not at all," Peter said, with all the tact of a sexually-aroused gorilla. "A hacker would leave behind some digital fingerprints, but those are generally hard to find. If I were in your shoes, I would—"

There, Peter's voice tapered. Lucia thought she heard a rapping in the background, followed by a muted voice, but she couldn't be sure. The quality of the connection wasn't great, to start, and the ambient noise around her only served to obfuscate the details.

When Peter spoke again, his words were laced with hisses, as if he were cupping his hands around the transmitter.

"Shoot. The cops are back," he said. "I better go; lay low for a while. I may be wrong about this whole hacker thing, but on the off-chance that I'm not...I'd suggest going off the grid. Completely. With your phone shut down and taken apart, no one can track you. Not me, not a hacker, not even the NSA."

"But what about Finley?" Lucia objected. "What if she tries to call me? Or text me? I'd rather not roll those dice."

"I know, but it's the safest course of action right here and right now," Peter pressed. "If my hunch is right and there *is* a killer out there, you may be in very real danger. He may be following you *as we speak.*"

"*May be,*" Lucia pointed out, even as she checked and double-checked her surroundings for unfamiliar characters. "As of now, we can't be sure about anything. The Labyrinth may be nothing but fiction—a game without an ending."

"True," Peter allowed. "But fiction isn't just *lies*. All fiction incorporates *truth*. And *good* fiction...? That incorporates *a lot* of truth."

That said, he advised Lucia to keep her wits about her—to avoid unnecessarily risky situations—and he muttered a clipped goodbye. He probably didn't mean for the farewell to sound brusque or for the intervening dead air to raise the hairs on Lucia's forearms, but he was successful on both fronts, regardless.

Chapter 35

With Peter's warnings reverberating in her head, Lucia drove to Dale's Pawn—which occupied a weed-infested lot across from an abandoned dollar store—and went straight to the service counter. She'd never been inside that particular pawn shop before, due mostly to its erratic business hours, but it had a familiar ambiance. It possessed buzzing fluorescents, cracked laminate tiling, overloaded utility shelves, dusty display cases, and, hidden beneath the tang of industrial cleaning solvents, the scents of metal polish and mildew.

The employee behind the register was no more aesthetically—or aromatically—pleasing. He was burly son-of-a-bitch with bulky green tattoos, a handlebar moustache, and prominent brows, which sheltered a pair of beady, shark-like eyes. She thought his name was Kevin Seymour and she was pretty sure he'd served two tours in Afghanistan—she could sure picture him on the back of a Humvee, cigar in hand—but she wasn't positive, and she didn't bother to ask.

With as much confidence as she could muster, she wrestled her wallet from her back pocket, set her feet, and said: "Hello, sir. I need something for protection. Can you help me?"

Even to her own ears, the phrase sounded unnatural, but it was the best she could come up with, given the circumstances. She'd never attempted to purchase a gun before, so she wasn't sure how to broach the subject. Was it normal for a person to walk into a pawn shop, to slap a wad of bills on the counter, and to demand a firearm?

To her chagrin, the employee didn't react, one way or another. He merely leaned forward, set his swollen forearms on the counter, and said, slow as January molasses: "Well, I reckon that depends. What—*exactly*—do you need protection *from*?"

It was a fair question, based on her own inquiry, but she suddenly found herself at a loss. She didn't *know* what she needed protection from. She didn't *know* if she was preparing to face a ruthless serial killer, a bunch of sex traffickers, or something else entirely. Her thoughts were so twisted, she could barely tell up from down.

Perhaps sensing her discomfort, the employee shifted slightly and said: "We got shotguns, rifles, mace, revolvers, knives.... Hell. We might even have a sword in the back. Care to take a look?"

"No. I think...I think one of those will do the trick," Lucia returned, jabbing a finger toward a collection of handguns, which slumbered within a Plexiglas display case.

If her tattooed friend was disappointed by her decision, he didn't show it.

"Want to see anything in particular?" he grunted, while he slogged toward the scarred-and-smudged case.

In response, Lucia bit her lip; glanced from one model to the next. There weren't more than a dozen guns on display, but she couldn't identify a single one of them. They all looked the same beneath the rapidly flickering fluorescents. They all looked like misshapen chunks of steel, wood, and fiberglass.

"How about that one?" she said, indicating the largest and shiniest of the bunch. She was tempted to ask about the gun's stopping power—about whether it would be able to drop a full-grown man at five, fifteen, or twenty-five yards—but she ended up keeping that question inside. She didn't want to rub the man the wrong way; make him think twice about selling to her.

For what it was worth, the employee fulfilled her request without hesitation. He drew the weapon from the case, turned it over once or twice, examined the tag, then placed it on the counter in front of her.

"That there is .44 Magnum Desert Eagle. Made in Minnesota," he said, without particular enthusiasm. "In my opinion, one of the best handguns ever produced. Reliable as hell."

"Good. I need something reliable," Lucia said as she hefted the weapon from the counter; as she held it at arm's length; as she closed one eye and sighted down the barrel. To be honest, she was surprised by the gun's weight—by how clumsy it felt in her palm—but she tried not to let it show.

Her act must have left something to be desired.

After a matter of seconds, her tattooed friend crossed his arms and said: "You don't shoot much, do you?"

"No. But I've always been a fast learner," Lucia returned, a kernel of defensiveness in her voice. "I didn't learn how to swim until middle school, but that didn't keep me from making the varsity swim team, freshman year. Or from—"

Her tattooed friend didn't care to hear her life story.

Before she could venture any further into her past achievements, he tugged another handgun from the case, slapped it on the counter, and said: "Here. Try this one. She's a Ruger LCR, model 5401."

"Which means...?" Lucia said, tentatively returning the Desert Eagle to its roost. She fully expected the man to segue into a fantastical sales pitch since she was an admitted greenhorn and since she was practically *begging* for more information, but the man frustrated her expectations. He held his peace until she had the revolver in her hands. And even then, he didn't say anything aside from, "Better?"

"Actually...yes. Much better," Lucia admitted, marveling at the difference in weight and balance. The thing still strained her muscles when she held it away from her body, but it was much less cumbersome than the Magnum. And much cheaper, to boot.

Determined to close the transaction and to get on with her preparations, she returned the revolver to the counter and immediately pulled her credit card from her wallet.

"I'll take it," she announced, with finality. "Along with a box of... well...whatever this thing takes. Can you do that?"

*****

Within an hour, Lucia was staged beside Cozzens Lake; a dozen .38 Special casings scattered around her. She was beginning to understand the Ruger's recoil, but she still wasn't able to knock the plastic bottle from the stump.

"Okay. Focus. You can do this," she whispered, while she sighted down the sleek, blued barrel. Her tattooed friend had given her a couple of tips before she'd left the pawn shop, but none of them seemed to be increasing her confidence or accuracy. The more rounds she sent downrange, the more she felt like an overgrown toddler.

Reminding herself to keep her feet set and her eyes open, she disengaged the Ruger's safety, drew a bead, and—

Bam!

—sent a large anthill straight to hell.

For a second time.

Disappointment burning at her core, she let her arms fall and focused on the revolver's report—on the way the sound rolled over the barren plains, spreading and tapering simultaneously. A mile to the northwest, the noise may have drawn some attention, but where she was standing…? Where she was standing, there was no one.

No one at all.

And yet…she didn't *feel* alone.

In the midst of the absence, there was a *presence*. Not a *human* presence, exactly, but a presence nonetheless. She could almost hear it in the silence between heartbeats; in the stillness that blossomed between gusts of hearty midday wind. She couldn't tell what it *wanted*, but she could tell that it was *there*. And that it was *watching* her.

Aware that the hairs on the back of her neck were standing on end, she shuffled in a circle and peered across Cozzens Lake. She would've paid a king's ransom to have the old Cozzens Lake back, as the old Cozzens Lake had been able to melt her cares like so much wet newspaper, but she didn't have a king's ransom. At the moment, all she had was a secondhand revolver, a box of hollow-point ammunition, and a desire to make her sister's kidnapper pay for what he'd done.

Chapter 36

According to the town elders and—perhaps more significantly—to a sixty-page paperback titled *Eaton: Through the Decades*, which annually sold a half dozen copies and which was available exclusively through the U-Fill It gas station on the south end of town, Collins' Crossing was a priceless historical landmark; a testament to the community's undying spirit. But in person, it was less than impressive.

In person, Collins' Crossing looked like little more than an ugly wooden bridge. Because it was an ugly wooden bridge. And it didn't span a river. It spanned a ditch. A *long-disused* ditch. A ditch that, for practical purposes, should have been leveled during the Nixon administration.

Remembering the time she and her friends had covered the thing in green water-based paint—to commemorate Saint Patrick's Day—Lucia pulled her Focus to the side of the road and shifted stiffly into neutral. She wanted to derive some measure of joy from the memory, but, in her bug-spattered and dust-filmed headlights, both the bridge and the ditch looked *diseased*—as if they'd been dredged from some manic-depressive's deepest nightmares.

Was she making the right call, coming out here on her own? Sure, she had the Ruger in her passenger seat and a can of mace in her glove compartment, but would that be enough? Would five rounds and spritz of oleoresin capsicum keep her safe from…well…from whatever lay in the all-encompassing darkness?

With fatigue pulling at her eyelids, she shifted back into gear and edged her Focus across the bridge. She was tempted to turn on the radio—if only to keep her attention from the dashboard clock—but paranoia kept her from following through. She was afraid the music would cause her to miss some important detail. Besides, she was close to her destination. In her rearview mirror she could see Mr. Potter's farmhouse. And up ahead...?

Up ahead, there was blackness.

Infinite blackness.

Where one layer of blackness ended, another began, creating the impression of a three-dimensional tapestry—of not-quite-formed plants and objects. And *people*.

A quarter mile past Collins' Crossing, Lucia began to see humanoid shapes amongst the walls of corn. None of the shapes remained for long, however. Each time she pressed ever-so-slightly on the brake pedal, they dissolved back into the ether. Like so many wisps of smoke.

Telling herself that she was allowing her fear and superstition to control her—to dictate what she saw and felt and heard—she adjusted her grip on the wheel. And she gradually became aware of a low-pitched hum.

No. Not a hum.

A buzz.

Skin prickled, Lucia returned her car to the shoulder and killed the engine. She couldn't tell where the noise was coming *from*, precisely, but she could tell it was *close*. She could tell—

Her phone.

She'd forgotten to turn the device off following her discussion with Peter, and now it was vibrating in the passenger seat: trapped beneath the box of .38 Specials.

Hoping against hope that her sister was on the other end, Lucia dug the phone out from under the box and examined the caller ID.

It wasn't her sister...but it wasn't a stranger, either.

It was Brian.

Or it was Brian's cell phone number, at least.

Against her better judgment, she answered the call.

"Hello?" she said, while monitoring the rows of corn around her. "Brian?"

"The one and only," Brian said, sounding equal parts pleased and exhausted. "Sorry I missed your calls earlier. Things have gotten… sticky."

"Yeah. I heard," she said, struggling to keep her voice neutral. "How are you holding up? Are they treating you okay?"

"For the most part," he said, with a small chuckle. "They were pretty harsh at first, but they changed their tone when my lawyer showed up. She's the reason I'm talking to you now, actually."

"She?"

"Donna Montgomery. She practices law over in Boulder," he said, by way of explanation. "She convinced that fat sack-of-shit detective—"

"Trotter."

"That's the one," Brian confirmed. "Anyway, she convinced him to give me ten minutes alone with my phone. You should've seen it. She had him so turned around, he was pissing from his asshole. She—"

"Sounds pretty amazing," Lucia interrupted. "Maybe you should take her out to dinner."

It was a kneejerk reaction—one she immediately regretted—but she didn't apologize for it. She wasn't in the mood to apologize.

For what it was worth, Brian didn't respond in kind.

"It's not like that," he said, calmly and collectedly. "You know how I feel about you. About *us*. I want—"

He cut himself short.

When his voice returned, his tone was less guarded.

"We'll talk later," he assured her. "In the meantime, keep your head down. And don't do anything rash. Can you do that for me?"

It was a simple yes or no question, but Lucia found herself at a crossroads, nonetheless. On the one hand, she wanted to tell him where she was and what she was about to do, but on the other…? On the other, she didn't want him to worry. Or to—God forbid—try and stop her.

Imagining police cruisers rushing toward her, lights flashing, painting the fields in garish shades of blue, white, and red, she cleared her throat and said, as convincingly as possible: "Yes. Of course. I can do that. Cautious is my middle name. Lucia Cautious Corvi." Then she bid him farewell and hung up the phone.

She regretted that decision most of all.

Without Brian's voice in her ear, the air in the cab was static. There were no minute little sounds to keep her mind from wandering—from painting maws and fangs in the margins. There was only silence: the music of the damned.

And the lost.

Afraid of the track her thoughts were taking, Lucia pocketed her keys, gathered up her revolver, collected her cane, and ventured outside.

While the night was cold, it wasn't a *wet* cold. It wasn't the type of cold she'd encountered in the Midwest. It wasn't the type of cold that enveloped you like a wet blanket and stabbed needles of ice into your bones. It was a merciful cold—a dry cold.

None of that mattered, though.

In a matter of seconds, Lucia felt like a human ice sculpture. Or—more accurately—like a cosmonaut who'd been sucked from her vessel; left to float through the vast vacuum of space.

Picturing a great void before her—a great density of hunger, suffering, and malignant intelligence—Lucia shivered and pulled her shawl more tightly around her shoulders. She shouldn't have felt like a forsaken deep space explorer since she was no more than two miles from her childhood home and since the night was alive with familiar chirps and rattles and hisses, but she *did*. She felt like she was on another planet. Not a distant planet, perhaps, but a parallel planet—a planet that existed in some neighboring reality.

Considering, then rejecting, the possibility that she'd driven further than she'd originally intended, she shut her driver-side door and focused on the rhythm of her breathing. She realized she was under-rested and over-stressed and was, therefore, liable to experience a flare-up, but there was little she could do to remedy the situation. Until her sister was safe…or until the person responsible for her abduction was dead…

Lucia shook her head. She couldn't afford to lose herself in the innumerable what ifs. She had to keep her mind in the present; take one step at a time. Self-control was the name of the game.

As long as you stay calm, everything will be alright, she assured herself.

Did she believe that, though?

No. She didn't. A primitive part of her was alive, and it was screaming that something was not right. It was urging her to climb back into the Focus and to hit the gas until she was far, far away.

Lucia refused it.

Making sure the revolver was fully loaded, she ventured around the car and cleared her throat. The weapon's grip was biting into her palm—leaving miniature diamonds in her sweat-softened flesh—but she found herself unable to relax her fingers. Or to tear her eyes from Mr. Potter's cornfield.

In the midst of the innumerable tassels and stalks and husks, she sensed a presence. A *physical* presence. Not something intangible. Not something that had emerged from her own sea of insecurities.

Within that rattling and swooning mass, she sensed something *real*.

Unsure how, exactly, to proceed, she took a solitary step forward, swallowed, and forced the word "Hello?" from her lips. She intended to say "My name's Lucia. I'm Finley's sister," in the subsequent silence, but that phrase was harder to conjure. With her larynx half frozen and her vocal chords pulled tighter than heavy-gauge guitar strings, two-syllable words were difficult enough.

Fortunately, a follow-up sentence wasn't necessary.

As Lucia watched her breath turn to vapor and dissolve into the cloying dark, a new noise arose from the field. It wasn't a loud noise, but it was distinct.

It was the sound of a stalk snapping in two.

Chapter 37

Suddenly unable to hear beyond the *thumpa-thumpa* of her own heart, Lucia lifted her revolver and surveyed the rows in her immediate vicinity. She was tempted to fire a round into the emptiness, both to assert her ability to defend herself and to dilute the feeling of helplessness that was uncoiling in the pit of her stomach, but common sense stopped her. For all she knew, her sister was the one in the field.

Picturing Finley with a bag over her head, a gag in her mouth, and ties around her wrists and ankles, Lucia took a second step forward and eked out her sister's name. She hoped to receive some kind of confirmation, in the ensuing seconds, but she was treated to something else entirely.

She was treated to a rush of dread.

Preternatural dread.

The type of dread she'd encountered only once before.

With a numbness in her extremities, Lucia crouched down and ran her free hand through the dirt. She wanted to believe that the numbness was a natural occurrence—that her body was angling for an attack—but she couldn't be positive. Her world was beginning to spin and shadows were beginning to writhe in her peripheral vision.

Locating a jagged rock among the bits of gravel and detritus, Lucia straightened, turned around three times, and reigned in a deep breath. She could hear Brian in the back of her head as she pressed the stone's edge against her forearm—could hear him saying "What are you doing?" and "Are you crazy?" and "You don't *actually* think Mr. Sticks exists, do you?"—but that wasn't enough to dissuade her. In one sharp motion, she drew the stone across her arm and winced at the pain that followed—at the rivers and tributaries of blood that slithered downward, toward the thirsty earth.

Disgusted by the sticky wetness of her own bodily fluids, Lucia tossed the rock down the road and awkwardly proceeded to take off her shoes. She expected to feel silly—foolish, even—as she set the sneakers aside and tugged at her socks, but she didn't. If anything, she felt a measure of *relief*.

Was that crazy?

Yes, she decided. It was crazy. But then, the *world* was crazy. Over the past nine days, she'd seen its true colors. She'd stumbled through its back alleys, slogged through its sewers, and peered through its soap-covered windows. And she hadn't liked what she'd seen.

Ruminating on the time she'd spent in the deep web, she shivered and worked her toes into the dirt. She knew Mrs. Janowski would have counseled her to pray, since Mrs. Janowski was a good Christian, but a lack of familiarity held her back. She couldn't quote any particular prayers, and she didn't think the Maker of All Things would appreciate a casual "Hey. I know you're busy up there, but I've gotten myself into a pretty fucked-up situation. I'd appreciate some help, if you're so inclined. Tootles!"

Wishing she'd paid more attention in her religious studies classes, she gritted her teeth and continued her advance on the cornfield. She couldn't see much, what with the moon hidden behind a bank of tumultuous gray clouds, but she didn't have to *see* to know where she was heading. She'd been in Mr. Potter's field before. She knew where all the access roads were located—where one drip line ended and another began.

It was what she *didn't* know that scared her.

Less than a foot from the perimeter, she caught a whiff of what might have been body odor—it was a ripe, fetid stench: a stench that made her nostrils flare and her eyes water—but she didn't let that slow her down. She used her forearms to part the first two rows and then—

She was elsewhere.

She was in a place devoid of sound. A place where the air was thinner, the clouds were thicker, and the corn was taller. She was in a place of near perfect darkness—a place where a person could easily wander too far and cease to exist altogether.

In that place, she was unable to distinguish her car, the road, the Stenson Company grain elevator, or even the Great Western sugar plant. All of them were gone—swallowed up by the vast maw of night.

But they weren't actually *gone*, were they?

Overcome by a feeling of *otherworldliness*, Lucia stopped in her tracks. She hadn't walked more than a dozen yards, and yet she already felt lost. She felt as though someone had blindfolded her, spun her around, and pulled a rug out from under her feet.

Reminding herself that dizziness, vertigo, and confusion were relapse symptoms, she gave her head a shake and pressed forward. She wasn't about to let her body get the best of her. Not now. Not when she was so close to the end.

The end.

Those words reverberated in her skull. Travis St. John had gone looking for The End, and his story hadn't concluded with "happily ever after." His story had concluded suddenly and violently. Much like Jenny Holtzmann's story.

Was Lucia's story going to follow suit?

Sensing eyes all around, Lucia dug her phone from her pocket and tossed it as far as she could. If Peter was right and there *was* a tech-savvy killer on her trail, he would have a harder time tracking her down.

Unless he was already watching her.

Feeling a light touch on her arm, Lucia spun; jabbed the revolver into the darkness. But there was no one there. The space beyond her sight was as empty as her stomach.

Reprimanding herself internally, Lucia lowered the gun. She may not have been thinking straight, but even so, she recognized the need for restraint. She realized that she was engaged in a high-stakes game of poker and that it was in her best interest to play her cards close to her chest.

"It's okay. You're okay. Everything's okay," she murmured, in the hopes that the sound of her voice might make her feel less like a character in a bizarre videogame.

The technique wasn't particularly successful.

Each subsequent step—hell, each subsequent *breath*—added a twist to the knot that had once been her gut.

Excruciatingly aware of the numbness in her hands and feet, she shuffled into the next row and continued east. Or…the direction she *perceived* to be east. In reality, she may have been heading north, south, west, or any direction in between.

Lucia wrinkled her nose.

There was that smell again.

That rotten smell.

It was stronger here. So strong, it cancelled out the field's natural perfume. It drove away the musk of pollen and the tang of earth until it was the only scent in Lucia's nostrils.

Had something crawled into the middle of the field and died? Lucia had encountered a number of animal carcasses in her lifetime, thanks in no small part to loose parental supervision and an adventurous spirit, but she'd never encountered anything so *sweet*.

It was the sweetness, she decided, that revolted her the most. It reminded her of a slow-roasted ham.

Anxious to leave the pocket of fetid air, she exhaled deeply and increased her pace. She used her cane to keep her upright and the Ruger to keep the protruding leaves and husks from slapping her face. But she was only able to maintain her balance for so long.

All at once, the ground beneath her fell away and she toppled forward, not unlike a de-stringed marionette. She did make a wild attempt to catch herself as she twisted through the arid dark, but the effort was ultimately in vain. When she finally hit the ground, she hit the ground hard. And she heard her right shoulder pop.

With pain radiating through her core, mingling with the numbness in her extremities, she rolled to her back, squeezed her eyes shut, and bit her lower lip. She wanted to scream—to unleash all her agony and frustration and confusion—but she didn't dare. A scream wouldn't only give away her location…it would reveal that she was injured; that she was easy prey.

Come on, you wuss. Get up, she ordered herself. *This is no time to throw in the towel. You may think this is the end of the line, but it's not. You have more fight left in you.*

What had her father said when she'd dislocated her wrist, the day before her debut swim meet at Eaton High? For one reason or another, she couldn't remember. She couldn't even remember the look on his face. Which only served to frustrate her more. Until she managed to sit up.

The second she leveraged herself upright, she forgot all about her father and her shoulder. Not because she discovered that her Ruger was missing, or because she found herself in the midst of a small clearing; because she wasn't *alone*.

There, no more than five yards to the east—or was that the north?—lay a humanoid shape. Lucia couldn't make out the shape's gender, as it was angled away from her and as it was partially concealed by dirt clods and cornstalks, but she could tell that it was, most definitely, the source of the stench.

Imagining the scene in broad daylight—turkey vultures circling overhead, beetles wriggling underfoot, the air thick with flies—Lucia grimaced and started toward the shape. She knew smiling was supposed to repress the gag reflex, but that knowledge was of little use to her. At the moment, she was physically unable to produce a *smirk*, let alone a *smile*. After all, there was a good chance the body belonged to—

No.

It's not her.

It can't be her.

Mind rushing, painting pictures of delicate blue lips, full-but-pale cheeks, and tangles of greasy red hair, Lucia pulled herself within a yard of the body and abruptly stopped. Half of her wanted to break down and sprint in the other direction, but the other half wouldn't let her.

It was that other half that prompted her to reach out and gently brush the debris from the body's bloated and lifeless face.

Chapter 38

Even though Lucia *knew* what time and bacteria could do to a deceased human body—during her high school tenure, a boy named Jordan Shaw had, in an extremely misguided attempt to impress her, shown her a number of pictures from a website called Rotten.com—she was, nonetheless, revolted by the visage that grinned up at her. She took one look at the desiccated lips, the yellowed teeth, the discolored flesh, and the maggot-eaten eye sockets, and she promptly threw up.

Had her sister been reduced to that *thing?* To that grotesque puppet? To that parody of a human form? To that greasy, gas-filled puppet?

No, she concluded, at long last. The remains before her, while definitely *human*, were not her *sister's*. They were the remains of a *man*. Beneath the doubled—and unnaturally distended—chin, she could see a prominent Adam's apple. And beneath the Adam's apple...?

Lucia frowned.

There was something shiny attached to the corpse's chest—to the *Built Ford Tough* T-shirt. It was small and rectangular and it winked at her, despite the meager supply of moonlight. As if it wanted her to take a closer look.

Lucia accepted the invitation.

With shaking hands, she cleared the debris from the corpse's thorax...and discovered a name tag.

At the top, the thing simply read: Lucky Lou's Gas and Auto. But the text didn't stop there. Directly underneath, in much bigger print, it read—

Gus Stansky.

The man who had been dating Lucia's mother.

The man who had preferred to masturbate in public while wearing women's lingerie.

Unsure how…or why…or *when*…the man had ended up in Mr. Potter's cornfield, Lucia teetered onto her ass and kicked numbly in the opposite direction. She didn't want to stay in the clearing any longer, but she couldn't summon the wherewithal to stand.

Hoping a moment of silent introspection would reset her synapses, she released an uneven breath and closed her eyes. She intended to count to ten, too, but the universe had other ideas.

As soon as the number three materialized in her thoughts, she heard a *snap!*, followed by a *voice*.

"Disgusting, isn't he?" the new arrival said, sounding—at least to Lucia's ears—both incredibly close and incredibly far away. "Smells like one of those portable shit houses. Not that he smelled much better when he was alive."

The new arrival proceeded to laugh, but Lucia wasn't remotely amused.

"Why?" she demanded, even as electric jitters arced up and down her spine; as shadows and ghouls danced in her peripheral vision. "Why did you kill him?"

"Kill him?" The new arrival emitted a self-satisfied chuckle. "I'm afraid you're confused. I didn't kill him. *He* killed *himself*."

"With his bare hands?" Lucia returned, searching the darkness for signs of movement. "Forgive me, but I find that hard to believe. Not long ago, someone told me Gus was harmless. I was assured—"

"Harmless?"

The entity in the corn laughed again.

There was something vaguely familiar about that laugh—about the cadence and pitch—but Lucia couldn't quite place it.

"Gus was *never* harmless," the entity continued, undeterred. "He was sick. *Deranged*. Do you have any idea what he would say when our mother was gone? When it was just the two of us? Do you have any idea what he would *do*?"

"I—" Lucia began.

She didn't get any further.

As she struggled to comprehend what her counterpart was talking about, the rows at the far side of the clearing shifted and a single figure emerged. It wasn't a stranger, either—some drifter she'd passed in the streets and promptly forgotten.

It was her *sister*.

"Finley? Is that…is that really *you*?" she managed, as soon as the waves of relief, joy, disbelief, and bewilderment began to subside.

In response, her sister lifted her arms, as if she were a magician who had just accomplished a feat no magician had accomplished before her, and said: "In the flesh. Happy to see me?"

"Are you kidding?" Lucia gushed. "I was worried sick. We all were. Me and Peter and Brian, we—"

"Thought I was dead? Yeah. I know," Finley said, taking a step forward, but remaining well outside of Lucia's reach. "I kept tabs on all of you."

"Then why didn't you reach out to us?" Lucia grimaced. "Why didn't you make contact? We were always on your side. We only wanted to help you."

"Oh?" Finley returned, tapping a finger against her lips, as though this were brand new information. "Is that why you slept with Brian on Sunday night?" And then, in response to Lucia's look of astonished puzzlement: "That's right. I was *there*. I saw *everything*. I saw the way you looked at him; the way you invited him inside; the way you led him to the bedroom. It was your goal to fuck him from the start."

"No. It wasn't. What happened that night…it was a mistake," Lucia stammered, while attempting to stand. She wanted nothing more than to throw her arms around her sister and to limp from that horrid, godforsaken cornfield, but she could tell her sister had different intentions. She could see the smirk solidifying on her sister's face; could hear the hostile undertones in her voice.

"Look. We can sort this out later," Lucia said, as evenly as she could. "Right now, we should leave. It's not safe."

"No. It's not," Finley agreed. "But we're not leaving. We're going to talk. We're going to settle our differences, right here and right now. Do you know why?"

Numbly, Lucia shook her head.

"Because, by morning, *you're* going to *no longer exist*," Finley concluded. "*He's* coming for you. And when *he* comes for you, there's no way out."

"And who, exactly, is he?" Lucia ventured. "Some guy you met on the internet?"

"Hardly," Finley sniggered. "I'm talking about *Mr. Sticks*. The Mr. Sticks."

"Okay. But Mr. Sticks isn't *real*," Lucia managed. "He's an urban legend. He can't actually hurt anyone."

"No?" Finley said, brows wrinkling. "Tell that to our friend, Gus, over there. He didn't believe the stories, either. He followed me out here, that Saturday night, thinking he could have his way with me—thinking he could fuck me one more time without our mother noticing. But Mr. Sticks took care of him.

"Mr. Sticks takes care of all his Believers," she explained, while moseying counterclockwise around the clearing's perimeter. "He's not some heartless beast. He's a shepherd. He keeps a constant watch over his flock; makes sure his sheep are happy at all times. And if something stands in the way of one sheep's happiness...well..."

Finley made a gesture toward Gus Stansky's sun-dried husk.

Then she shifted and made the same gesture toward *Lucia*.

"I wish I could say it's not personal, but it is," she continued, kicking at a loose bundle of roots and dirt. "After all, *you're* the reason Mom and Dad broke up. *You're* the reason they started drinking and sleeping around. *You're* the reason they can't stand the sight of each other.

"You may think you're some kind of saint because of your disease, but you're not. You never have been," Finley said, with a deepening frown. "All through high school, you were a nightmare. You expected everyone to bow to your every whim. You were rude and angry and endlessly demanding."

"Maybe at the beginning," Lucia allowed, in the most courageous voice she could conjure, "but I was coming to terms with...well... with *everything*. You have to understand that—"

"I don't *have to understand* anything," Finley snapped, revealing a measure of the molten hatred that was bubbling just below her surface. "I was there for the tantrums and the outbursts. I got to *see* everything. The day you went off to college, I was *so* happy. I thought that things might go back to normal. But I was wrong.

"No matter how many times you leave, or how far you run, you always end up coming back," she fumed. "And every time you come back, you fuck things up even more. Hell…even when you're *not* here, you fuck things up. Why is that? Why can't you just *stay gone?*"

There, she stopped, and she curled her fingers into fists; squeezed until her knuckles were white. It was clear that she didn't expect an answer to her question, but Lucia chose to supply one, regardless.

"Why?" Lucia said, unsuccessfully fighting a tidal wave of tears. "Because we're *family*, that's why. Because I *care about you*. I always have, and I always will. We may not see eye to eye on everything, but we're *sisters*. We *need* each other."

"No. We don't. And we're not sisters. We're *half*-sisters," Finley corrected, with a smile that communicated equal parts sadness and loathing. "You're the only genuine article. Me? I'm the runt. The bastard. The *mistake*. The reminder that—"

She didn't go on. Instead, she gave her head a shake, choked out a laugh, and said: "You know what's craziest of all? Up until I was six or seven, I looked up to you. I saw you the way our parents saw you—the way they *still* see you. I thought you were *perfect*. I thought you were God's gift to humanity. Ridiculous, right?"

In response, Lucia swallowed; used her good arm to wipe at her cheeks. Her sister's words hurt more than she cared to admit. They were sharp and hot, and they burrowed into her flesh like deer ticks—like starved and ravenous leeches. She could feel them working in her stomach, throat, and temples.

"Look…" she sniffled, at the tail end of a long and uncomfortable silence. "I'm sorry for all the ways I've hurt you. I didn't mean to… well…I didn't mean for things to go the way they did. If I'd known the way you felt, I would've done something. I would've fixed it."

"Maybe. But that's the point, isn't it?" Finley said, in a slightly more controlled tone. "You didn't notice. You *never* notice. You're the center of your own galaxy. You only look outside of yourself when it's convenient. Like right now."

That said, Finley turned away and started for the perimeter.

Chapter 39

"No."

The word slipped from Lucia's vocal chords with almost zero forethought, but it did wonders for her lagging spirits. It injected life into her slumbering muscles; into her discombobulated inner ear; into her pounding head. It reminded her, if only for a second, that it wasn't The End; that her heart, though damaged, was still beating. And she used that split second of clarity to rise from her knees.

Finley was less than impressed by her determination.

"No?" the girl said, pausing a foot from the fibrous barrier. "What's that supposed to mean?"

"It means that we aren't done," Lucia said, using her arms to keep herself upright. "It means that we're going to work things out; that it's not too late to turn things around. All we have to do is—"

"What? Love each other?" Finley said, edging once again in Lucia's direction. "Love is all Mom and Dad had, and look how they turned out. They can't be in the same room, let alone the same *house*."

"No…but we're not Mom and Dad," Lucia said, in spite of her trembling legs. "We don't have to turn out like them. We have control over our own lives. We can make things better. We can make *ourselves* better. Don't you want to *try*?"

It wasn't a particularly eloquent entreaty, but what it lacked in pageantry, it compensated in *honesty*. There was nothing remotely artificial about it. Every word—every *syllable*—was straight from the heart. And Finley must have recognized that.

"Is that what you truly believe?" she said, drawing—for the first time—within arm's reach. "Do you really think we can overcome our problems and get back to being a *family*?"

"Yes. I do," Lucia said, with tears in her eyes. She could smell her sister's perfume from where she stood—Donna Karan's Be Delicious: a scent their mother called "whorish"—but she resisted the urge to wrap her sister in a bearish hug. She didn't want to force the issue.

In the end, she didn't have to.

Following a moment of silent introspection, Finley swept forward and pulled Lucia to her chest. But the Finley who exited the embrace looked *different*. The Finley who exited the embrace had a strange glimmer in her eyes.

"If that's what you truly believe," she said, fingers tightening around Lucia's biceps, "then you must be one hell of a stupid bitch." Then she made a jerking, *thrusting* motion with her lower half, and gave Lucia a shove.

Lucia made an attempt to right herself, of course, but it was no use. Until she hit the ground, she didn't realize that her left leg was broken; that her kneecap was pushed violently to the side.

"Why?" she managed, an instant before her nervous system responded and sent laces of molten pain through her body. "We're *family.*"

"In the eyes of the law, maybe," Finley returned, with a self-satisfied sniff. "But none of that matters anymore. The Saturday before last, I became a part of a better family. I became a part of *Mr. Sticks'* family. He accepted me, flaws and all, because he *loves* me. He loves me so much, he's willing to *kill* for me. No one else on this earth loves me that much. No one. Not Mom, not Dad, not Brian, and definitely not *you.*

"It's sad, really," she said, between Lucia's moans. "If you'd just stayed away, Mr. Sticks might've spared you. He might've allowed you to keep living your sad little life. But you couldn't stay away. You had to stick your nose into my business. Into *our* business. And now you're going to pay the price.

"Do you hear that?" she said, tilting her chin toward the sky and cupping a hand around one of her ears. "That's Mr. Sticks. He's on his way. I don't think it'll take him long to find you, either. You're making a lot of noise. More than Gus, actually. The only difference is…you're not begging for your life. Yet."

It was an unnecessarily cruel way to say goodbye, in Lucia's opinion, but she wasn't in any condition to retaliate. Her body was on fire, and her mind was in a fog—beset by tendrils and shadows; by sadness and regret.

Finley wasn't moved by her agony.

With a flat and emotionless "Farewell," the girl pivoted and made for the wall of corn. Lucia hoped, in some faraway part of her consciousness, that her sister might have a last-second change of heart and return to her side, but she was disappointed. She heard her sister pass through the perimeter without pause. And she felt another presence take her sister's place.

Unable to compose herself enough to speak, Lucia anchored her good hand in the dirt and dragged herself in a circle. She made an effort to examine the perimeter as she went, but her eyes were no longer up to the task. Each time she blinked, she saw new shapes within the stalks; within the blackness swarming in her peripheral vision.

Come on. Pull yourself together, she told herself, even as she bumped up against Gus's corpse; as her fingertips brushed his cold and leathery flesh. *You can get yourself out of this mess. You're a Corvi, and Corvis are tough as nails. Your grandfather—*

Lucia's internal pep talk ended there.

As she sat, breathing in through her nose and out through her mouth, she became aware of a peculiar *swelling*. Not a swelling *within* her, but a swelling *without*. The air seemed to be thickening, and the ground...? The ground seemed to be *vibrating*.

Was her mind playing tricks on her, or was she experiencing some kind of—dare she think it?—*supernatural phenomenon?*

Determined to get to the bottom of the matter, she shut her eyes tight, and forced the word "Hello?" from her throat. Or...she intended to force the word "hello" from her throat. The word that actually slipped from her vocal chords was not, strictly speaking, a *word*. It was, rather, a collection of garbled *sounds*.

Frustrated—and more than a little *scared*—she pulled herself toward the center of the clearing. She wanted to move as far away from the *presence* as possible, but she was having trouble pinpointing its location. It seemed to be *all around her*. She could feel it to her left, to her right, ahead of her, and behind her.

Glimpsing innumerable disparities in the darkness—in the spaces between the trembling, *writhing* cornstalks—she stopped and drew her good leg to her chest. She figured the Ruger was somewhere close, but she seriously doubted that she would be able to find it. Not within the next two minutes, at least. Not before the thing in corn tired of watching her and—

Lucia shook her head. She didn't want to turn her mind's eye toward the afterlife. She didn't want to, because she knew what she would encounter. She knew she'd see an abyss. And within that abyss, she'd see the souls of the lost. She'd see countless bruised bodies, swarming through the darkness, begging for a glimmer of light; for an instant of warmth. She'd see distended bellies and sagging breasts; flabby legs and gnarled, soot-blackened feet.

And that wasn't the worst thing she would see.

Within—or perhaps *below*—the endless folds of darkness, she would see a hunger. An old hunger. A hunger which had existed since the beginning of time. She would see it slither amongst the naked masses, not unlike an eel; not unlike a recently-awoken predator; not unlike the god of a submerged and forgotten civilization. And she would be unable to look away.

Overwhelmed by a rush of existential dread, Lucia straightened; pawed at her throbbing temples. She hoped the action would reset her neural network and—secretly—keep the Hunger from manifesting in the material world, but the measure was ineffective.

When Lucia finally lifted her gaze from the husk-laden earth, she discovered that the Being was *there*. *In the flesh*. She could see it standing just beyond the perimeter—an extension of the darkness itself. It seemed to favor the height and build of a man, but it wasn't limited to a single shape. Each time she blinked, she saw a different form. One second it was tall and thin, and the next it was short and squat. The only constant was the veil of living shadow that surrounded it; that encapsulated it; that wove to and fro like sentient fibers.

Lucia made an effort to focus on those shadows, if only to prove to herself that she wasn't losing her grip on reality, but she quickly found that it was impossible to isolate them from the whole. Under a direct gaze, they simply ceased to exist. They dissipated into the blackness, as if they were nothing more than puffs of vapor.

But they weren't puffs of vapor. They were real, and they exuded a preternatural energy. Lucia could feel it in her fingers and toes; could taste it on her tongue. It was heavy and it left a copper tang on her palate.

Much like blood.

Gorge bobbing in the back of her throat, Lucia lurched forward and retched. She retched until her stomach was empty—until her lips were spattered with acidic bile. And when she straightened...?

When she straightened, there was a new figure in the clearing. It was a small figure, with round hips and long hair, and it was crawling toward her. Slowly. It was making odd noises, as well, as if it were a toad, drowning in a pool of mud.

Frightened and disgusted, Lucia used her good leg to propel herself in the opposite direction. But she stopped as soon as she registered the face beneath the mop of hair. She wasn't being pursued by some undead acolyte or some gremlin from the depths of Hades.

The figure on the ground was *Finley*. And she wasn't in good shape.

"Help me," the girl managed, between blood-foamed lips. "Please. Help me. I—"

She didn't mean to end her entreaty there, but any subsequent words were stolen by her second mouth—by the wet smile that stretched across her trachea.

Five minutes earlier, Lucia would have advised her sister to stay calm, but she'd since lost the ability to form a sentence. She could only watch as her sister choked and gargled, choked and gargled—as blood and saliva and hot, fetid breath bubbled from the gash in her neck.

Just...don't. It's no use, Lucia thought, in a deep and secluded part of her psyche. *The sooner you give in, the sooner the pain will go away.* But her sister wasn't attuned to the same psychokinetic frequency.

With a hoarse whimper—a whimper that escaped first from her throat, then from her lips—Finley dug her fingernails into the dirt and resumed her crawl. She didn't seem aware of her cracked palms, her lacerated breasts, or the pool of blood that was rapidly spreading beneath her. Her eyes were locked on Lucia, as if Lucia was a lone life raft amidst a tumultuous sea.

You can do it. You can help me. It's not too late, Finley's pupils screamed, even as her movements began to slow. *We're sisters, remember? And sisters stand up for each other, no matter what. Though it may wind and hail and snow and rain—*

The bond of sisterhood will always remain, Lucia concluded internally. It was a stupid rhyme from a stupid picture book, but it still brought a tear to Lucia's eye. It was a reminder of the relationship they had once shared—a reminder of the relationship they would never rekindle.

Overcome by emotion, Lucia pivoted, and reached for her sister's hand. It was her way of saying "I'm sorry" and "I forgive you" and "I wish I could go back in time and prevent all of this shit from happening." But her fingers never found their mark.

All at once, Lucia became aware of a *shifting* amongst the darkness. And then—

Chapter 40

Light.

Unsure where the radiance was coming from, or why she was suddenly lying on her back, with her legs twisted beneath her, Lucia rolled; buried her face in the crook of her arm. She knew she was in Mr. Potter's cornfield—her memory of the drive was clear—but any subsequent events were muddy, at best.

Had she wandered into the field, only to fall and to pass out from the pain?

No.

She had fallen…but the fall hadn't broken her leg. She'd seen something. In the clearing. Something grisly and gory and terrible.

She'd seen a body.

Gus Stansky's body.

And after that…?

Lucia frowned; fought against the fog that had gathered in her prefrontal lobe.

After Gus Stansky's body, she'd encountered a person.

Her mother?

No. Not her mother. Her *sister*. Except…her sister hadn't been alone. Something else—a *Hunger*, a *Disparity*—had accompanied her. And that *Something* had grown. It had woven itself into the very fabric of darkness until…

Until what?

Lucia couldn't say.

Wondering whether her mind wasn't shielding her from what had actually happened, she lifted her head and gradually exposed her pupils to the light—to the early-morning sun and the rows of vibrant, green-

and-yellow cornstalks. She could see Gus's body across the clearing, but her gaze wasn't drawn toward his leathery, fly-spackled corpse. Her gaze was drawn to the trail of blood that zigzagged its way through the dirt—through the cicada husks, the dried leaves, and the tufts of greasy raccoon hair.

Certain the blood had, at one time, belonged to her sister, Lucia crawled to where her cane had fallen, and used the implement to rise to her feet. Her left leg was still useless, and her right arm was still throbbing—vying for control over her central nervous system—but she refused to let the pain overtake her.

With her teeth gritted and her fists clenched, she followed the trail of blood to the edge of the clearing, took a deep breath, and waded into the forest of green and yellow. She wasn't sure where the trail would lead, or what she would discover at the end of it, but she wasn't about to allow the *where* or the *what* to slow her down.

As quickly as possible, she hobbled through the corn, pausing only to regain her balance or to change direction. She was heartened by the uprooted stalks that she passed, now and again—they proved that a struggle had taken place—but she was dismayed by the amount of bodily fluids underfoot.

Counting to ten repeatedly, to keep her mind occupied, she passed the remnants of an old scarecrow. And then she stopped.

She'd reached the field's eastern perimeter.

She'd reached County Road 43.

Ahead, the earth gave way to gravel, which gave way to pavement. There were more cornfields beyond—fields which bled into fields, which bled into feed lots—but the trail of blood didn't stretch that far. The trail of blood only stretched onto the gravel shoulder. There, it abruptly ended.

Stomach seizing, Lucia hitched from Mr. Potter's cornfield. She intended to examine the place where the sticky residue tapered, but her muscles weren't up to the task. After three meager steps, she collapsed.

*****

When Lucia finally came to, she was no longer alone. Peter was standing over her. And he was asking one question, over and over.

He was saying: "Lucia. What the hell is going on?"

It was a perfectly straightforward question, but Lucia didn't have an answer to match.

She could only shrug and say: "I don't know."

Because she didn't know.

And she strongly suspected that she never would.

About The Author

Jeffrey Hale is no stranger to suburban horror. He's been accosted by goat-human hybrids, chased by inbred wenches, attacked by giant killer bees, and survived countless hours of prime-time television. When he isn't busy fighting for his life, he can be found reading, writing, playing the bass guitar, or otherwise making a damn fool of himself. You can stalk him (digitally) at twitter.com/jhalehorror or at facebook.com/jeffreyhalehorror. To stalk him in real life, you can find him at *address, city, and state redacted*.